THE
LOST
CHILDREN

MO
OR

ALSO BY HELEN PHIFER

The Ghost House
The Secrets of the Shadows
The Forgotten Cottage
The Lake House
The Girls in the Woods
The Good Sisters

THE
LOST
CHILDREN

HELEN PHIFER

bookouture

Published by Bookouture
An imprint of StoryFire Ltd.
23 Sussex Road, Ickenham, UB10 8PN
United Kingdom
www.bookouture.com

ISBN: 978-1-78681-175-2
eBook ISBN: 978-1-78681-174-5

This book is a work of fiction. Names, characters, businesses,
organizations, places and events other than those clearly in the
public domain, are either the product of the author's imagination
or are used fictitiously. Any resemblance to actual persons, living or
dead, events or locales is entirely coincidental.

This book is dedicated to my amazing, gorgeous Dad,
who I miss every minute of every day.

PROLOGUE

October 1975

'Alice? Alice?' Lizzy hissed.

Ward thirteen was unusually quiet. In fact, it was too quiet, and this was what had disturbed Lizzy. She lay on the too-firm mattress, afraid to move because her bed creaked louder than anyone else's. Alice, who had been there much longer than Lizzy and was almost fifteen, was asleep.

Looking around to see who was still awake, the first thing Lizzy noticed was that Tommy's bed was empty. This afternoon he'd gone berserk and he'd been taken away for treatment. When they'd brought him back he hadn't said a word. He'd lain on his bed, staring into space with even more dribble than usual running down his chin. Treatment – the very word struck fear into Lizzy's heart. She was only nine years old, but she knew well enough that if you didn't behave they would inject all sorts of poison into your veins and call it medicine. Where was Tommy? It was quarter past four in the morning now, and there were no nurses behind the desk like there usually were. Lizzy pushed herself up on her elbows so she could see into the small staffroom behind the desk. This was shrouded in darkness as well. Where was everyone?

Feeling braver now, she tiptoed out of her bed across to Alice's and tugged her arm. Alice groaned, then turned to look at her.

'What's up?'

'Where's Tommy?'

Alice sat up. 'What do you mean?'

Lizzy pointed to his empty, still-made bed.

'Maybe they let him go home? Go back to sleep, Lizzy.'

'Then why didn't he take his teddy? And his pyjamas are still on the end of the bed.'

Alice rubbed her eyes, threw her legs out of the bed and walked barefoot across the cold floor to Tommy's bed, which was opposite hers. She picked up his teddy, then looked back at Lizzy, who was watching her, and shrugged.

'I don't know; maybe he got sick.'

'This is a hospital; we live here. If he was sick, he'd still be here, wouldn't he?'

'I don't know, Lizzy. Yes, I suppose he would.'

'They've hurt him.'

Alice looked at her carefully and nodded. 'Yes, they probably have. And we should get back into bed before the nurses come back and catch us, or they might hurt us as well. Best not to ask any of them where he is either.'

Lizzy turned and climbed onto the chair next to her bed to peer out of the large window, which looked out onto the back of the hospital grounds. There were fields, which were nice, and there was a cemetery for the patients who had died here. That wasn't so nice. It was scary: there were rows and rows of simple wooden crosses, each one marking someone's grave. On each cross was a number, and Lizzy had asked one of the nicer nurses what the numbers meant. She'd replied that they were the patients' hospital numbers, so they knew who each one was. Lizzy had wanted to ask her why they didn't just put the patients' names on instead, but had been too scared.

A small pinprick of light moved across the path that led from the hospital towards the cemetery.

'Alice? There's someone outside with a torch.'

Alice climbed on the chair next to her, pressing her face against the glass. They watched as the beam moved slowly. They could make out a shadowy figure in the dark. Whoever it was moved as if they were dragging something heavy behind them. Lizzy's small hand slipped into Alice's and she whispered, 'What are they doing?'

Alice jumped down off the chair, pulling Lizzy with her before they got caught peeking.

'I don't know, but you should get back in bed and don't say a word to anyone. Or you will end up like Tommy.'

Lizzy clambered back into bed, her heart thudding so fast it was all she could hear. She lay on her side and pulled her covers over her head. What did Alice mean, she would end up like Tommy?

Then she realised what it was that was being dragged behind the person with the torch. She rammed her fist into her mouth to keep herself from screaming.

CHAPTER ONE

The bright green Citroën with 'ARNOLD'S ESTATE AGENTS' emblazoned across the side stopped outside the huge, rusted gates. Cheryl Tate shuddered; she hated this place and cursed Adrian, the agent in charge of business sales, for ringing in sick today of all days. He had done nothing except brag all week about what a killing he was going to make on the sale of The Moore, and now he wasn't even going to be showing the potential buyer round the place. Instead, the task had fallen to Cheryl.

The Moore had once been the county asylum, serving the whole of this part of the north-west. It had originally housed thousands of patients, but over time the adults had been phased out until only the children were left. Every child with mental health or learning difficulties from all over the county had ended up in there. It had finally shut for good amid a patient abuse scandal in the seventies.

Why anyone would want to buy this place was beyond Cheryl. The pictures in the file showed a grand building, which had probably been deemed one of the finest mental institutions in the country when it was built. Now, however, it was a wreck, the windows all broken and boarded up. The limestone exterior was covered in moss. There were weeds growing all around the outside, making it look scruffy. The roof had huge, gaping holes that were sprouting trees or bushes of some kind. It looked like a huge mausoleum. And perhaps that was fitting: the number of patients who had died from tuberculosis in here was legendary. No mat-

ter what you turned it into – a five star hotel, luxury apartments
or a grand house – you would never be able to get away from
what it once was. No one could ever be truly happy living there,
could they? It would always have the dark, sad, atmosphere that
lingered around it, clinging to the building. A mental asylum was
not a happy place to develop, Cheryl thought, no matter how
much money you might throw into it. However, this was only
her opinion, and it wasn't her place to say anything. Her job was
to show this buyer around the parts of it that were deemed safe,
and then she would get the hell out of there.

She got out of her car, the keys for the new padlock in her
hand. She unlocked it, pushing the heavy gates wide open so
she could drive through. The gates were damp and smelt of rust.
Wrinkling her nose, she wiped her hands on her black trousers to
rid them of the brown particles. She drove along the bumpy, overgrown drive until she reached the wide steps, where she looked
up at the entrance and the imposing oak front doors and sighed.

Forcing herself to get out of the car, she grabbed the large
torch she'd brought with her, and the huge key ring that opened
the many doors to the building, then walked up the steps. At
least Adrian had had the sense to put a sticker on the key which
opened the building, otherwise she might have been here until
tomorrow figuring out which one to use.

Trying to think about what she was going to make for tea to
take her mind off where she was about to go, she twisted the key
in the lock. The door opened effortlessly. It swung open, revealing the dim entrance. Turning on the torch, Cheryl swept the
beam around to make sure there were no homeless people sleeping inside. Although if they were brave enough to sleep in here
on their own, God forbid, who was she to turf them out? She
stepped inside, her feet crunching on a carpet of broken glass.
The torch beam picked out the faded blue graffiti which covered
the walls. There was a faint smell of something gone bad.

Cheryl heard the rumble of car tyres on the drive. Relief washing over her, she turned and walked briskly back outside. A huge, shiny black Porsche Cayenne came into sight. It looked expensive, with its privacy glass and personalised number plate. As it pulled up alongside her car and she saw the size of the man who was driving it, she felt a lot better about going inside the asylum. He got out of the car and smiled at her, his brilliant white teeth almost dazzling. He was at least six foot tall and had a very muscular build. She felt her stomach flip: he was so attractive she didn't want to take her eyes off him.

'Hello, you must be Mr Phillips? I'm Cheryl Tate.' She held out her hand towards him and he took it, shaking it firmly.

'I am, and it's a pleasure to meet you, Ms Tate.'

She felt her cheeks begin to burn. 'Please call me Cheryl. Well, I suppose we should get it over with, then.'

As soon as the words left her mouth she could have kicked herself; she was supposed to sound excited. Enthusiastic, not scared shitless. Mr Phillips didn't say anything, just nodded. Cheryl turned around to go back inside the building, wishing she'd worn flat shoes instead of courts. Leading him inside, she looked at the thick, peeling chunks of paint that were hanging down. The walls underneath were covered in furry black mould.

'I'll spare you the sales talk; I think you can see for yourself it's in dire need of serious renovation.'

He nodded, walking on ahead of her. 'Thank you; I appreciate that. I knew it was going to be bad; I just wanted to see how bad. If I'm going to be asking my investors to back me, I need to be able to tell them I've seen it for myself. Do you know how long it is since anyone has been in here?'

She tried to remember what Adrian had told her. Was it three or six months? She couldn't remember.

'I think it's been around three months.'

He sniffed the air. 'What's that smell?'

'I don't know; I could smell it when I walked in.'

'There must be a dead animal somewhere.'

He walked towards a set of closed double doors at the far end of the entrance area. She followed him, trying her best not to trip over the glass and debris on the floor. He pushed the doors open. The smell which came out was vile, and she gagged. Lifting a hand to cover her mouth, she noticed that Mr Phillips did the same.

'Wow, that's bad,' he said through his fingers, his voice muffled.

Taking the torch from her, he shone it inside the entrance to the ward, the light reflecting off the worn metal patient trolley directly in front of them. It was the only object in the middle of the large corridor which led into what was an otherwise empty room. Mr Phillips lifted the torch higher – and the sound that erupted from Cheryl's mouth was not one that she'd ever heard herself make before. Unable to register what she was looking at, she simply knew it was bad.

Mr Phillips jumped at her screech, then he stepped forward. One arm lifted to cover his nostrils against the foul stench that was permeating the air, he slowly moved the light over what was strapped onto the trolley. A body. A pale, bloated body. Cheryl couldn't take her eyes away from it. It was fully clothed, but the hands which were strapped down were purple and black. The worst thing was the face: the poor man, who had still had a head full of thick, silver hair, looked terrifying. His head was tilted in their direction, and where he should have had an eye, there was a metal spike sticking out of the socket.

Dropping the torch in shock, Mr Phillips stepped backwards. Grabbing hold of Cheryl's hand, he tugged her and ran towards the main doors. Cheryl was still screaming. Once they were outside, he gently slapped her cheek. Tears were falling from her eyes and he led her to his car, where he opened the door and helped her inside. She sat on the soft leather seat and he passed her the handkerchief from his suit pocket. Then he shut the door to drown out the sound of her crying, and phoned the police.

CHAPTER TWO

Detective Inspector Lucy Harwin drove through the quiet streets of Brooklyn Bay, once again thinking how sad it was that the once-thriving seaside resort was now more of a ghost town. She pulled up outside the row of large, brightly coloured Victorian townhouses, relieved she could park so near to where she was going, considering it was Thursday morning.

She no more wanted to go inside and speak to Sara Cross about her personal problems than she wanted to tell Browning who she worked with. However, she had no choice, because it was what the doctor from headquarters had ordered. She would go through the motions as best as she could, although she'd rather be sitting in the studio getting her tattoo finished than being here. It would be far less painful than having that strange woman probing into the darkest depths of her mind.

Lucy got out of her car and pulled her hood up, briskly walking across the road, afraid in case a police car turned into the street and one of her colleagues saw her going into the psychologist's office. Some things were too private for public knowledge. Not that she knew half of the response officers now; they seemed to have had an influx of student officers, all under the age of twenty-five.

She walked in and took a seat in the waiting room, which had once served as someone's living room. Picking up a magazine from the impressive display on the coffee table, she began to flick through it, not taking much notice of its contents. The waiting room was sparse: some chairs that weren't exactly comfortable, a coffee table, and some black and white prints of the older, more striking Victorian buildings that were the town's landmarks. The walls were painted in what she supposed was a calming duck-egg blue, and the chairs were all cream. Lucy didn't like it. It was too much like the woman who she was supposed to tell her innermost fears to – far too friendly. There was something about Sara Cross that Lucy didn't like. Then again, Lucy didn't really mix with most people; she'd never been one of the popular kids at school. It wasn't that she didn't like people, because she did. What she objected to was getting too close to them, and the inevitable hurt that always seemed to follow. They either moved on or died – and she hated the thought of anyone that she cared for dying. Her years working as a response officer had only confirmed her belief that the human race was destined for disaster. This had resulted in her growing even further away from anyone in her close circle.

'Lucinda, you can come through now.'

Lucy jumped; she hated her full name but Sara Cross insisted on using it, much to her annoyance. She stood up, pulling down the sleeves of her sweatshirt so her tattoos were hidden. That was a part of her she only showed when she was off duty; she never had them on show for work, and this was technically work. She always wore long-sleeved shirts or blouses, even in the summer. Lucy was very proud of her ink, but she didn't like to mix work with her private life. As far as she was concerned, the two couldn't be further apart if she tried.

As she followed the woman into her office, her phone began to ring: she'd forgotten to switch it to silent. Sara frowned at her.

'You know the rules, Lucinda; no phones whilst we're in session. Please switch it off.'

Lucy muttered an apology then tucked the phone back into her jeans pocket, where it vibrated to tell her she had a voicemail message.

Both women sat down – Sara behind the big white desk, which had a vase of crisp white lilies and a huge black notebook placed on it. Lucy tried not to sigh as she wondered what crap she could tell her today without actually revealing anything about her life.

'How are you this week?'

'Fine.'

'How's your daughter Ellie?'

'Fine.'

'So. Today's the big day; it's been three months since that tragic incident. Are you looking forward to going back to work this afternoon?'

Lucy looked up at the large cream clock on the wall behind the desk. This was going to be a very long hour. Her phone began buzzing and vibrating in her pocket. She looked at Sara, who was watching her every move. The woman was waiting to see if she took the phone out of her pocket. Lucy tried to ignore it, then thought: *Fuck it.* She pulled out the phone and looked down at the screen.

'I have to take this call.' She turned away from Sara.

'Boss, you have to come down here and see this. It's really bad.'

'Come down where, Mattie? You have to be a little more specific.'

'The Moore – you know, the old county asylum. It's up for sale, would you believe it? One of the estate agents was showing a potential buyer around when they found him.'

'Found who?'

'Well if we knew that, I'd tell you.'

'I'm on my way.'

'Thank god for that. Browning said if I couldn't get hold of you that he would deal. I can't work with him all day, not on something like this. Please don't do that to me; you know what a miserable git he's been lately.'

Lucy laughed and ended the call; she didn't know about Browning because she hadn't been in work. She turned around to look at Sara, who was sitting there staring at her with her piercing blue eyes, drumming her fingers against the shiny surface of the desk. She stopped now, and clasped her fingers together.

'You heard that,' Lucy said. 'I'm very sorry, but I really have to go to work.'

'Lucinda, I know you don't relish the thought of our sessions, but can I remind you that it was a part of your action plan? As part of your managed return to work, you should attend the counselling sessions offered to you. I'm very busy and had to do my best to squeeze you in; if you leave now, I can't guarantee another appointment for a while.'

Lucy thought this was the best news she'd heard all day. 'I'm well aware of that; however, work comes first.'

'Work is tearing you apart; you need to engage with me. I'm not that bad. If you just opened up a little, I'm sure we could become great friends. There must be someone else in that big police station apart from you who can deal with a crime scene?'

Lucy shook her head.

'I'm sorry, Sara, no, there isn't. I'm needed by my team.'

'Then you leave me no choice and I'm sorry to have to do this. I'll have to inform your superiors that you're not engaging with me.'

Lucy shrugged, trying her best not to laugh. Was that supposed to be some kind of threat?

'That's your decision and if that's what you believe, then I'm fine with that.'

She turned and walked out of the door, letting it slam shut behind her. She'd been hauled in front of her boss for far worse. And although she didn't welcome the thought of being sucked into a murder investigation so soon, there were only so many weeds she could pull and seeds she could plant in her small back garden. As much as she loved pottering around out there, she loved her job more.

She reached her mint green Fiat 500 that was parked across the street and climbed inside. Her phone beeped and she looked down to see another message from Mattie.

Glad you're back, this is a bad one. Right up your street.

Lucy typed back. *Yeah, cheers for that. I wouldn't have wanted you to go easy with me on my first day back.*

Lucy pulled the large pair of Chanel sunglasses out of the glove compartment and slipped them on – a present from George. And the one and only thing from him she'd kept after he'd left her for a girl who worked behind the beauty counter in a department store. The rest of the stuff she'd bagged up and given to the charity shop; they would have had a field day rooting through it. She wondered how much of it had actually reached the shop rails.

As she drove away, she didn't notice Sara's tall figure watching her from the upstairs window, shaking her head. Even if she had, she wouldn't have cared. Counselling was never going to get rid of the memories of that dusky, cold afternoon. They would always be there, tucked away for now – but still there, and liable to sneak out of their corner of her mind when she was least expecting it.

As she started on the fifteen-minute drive to the long-abandoned mental asylum, she pushed the memories back into their corner. She had no time to dwell on her own self-pity. She needed to be focused and ready for whatever horror Mattie had decided was worthy of sharing with her.

As she drove through the run-down seaside town of Brooklyn Bay – her home – she sighed. It had once been a bustling place, full of picture houses and music halls, and the funfair along the south end of the promenade had once been thriving. It was sad that all that was left of the fair now was the huge tower that had once been the main support for the biggest ride. The land was boarded off and overgrown with weeds. It was waiting for the council to secure enough funding to do something with it. Lucy thought they should have just left it as it was. She loved it here, though; she loved walking along the promenade and past the old pier, reminiscing about her teenage years spent in the amusement arcades with the few friends she'd had back then.

She was glad that it wasn't school finishing time; the roads around here only really got busy between three and five. She left the town and drove along the coast road, which led to the beach and all the small hamlets and villages that ran along it. The asylum had been built far enough away from the town centre that the patients would have quite a walk to reach civilisation. Yet not too far, in case anything should go wrong and need police intervention.

It was a cold morning. The sea had gone out, leaving the sands glistening in the sunlight. There were only a couple of cars parked up along the beachfront. In the summer it would be crowded, as cars full of parents and kids tried to find somewhere to park up and buy an ice cream. Roy's Ices were famous throughout the area, and as she passed, Lucy thought she could just do a home-made apple crumble ice cream in a waffle cone. She'd had a terrible sweet tooth since she was a kid; now her vices were sugary vanilla lattes, chocolate and ice cream. Luckily, she'd inherited her gran's genes which meant she could eat and drink whatever she wanted and not gain any weight, unlike her poor sister, Lydia, who had been cursed with their dad's genes, meaning she only had to think about an ice cream and she'd pile on the pounds. Lucy had always been grateful that she wasn't Lydia, who the kids at school had teased over her size. Lucy had got into a fair few fights sticking up for her older sister.

She reached the small, tree-lined lane which signalled the turn-off for the asylum, and began to indicate. Turning the corner, she could see the imposing one-hundred-foot clock tower of the hospital peeking through the bare branches of the trees. It was built in the same limestone as most of the other grand buildings in the area. As she drove nearer, it struck her how scary and desolate it looked. It was the kind of place that you would want to go ghost hunting in, if you liked that kind of thing. The huge 'for sale' sign filled a large chunk of the metal gates, which were wide open. She hadn't realised it was being sold – not that she'd had any reason to. Who in their right mind would want to buy it? It was far too creepy; the number of people who'd died here didn't bear thinking about.

As she drove through the gates, she tried to push down the butterflies that had begun to fill her stomach and make her heart race. She could do this; she lived to do this. Since coming out of her probationary period, she had worked hard to climb the ranks as fast as she could, making detective inspector by the age of thirty-four. They'd promised that when she came back from her time out – gardening leave; whatever they wanted to call it – she could have the chance to take on the role of detective chief inspector. She'd declined. She didn't want to be the one who spent all her time worrying about how much money an investigation was costing. She much preferred to be the one out there, catching the criminals.

The assortment of police vans and the single Ford Focus looked out of place against the backdrop of the hospital. There was also a vile green car which had to belong to the estate agent – this was parked next to a very nice Porsche. Lucy nodded at the paramedics leaning against the side of the ambulance. She parked her car alongside them and took her sunglasses off, inhaling through her nose and breathing out. *You can do this, Lucy; you're good at this. It's what you were born to do, so pull yourself together and go inside.*

There was a copper who looked even younger than Mattie standing at the bottom of the steps, with a scene-guard booklet in his hands and a pen. Striding across towards him, she smiled.

'Morning. DI Lucy Harwin. Where is everyone?'

His cheeks flared red as he nodded towards the open doorway. 'Inside.'

He began to squirm and stutter as he forced the next question out. 'Can I see your warrant card? Sorry. It's just, I don't know you, and for all I know you could be a reporter.'

Lucy watched as he looked her up and down. She supposed she didn't exactly look like a DI in her tight faded jeans, Nike hooded sweatshirt and bright yellow Converse. Her pillar-box red hair was pulled up into a tight ponytail, and her sweatshirt sleeve had rolled up to expose some of the almost-finished intricate black and grey tattoos on her left arm. She hastily tugged the sleeve down.

'Ah, you have me there; I'm not due to start work until two and I've been called out to come and take a look at the scene. So I haven't got my ID with me. You're going to have to take my word for it.'

To give him his due, the poor lad looked as if he wanted to crawl into a hole and die.

'I can't, I'm sorry. I'll get in trouble.'

'Boss, what took you so long?'

The officer turned to see Mattie standing in the open doorway, and the look of relief on his face was one that Lucy would remember for the rest of her life. He'd just been saved from looking like a complete arse.

'I was busy, Matthew; some of us have a life outside of work.'

Mattie blushed; Lucy only used his full name if she was reprimanding him. 'Yeah, I am sorry about that. You need to see this, though. There's some protective gear in the boot of the Focus.' He lifted his hand to point in the direction of the car he'd arrived in, and a loud ripping noise filled the air as his white paper crime scene suit tore underneath his armpit.

Lucy walked across to the car and opened the boot. 'Have you been hitting the gym again?' She winked at him. An expert at getting dressed in the strangest of places, she ripped open the packet and deftly climbed into the suit, then added shoe covers and latex gloves. Catching sight of her reflection in the car window, she nodded: now she looked like a detective inspector. Walking over, she ducked under the blue and white tape the officer had just finished tying across the front door.

'Nice hair,' Mattie said. 'Get fed up of being blonde, did you?'

'Yes, thank you. I did. I wanted to go pink, but I thought that might be pushing it a bit.'

'Nah, red suits you. I like it.'

'Oh good, I'm so glad you approve.'

She turned away so he couldn't see the grin which had spread across her face. She'd known that dying her hair this particular shade of red might get a reaction from her superiors and she didn't care. They were all pussyfooting around her because they knew that if they'd done what she'd told them to that afternoon, things wouldn't have ended the way they had.

She had waved away the face mask Mattie had offered her, but now that she'd stepped inside the damp, draughty building and inhaled she wished she had accepted it graciously. The smell of decomposition was bad: the body had been here some time. Mattie passed her a torch, which she did accept. He pointed ahead of them towards the open doors, and she walked on in that direction. She shone the torch on the body strapped to the metal gurney, and took a sharp intake of breath. Whoever it was had been fastened down with thick, cracked leather restraints so that they couldn't move.

Mattie was talking to Detective Constable Colin Davey behind her and she blocked out the sound of their voices. She needed to think. She stepped closer to take a look at the bloated, mottled black and purple face staring at her.

'Is Dr Maxwell on her way?'

'Yes, boss, she said she'd be here as soon as.'

'Not that we need her to tell us the cause of death.' Lucy looked at the eight centimetre steel spike, which was attached to a wooden handle and protruding from the man's left eye socket. It appeared to go straight up into his brain. His other eye was the cloudy, milky colour which only happened some hours after death. The man's entire body was bloated, due to the bacteria from the intestines and bowel having escaped into the other body tissues after death. Lucy knew that it was these bacteria starting to grow that had produced the gases causing the foul smell which was now permeating the air.

'Nope, I'd say cause of death was quite obvious.'

CHAPTER THREE

Lucy walked around the gurney, shining her torch over the body. She couldn't help feel sad for whoever this was. What a scary place to die, and left here all alone afterwards. She couldn't see any other injuries, although that didn't mean that there weren't any. Despite what she'd said, it wasn't her place to say or to assume the cause of death. If Dr Maxwell heard her surmising, she'd give her a proper telling-off.

The torch light reflected off the metal band on the corpse's swollen, blackened wedding finger, and she sighed.

'Bollocks, he's married – and what a horrible way to die.'

Mattie took a step closer. 'That's what I thought; I've never seen anything like this before. What do you think that is sticking out of his face?'

Lucy shrugged. 'I don't know. It looks like some kind of ice pick, or maybe a chisel.'

Footsteps began to echo throughout the building behind them and Lucy straightened up.

'Ah, Lucinda and Matthew. If it isn't my two favourite detectives! What have we here then?'

Lucy and Mattie smiled at each other in the darkness, then moved away, giving Dr Catherine Maxwell room to take a closer look. 'You tell me; you're the doctor.'

'Gosh, are you feeling OK? Usually you're the first to tell me what's happened. You know, a little bird told me you were the DI in charge of this case, so soon after you've returned to work. I do worry about you, Lucy. Are you ready for such responsibility and all the bullshit that goes with it?'

'Ready as I'll ever be. How are you, Catherine? It's been a while.'

'I'm not too bad; still slicing and dicing for a living.'

Catherine walked around the body, her torch examining every inch of it. 'Well, well, well. This is a turn-up for the books. I can't say I've ever dealt with anything of this nature before. It's really quite brutal, isn't it?'

'So you know what it is, then?'

'Off the record, I think I have a pretty good idea.'

'And?'

'Don't quote me; this is strictly between us. But on first impressions I think that our victim has approximately been dead for around six to eight days. I also think that he might have been lobotomised – probably the first such procedure to be carried out in this country for a very long time.'

Mattie looked at the body, then back at Catherine. 'What's "lobotomised" when it's at home?'

She turned to stare at him. 'Seriously, you've never heard of a lobotomy? Have you never watched *One Flew Over the Cuckoo's Nest?*'

He shook his head.

'You youngsters. I guess I'm showing my age now. Basically, it's quite a simple procedure, not too complicated at all. It was hailed as a miracle cure for all sorts of mental illnesses back in the forties. I think it was first carried out by a Portuguese neurologist who thought that mentally ill patients were suffering from fixed circuits in the brain. It was then picked up by the US and then us Brits.'

'What exactly was it used to treat?' Lucy asked. 'I can't imagine doing that to someone would cure anything.'

Mattie, unable to speak, was listening to the conversation with his mouth open and a grimace on his face.

'It became a common part of psychiatric medicine,' Catherine said. 'They used it to treat depression, compulsive disorders and schizophrenia. The whole procedure only took around five minutes and was generally performed under a local anaesthetic.'

'So they were awake?'

'Yes. They would force a pick-like instrument – very much like the one protruding from our victim – through the back of the eye socket, to pierce the thin bone that separates the eye socket from the frontal lobes. Then they would give it a good old jiggle around until the frontal lobes were severed from the rest of the brain.'

Mattie groaned. 'Oh fuck, I can feel my eyeballs squelching just thinking about it. That's horrific. Thank god for Valium.'

Lucy smiled, but Mattie was right. It was barbaric, and it must have been agonising. There was a lot to be said for modern medicine.

She looked back at the corpse. So, who in their right mind would want to perform a lobotomy in a long-abandoned mental hospital?

'Do you think they meant to kill him? Or could it have been an experiment gone wrong?'

Catherine was leaning directly over the man's face, shining her torch around the entry wound. 'Judging by how far this has been pushed in, I think it's safe to say that they meant business. I'll know more when I complete the post-mortem. Oh, and none of this is official. You know that, right?'

'Yes, we know. Thank you, it just gives us something to go on for now.'

Catherine stood up and snapped off her blue latex gloves. 'I'll look forward to this one; I'm intrigued as to why anyone would use a lobotomy as the cause of death.'

'You and me both. Do you know when the post-mortem will be?'

Catherine looked at her phone. 'Not today; I'm finishing early to spend the day with my dearly beloved. It's our wedding anniversary and I'm not working any later than I have to. He made me promise that I'd be home early – he's offered to take me out, and he's paying, which is a very rare occasion. I have no intention of letting him get away with it.'

'Happy anniversary. Tell Mr Maxwell I said hi.'

Catherine smiled. 'I will, thank you, Lucy. I'll be in the mortuary at eight o'clock tomorrow morning, so get there for no later than nine. You know, as far as murders go, this has to be one of the most original I've ever come across.'

'What do you mean?'

'Well, to lobotomise someone inside what was once a state-of-the-art mental institution, which no doubt carried out these operations back in its heyday, is pretty ingenious if you ask me.' She turned and walked away, leaving Lucy's mind overflowing with ideas.

Mattie looked at her. 'I wonder how long they've been married.'

'Too bloody long!' Catherine's voice echoed around the empty entrance hall and then she was gone – back out into the fresh air to sign herself out of the scene.

Lucy began to laugh. 'You really need to work on your whispering skills; you're crap at being discreet. Come on, there isn't much more we can do here. She's right, though, this crime fits the scene perfectly. Let's get Forensics in to sweep the entire area and get it all documented. I need coffee so I can think about what a mess this is going to turn into with a fully functioning brain.'

'Coffee sounds good to me, boss.'

As Lucy left, she paused inside the entrance area to look at the huge number of corridors that led off from it. The building was a maze of corridors and rooms. Shining her torch down the one without wooden fire doors blocking the view, she inhaled. It went on forever. This place was huge, and for all they knew there could be more bodies hidden around. They could have stumbled upon someone's killing ground. The thought made her shiver. She actually found herself crossing her fingers and praying to god that this was the only body.

Before she went out into the open, she made a silent promise to the man who had been left here to rot. She would find whoever had killed him and bring them to justice. She could feel the familiar fire in the pit of her stomach, signalling that she was about to throw herself into this investigation and let it take over her life until the killer was caught. And she would: wholeheartedly, and with no regrets, because she was passionate about her job. She would get justice for this victim, no matter what the personal cost to her was.

CHAPTER FOUR

Lucy stepped out into the fresh air and took a huge gulp of it to clear her lungs. She should definitely have taken a mask from Mattie. The smell of the body, mixed with the dust and mould spores that must be floating around in there, had been enough to make even a hardened copper want to throw up.

Mattie stepped out behind her, pushed his mask down and whispered in her ear. 'The monkeys have arrived in force.' He pointed to the cluster of what must have been every CID officer who was on duty. Tom Crowe, the detective chief inspector, was standing deep in conversation with Detective Sergeant Peter Browning. Tom lifted his hand and waved at them. Detective Constable Colin Davey was also standing next to them, along with several of the other DCs. Lucy headed towards them, and Tom broke away to meet her.

'How are you, Lucy? I'm sorry about this. Talk about throwing you back in the deep end on your first day.'

'It's fine, boss; I suppose I wouldn't want it any other way. It's nice to be back doing my job.'

She tried not to be bitter with Tom; he was a good man and a decent boss. He'd been to visit her a couple of times whilst she'd been off work. Mattie had told her that he'd got himself into a spot of bother with the big bosses by defending Lucy's actions. It hadn't been his fault that they'd had to suspend her; he'd only been doing his job.

'And it's good to have you back,' he replied. 'So, what have we got then?'

'Will it be easier to speak to everyone and save repeating myself?'

He nodded. 'Of course.'

They walked over to join the small group, who stopped chattering. Lucy explained everything to them, watching to see who was listening and taking note. Relief washed over her to see that all of them were; she'd been worried that they wouldn't take her seriously. Mattie was loyal and she'd never doubted him, but Browning could be a pain in the arse and mouthy with it. However, as she spoke, he didn't say anything – which was a big surprise. Maybe her suspension wasn't going to cause a pissing contest after all.

'There are lots of lines of enquiry to follow. Who is our victim? I want that to be your priority, Browning. We need to figure out how and where the killer gained access to the perimeter and the actual building, which as you can see has been closed for years. Then we need to cordon the asylum off. There must be some forensic evidence somewhere. It's too far to walk here, especially with the victim in tow.'

She stood with her hands on her hips, looking around. As she surveyed the massive buildings and acres of overgrown gardens, a groan escaped her lips. The place went on forever; they didn't have the kind of manpower necessary for this.

'We're going to need a search team to go through the rest of the hospital. He might not be the only victim.'

Mattie looked down at his notebook. 'The estate agent said the place was locked up tight when she arrived. She had to open the gates so she could drive through, and she used a key to get through the front doors. It was all secure.'

'So are we assuming that our killer had a time machine or a magic Santa key then?' Lucy said. 'Perhaps they can teleport? I want a search team here now to clear the rest of the building, and we need to establish just how the killer got inside. We need to stop anyone coming anywhere near; the road outside only leads two ways. Radio for more patrols, PCSOs, any available staff to come and block it off until we know which route the killer took. Colin, can you start researching this place? I want the usual checks, plus I want to know when it shut down. When the last patients left, a list of patients and staff that worked here. Oh, and I need to know if they performed lobotomies on any of the patients here. Actually, also, why did it shut down? I want you to find everything out that you can. Can you get back to the station and get started?'

'Yes, boss, I'll go now.' He held his hand out to Mattie for the car keys, who threw them across.

In less than a minute Colin was driving away, no doubt relieved to be getting out of there. Mattie shook his head and stared at Lucy. 'That's favouritism, you know. For once it would be quite nice to have the cushy inside job. Sitting on my arse all day would make a lovely change.'

'Ah, but I like working with you,' Lucy said. 'We make a pretty good team, and let's face it, your computer skills are sadly lacking compared to Col's. Being a top scorer on FIFA doesn't make you a cyber whizz, does it?'

He grabbed his chest. 'Oosh, right through the heart. You're a hard woman, you know that? Hitting a bloke where it hurts the most. OK then, what are you going to do?'

'I'm going to speak to those two.' She nodded in the direction of the Porsche and began to walk towards it.

CHAPTER FIVE

Edwin, Edwin, Edwin; what a silly man you were. After all these years of living in obscurity, you couldn't resist one last chance, could you? One last chance to have your moment in the spotlight. Well, you're certainly about to have it now.

To think that you actually believed I was writing a book about the great pioneering work you were responsible for at The Moore. You actually believed that after all this time, your evil deeds would be long forgotten. That people would not remember the barbaric procedures you carried out under the guise of a mental health professional. You even supplied your own instrument of death. After all this time, you were still keeping souvenirs from back in the day, back when you were happy to ruin the lives of teenage girls and young children without so much as a second thought.

On our second meeting, in the small internet café near to the market hall, you sat telling me proudly of how you'd changed so many young lives for the better. How they would all be living normal, happy lives now because of your willingness to carry out these procedures. Are they though, Edwin? Had you spoken to any of them in the last thirty years? No, I thought not. You'd hidden yourself away since the scandal that closed the hospital for good. I'd watched you pottering in your garden, with your poor unsuspecting wife at your side. Do you think she'd have been by your side if she'd known what kind of monster you really were?

Did you think that coming with me to the hospital was going to make you famous? You were so full of yourself that you never questioned why we were sneaking inside a building that said 'No Trespassing'. You followed me through that door, marvelling at how wonderful the hospital had been until those last few weeks.

You seriously believed I was enthralled with how bold you had been with your pioneering treatment. You even climbed onto the trolley of your own free will, trying to demonstrate your amazing procedure to me so I could describe it in its full glory on paper – only you didn't look too sure about it when I strapped your hands down. Your face soon turned to a mask of horror when I stood and asked you to repeat what that metal pick was used for. Only, it was too late. For the rest of my life, I shall treasure the flicker of recognition in your eyes when I asked if you remembered me.

You were so easy to fool, so gullible – although why wouldn't you be? I'm a mature adult; I've done incredibly well for myself, if I may say so, and none of it has anything to do with your pioneering skills. I'd almost been prepared to let it all go; you were so close to living out the rest of your days peacefully. Then the headlines broke that they were digging up the asylum cemetery, and it was too much. Every single smell, incident, mistreatment that I'd suffered came rushing back. That short news clip opened up a floodgate that I'd kept closed all this time, and now I can't stop the dirty grey water that has filled my mind. I'm drowning in the memories of that awful place. And I'm taking you and her down with me.

CHAPTER SIX

September 1975

Nine-year-old Lizzy Clements was trying to watch the television, but her baby brother wouldn't stop screaming. Her mum had carried the small, angry bundle of baby upstairs to lay him down for a nap, and Lizzy hoped he would shut up soon. Lizzy hated John – what a stupid name to call a baby. All he did was cry and scream; her mum used to smell of roses and now all she smelt of was baby sick. Lizzy couldn't remember the last time her mum or dad had sat her on their knee for a cuddle, or the last time they'd tucked her into bed and read her a bedtime story. *Carrie's War*, which she sometimes watched at school, came onto the television now, and she tried to block out the screaming as she began to watch the latest instalment.

Half an hour later, as the programme finished, Lizzy put the last of her ham sandwich into her mouth and leant forwards to put the empty plate onto the coffee table. It suddenly struck her how quiet the house was. Where was her mum and that horrible, noisy baby? A feeling of terror filled her chest and she wondered if her mum had taken the baby out in his pram and left her on her own.

She stood up and shouted: 'Mum?'

Normally, her mum would shout back, 'What?' But there was no reply.

Lizzy went and checked the kitchen. John's pram was still there, so her mum hadn't gone out and left her on her own. She went into the dining room, which was also empty, so she began to creep upstairs. It was so quiet that the creak from the top step filled the house. A gentle snore came from her mum's bedroom. Lizzy crept along to take a peek. As she opened the door, she saw her mum, who was lying fully clothed, curled up on the bed fast asleep. Next to her, in his cot, the small, chubby figure of the baby began to squirm around beneath his bright blue crocheted blanket.

Lizzy walked towards his cot and looked down at him. He was bright red, and the ugliest thing she'd ever seen. He opened his eyes and looked up at her. She stuck her tongue out. She hated him.

At half past five, Lizzy heard her mother scream upstairs. She wondered what the screaming was for. Moments later, Mary, the next-door neighbour, was hammering on the door, calling to see if everything was OK. Lizzy heard her mother run down the stairs and open the door. Through the window, she watched her run out into the street, clutching the baby.

Lizzy could hear her mother and wondered what she was screaming for. Within minutes, the sound of sirens filled the air. Lizzy stood and turned up the sound on the television. She wished her mother would stop screaming. She was almost as bad as the baby.

Mary came into the house. Lizzy smelt her before she saw her. She didn't like Mary because she always smelt of cigarette smoke and swore a lot.

'Lizzy? Your mum has gone up to the hospital with John. Are you OK, pet?'

Lizzy stared at her. What sort of question was that? Of course she was OK. She nodded her head at Mary, then turned back to the television.

Before long, the front door flew open and Lizzy's dad ran in. He didn't even look at her before he rushed upstairs to get changed out of his dirty, grease-stained overalls. Heavy footsteps came thundering back down. He went into the kitchen, where Mary was smoking.

'I'm so sorry, Ian. I can't imagine how upset you are. I think you should get yourself up to the hospital; Sandra needs you. I'll watch Lizzy.'

His eyes began to stream with tears and he nodded. 'Yes, I should go and see Sandra and John.'

He turned and left.

Mary watched Ian go, then turned around and jumped to see Lizzy standing there.

'At least we can get some sleep tonight.' Lizzy smiled at her before skipping off to her bedroom.

There was a loud knock on the front door. Mary opened it to see a policemen standing there.

'I need to see the baby's cot,' he said, 'if you could be so kind as to show me.'

Mary nodded and led the way upstairs. 'It's so tragic,' she said. 'Why do things like this happen to all the good people?'

The policeman shrugged his shoulders and walked across to peer into the cot. He examined a small white cushion which looked out of place. Taking his pen from his pocket, he pushed the cushion over to reveal a small pinky-red stain in the middle of the fabric. He let out a huge sigh. Wearing his leather gloves, he picked up the cushion and placed it into a brown paper evidence bag, taking it out to the waiting police car. Mary ran after him.

'What are you doing with that?'

'I'm sorry to say that it looks as if this might have been used to suffocate the baby.'

Movement from the upstairs window made them both look up. Lizzy was standing there, smiling at them.

Some hours later, Lizzy was curled up on the settee under a blanket, wondering how much longer her mum and dad were going to be at the hospital. She was hungry and tired. She was just drifting off to sleep when the front door opened. She sat up, and smiled to see her parents. Behind them were two policemen, a doctor in a white coat and two other men who she thought looked like ambulance drivers.

The smile left her face as neither her mum nor her dad looked at her. Instead, they put their heads down.

The doctor spoke to her dad. 'Mr Clements, why don't you take your wife upstairs and put her to bed? She needs some rest; it's been a terrible day and we don't want to add to her suffering any more than we need to.'

Lizzy stood up. She had no idea why these people were in her house, telling her dad what to do. Her dad took hold of her mum's elbow and pushed her towards the stairs.

'Mum, where are you going?'

Her dad didn't even look back at her. She watched them with her stomach churning as they walked upstairs, leaving her with these strangers. The doctor smiled at her and nodded at the two ambulance men. Lizzy felt her heart begin to race as the two men lunged towards her and grabbed an arm each. She began to struggle and kick out at them to make them get off her. What were they doing? She didn't understand.

The doctor came towards her, holding a large syringe filled with a cloudy white liquid. Lizzy strained against the men, who were holding her arms so tight she couldn't feel them. She carried on kicking her feet and the policemen rushed over to grab her legs. Lizzy tried her best to fight them off, but they were much stronger than her. As the huge needle pricked the soft skin of her forearm, sinking into the vein, she screamed at the top of her voice.

'Daddy! Help me!'

CHAPTER SEVEN

Lucy had spoken to the estate agent first, which had been quite difficult because the woman kept on sniffling and dabbing her eyes with a scrunched up cotton handkerchief. The handkerchief looked expensive, and Lucy guessed it must belong to the man who owned the Porsche. It must have been a terrible shock for them to find the body, but the man seemed to be coping much better than the estate agent. His tanned face was, Lucy assumed, a little paler than when he'd arrived, but at least he could string a sentence together.

Lucy knew that for the next few days at least, all she would think about would be the victim. However, she wouldn't lie awake at night like poor Cheryl Tate probably would, distressed by having seen that mutilated eye socket.

Lucy had seen some terrible things in her time, but it was all part of the job; she wouldn't change it for the world – catching criminals was all she ever wanted to do. And it had taken some work on her part to get where she was today. At fifteen she'd gone off the rails, causing her parents all sorts of worry. By seventeen, she'd been pregnant with Ellie.

As if she'd summoned her daughter by thinking about her, the phone in her pocket vibrated. Excusing herself from her two witnesses, she walked away, wrestling the phone out of her pocket. Reading the text message, she smiled.

Hi mum, off to Danny's party tonight. So won't be ringing later.

Don't drink too much and have fun. Love you xx

Repocketing the phone, Lucy looked around and noticed the field at the back of the asylum, which held an assortment of bright orange diggers and forklift trucks. Behind the vehicles were rows of wooden crosses. All of the vehicles were stationary. Lucy lifted her hand to squint and try to see what they were doing.

An elbow nudged her side. 'Are you all right, boss?'

'Yes, thank you. So, have we any news about the search teams?'

'They should be here any minute,' Mattie said. 'There's even a dog handler on shift today; she should be here shortly too. Hopefully the dog will pick up the trail and lead us straight to our point of entry. Both exits have been cordoned off and the workmen who are digging up the old cemetery have been sent home.'

'The cemetery in that field? Did it belong to the asylum, then?'

'It's where they buried the patients. Some developer bought it years ago to build houses. Apparently they didn't bother buying the hospital because it was in such a state, but they didn't mind building next to it.'

Lucy looked at him, frowning. 'They didn't bother with the hospital, but have no problem digging up a cemetery? That can't be cheap. Where are they putting the bodies?'

Mattie shrugged. 'I don't know everything. I just know that it caused quite an outrage with some of the older residents of the town. There were lots of upset people who had loved ones buried in there, and they didn't want them disturbed, hence why it's taken the developer so long to get around to it.'

'I bet they didn't. There are some things that you shouldn't mess with, and moving people from their final resting places is pretty high on that list.'

Mattie shifted from one foot to another, trying to hide his unease. Lucy knew what he was going to ask her next and she wanted to tell him not to say a word. She didn't need treating like a piece of fragile china.

'I was, erm… just wondering how you are. I mean, how you're holding up?'

'I'm good thanks, you?'

'Great, but that's not quite what I meant…'

The arrival of the search teams stopped the conversation before it became any more difficult. Lucy went over to talk to them.

After she'd discussed how the search should be carried out, she went over to join Mattie at another, much smaller, van with 'Police Dogs' written across the side of it. He was standing with Kim, the dog handler.

'I'm hoping Kim's going to make everyone's lives a whole lot easier,' he told Lucy.

'This a huge site to cover,' Kim said, 'but yes, fingers crossed we'll find the killer's point of entry and exit.'

'I hope so,' Mattie said. 'Otherwise we're going to be here until we retire.'

Kim unlatched the cage to let the huge black Labrador out. The pair of them set off, the dog sniffing around and straining at its lead, relieved to be released.

Lucy smiled at Mattie. 'Looks like we're almost good to go; as soon as the dog has finished, the search teams are going to go in and take a look. Blondie – the estate agent over there, currently messing up the leather seats in the Porsche with her leaky eyes – has requested someone from her office brings the blueprints for the entire building up, as well as all the information that they have regarding the hazardous parts. As soon as the search team has been in, I want to go back inside for another look.'

'Should we not go back to the station? It's going to take ages.'

Lucy shook her head. As tempted as she was, she couldn't leave. When she turned back to look at the imposing, sad, neglected building, she felt as if she was being drawn back to it. She didn't want to leave whoever their victim was lying all alone on that trolley in the dark any longer than she had to.

'No, we can go in and help out with the search. In fact, that's a good idea; let's get as many staff as can be spared here now. We can let the task force sergeant brief them, and if we all go in together to do an initial search to make sure there are no more bodies, I'll feel a lot happier.'

'Do you think whoever did this knew that the estate agents would be showing potential buyers around, and left him there for them to find?'

'I don't know, Mattie. How long has it been for sale?'

'At least a couple of years that I know of.'

'It's hard to say anything. There's only one person who knows at the moment.'

'Yeah, and I can't see them coming forward to tell us the answer, can you?'

Lucy shook her head.

Finally, one of the estate agents arrived with the blueprints for the building. He was sent in the direction of the task force sergeant, James Roberts. Lucy had been thankful for small mercies to find that it was Robbo who was on shift, rather than the arse of a sergeant who had fucked up big-time three months ago.

There was a large group of officers assembled, all ready to go in and search, armed with torches and small yellow cones to place by any evidence they may come across. They were split up into small groups and each allocated a section of the building. By this time, the dog handler had found what they believed to be the killer's point of entry. It was a small side door which was open, allowing access into the hospital. This had been sealed off and Jack Forbes, the lead crime scene investigator, was currently dusting for prints, footprints and DNA.

Jack's partner both in and out of work, Amanda, had put down some metal plates leading from the front door into the foyer area. The search teams would use them to walk across to the different wings with minimal disturbance. The area surrounding the room where the body had been found had been taped off so that a thorough investigation could be carried out. Lucy didn't envy the mammoth task that both Jack and Amanda faced; two more CSIs had been requested to be called in early to come and help them. Lucy hadn't even given a second thought to the budget when she'd given Control the go-ahead to ring them at home. Everyone knew that time was of the essence, and they couldn't afford to not bring in any extra help.

Robbo, as everyone called him, barked at the large group standing in front of him. 'Right, as you can see for yourselves this is a big fucking job. I've studied the plans of the building and decided that the ground floor is safe to search. I'm not convinced by what the estate agent has told me that the upstairs is ready for a herd of stampeding coppers. So for now, we'll focus on the ground floor. What we are looking for are any obvious signs of areas being recently disturbed. If you find an area that you think needs checking out, mark it and flag it up for CSI. Obviously a telltale sign would be a decomposing body, but Jack said to mark anything that stands out. It's vitally important that nothing is overlooked.'

Robbo began to call up groups of two and three, giving them their directions and ward numbers to search, pointing them out on the plans in front of him. Lucy and Mattie paired up together. Browning, who was sweating and huffing at the back of the group, followed them.

'I'll come with you two. I can't be arsed going with those lot; they'll be pissing around.' He pointed to the newest group of officers who were all chattering excitedly between themselves. Lucy groaned, although she couldn't blame him. All three of them made their way towards the building to search for more bodies.

Lucy found her heart racing at the thought of going back inside the asylum so soon. The thought of the cemetery in the field beyond, of how many people had died awful, lonely deaths inside the asylum, made her stomach churn. She let Mattie lead the way.

Browning, who hadn't stepped inside the building before, took one look around and shook his head. 'What an awful place to die.'

'You can say that again,' Lucy agreed.

'Poor bastard. I wonder what he'd done to piss someone off this much?'

Mattie opened a set of double doors, which groaned so loudly that Lucy and Browning – not to mention everyone else in the area – jumped.

'Sorry; it's just the doors.' Mattie held one of the doors open for the other two, then let go as Browning passed him. This left Lucy in front. She wondered if Mattie was more than a little bit spooked. It was dark down this corridor; all three of them switched on their torches. It smelt earthy, damp and fusty. However, there was no smell of decomposition, which made Lucy feel a little better. She led the way, walking for quite some distance before coming to another set of double doors. She shone her torch around, and felt her heart sink to see the faded teddies and flowers that had once brightened the walls around the doors now covered in graffiti.

Shining her torch above the doors, she read out loud: 'Welcome to Ward Thirteen.'

Mattie looked at Browning. 'Fuck; they kept kids in this hospital. This is wrong. It's so wrong.'

Browning looked around at the murals on the walls. 'I can't begin to imagine why you would leave your kid in a place like this.'

The search of the ward proved negative. Nothing in there looked as if it had been disturbed in years. There were no fresh footprints in the dust and debris that littered the floors. Mattie and Browning spent most of their time staring at the assortment of cots and beds, both of them wide-eyed, open-mouthed, shaking their heads. Some of the rusted bed frames had worn leather restraints dangling from them, similar to the ones on the trolley the body had been found on. As they turned to leave, Lucy gave the ward one last look. She knew this place was firmly embedded in her mind now. She might not have nightmares about the victim with a spike through his eye, but she would definitely have nightmares about the wards and the poor kids who'd lived on them.

The three of them emerged back outside into the fading autumn sunlight. Lucy didn't stop with the others. Instead, she carried on walking towards her car. She needed to clear her mind and get these awful, constricting overalls off. Tugging them down, she felt slightly better to be out of them. She hadn't realised how hot she'd been inside them until she felt the damp patches of sweat under her armpits. Lifting one arm towards her she sniffed, wrinkling her nose. Not as bad as it could be, but bad enough. She leaned back against the boot of her car and tried to decide what to do next.

She heard Mattie's voice not too far away. 'Now can we go for coffee? I need something. Actually, I think I need alcohol and lots of it.'

'Coffee is the best I can do,' Lucy said. 'You know that we're not going to the pub any time this year, don't you?'

He shook his head.

'Come on, I'm buying,' Lucy said. 'I need a double-shot vanilla latte to get my brain in gear. I feel as if I'm numb from my head down.'

'Thank fuck for that; I thought you were never going to say we could leave this place.'

Lucy got into her car and watched as Mattie tried to manoeuvre his six-foot-four frame into the front passenger seat.

'I hate this car.'

'I know you do. Just as well you don't have to drive it then, isn't it?'

'I'd rather drive a tractor.'

Lucy laughed and started the engine. 'I don't quite know how, but we need to solve this case, and fast. I don't want lobotomised old people turning up dead all over the place. It's not good for the tourism industry – and you know what that means.'

'It means the bloody council will be putting pressure on the chief to get it solved so it doesn't interfere with what little tourist trade there is,' Mattie said. 'I get it. Surely this is a one-off, though? It's so bizarre; I've never come across anything like it.'

'I hope so,' Lucy said. 'I really do.'

CHAPTER EIGHT

September 1975

Even with her eyes shut, Lizzy knew she wasn't at home in her soft, squishy bed. She was lying on a mattress that was much harder than her own. She tried to open her eyes and couldn't; they felt as if they'd been glued shut. Panic filled her chest, making it hard to breathe.

'Mum! Where are you? I can't see!' she screamed. She heard footsteps come rushing towards her. Relief flooded her small body – until she felt someone lean over her, and she realised it wasn't her mum. They seemed much too big, and they didn't smell like her mum did.

'Hello, Lizzy,' the person said. 'I'm Nurse Stone. You're in hospital. Do you remember coming here?'

She shook her head frantically from side to side. 'Where are my mum and dad?'

There was a slight pause. 'At home. I suspect they didn't want to come here with you.'

Lizzy's heart began to pound inside her chest. 'Why? Am I poorly?'

The nurse began to laugh. 'Well now, that's down to you and the doctor to decide. I would say that you were. Can you remember what happened?'

Lizzy felt her eyes begin to open, although she couldn't see properly – everything looked fuzzy. She saw the white cap on the nurse's head and tried to focus on that until it became clearer.

'Nurse, why didn't you tell me our patient was awake?' A man's voice came from the other side of the bed. He sounded strict, a bit like the headteacher at Lizzy's school. 'Blink your eyes a couple of times, girl,' he said now, 'and you should be able to focus a bit better.'

She did as he said and her vision began to clear. She could now see the short round man standing beside her bed. He was wearing a white doctor's coat with a stethoscope around his neck. Lizzy turned and saw the stern-looking nurse on her other side, who was watching her every move. Lizzy didn't like her; she didn't have a kind, smiley face like her mum. The doctor looked a bit friendlier, so she chose to speak to him.

'Why am I here? I want my mum.'

'Your mum will be here tomorrow; she's had a very sad and tiring day. She will be tucked up in bed by now. If we sit you up, you can have something to eat and drink, then you can go to the toilet and get back into bed. You've had some very strong medicine so your legs might feel a little like jelly.'

'Am I poorly?'

'Sick in the head, more like,' the nurse said.

The doctor turned to the nurse. 'If I hear you talk like that once more, Nurse Stone, I will move you to the men's ward for the rest of the week.'

The nurse rolled her eyes and Lizzy decided she definitely didn't like her. She was rude and nasty. And what did she mean, Lizzy was sick in the head? She hadn't felt ill this morning when she'd woken up, all she'd felt was tired because that baby had kept her awake again most of the night.

A picture of her tiny brother's lifeless body suddenly filled her mind and she began to scream, flailing her arms around. What had she done? While the nurse tried to grab her hands, the doctor hurried over to the wooden trolley behind the bed next to her. Still screaming, Lizzy looked in the bed and saw a girl who was a lot older than her. The girl lifted her finger to her lips, telling Lizzy to be quiet, then pointed to the doctor, who was holding a big needle filled with some cloudy white medicine. Lizzy realised that if she didn't shut up, the doctor was going to stick the huge needle into her arm again. She stopped. The girl smiled at her and nodded. The nurse let go of Lizzy's arm and the doctor paused.

Lizzy whispered, 'Sorry.'

The doctor placed the cap back on the needle and put it into his pocket. 'I know this is a bit of a shock for you, but you need to stay calm, otherwise I'll have to give you another injection to make you sleep. And you don't want that, do you?'

She shook her head.

'Good. That's a good girl. You do what the nurse tells you and you'll be just fine.' He turned and walked away.

The nurse, who had hit her leg on the metal cot sides of the bed while trying to hold Lizzy down, looked at her in disgust. 'You little shit; look what you've made me do. I've laddered my tights and they were new on this morning, fresh out of the packet.'

The girl in the bed next to Lizzy began to laugh, and the nurse turned to glare at her.

'You can shut up.'

The laughter got louder and the scary nurse strode towards the girl in the bed.

'I said shut up, you little bitch, or you'll be sorry.'

The girl lifted her hand to cover her mouth so the nurse couldn't see the grin underneath it.

'Carry on and you won't get any supper, do you hear me?'

The girl nodded and the nurse strode away. The girl looked at Lizzy, but pointed to the nurse. 'She is a bitch. No one likes her and she loves being mean. I'm Alice and I've been here for too long. So what did you do, kid? It must have been pretty bad to end up in the asylum.'

Lizzy had no idea what the asylum was. 'I don't know what you mean.'

'You must be pretty crazy to end up here, in The Moore,' the girl explained. 'This is the asylum. They call it a hospital, but it's not a proper hospital. It's where they put the crazy people, including the nutty kids. I'm here because they said I'm out of control. I hit my mother – who totally deserved it, by the way. She's a head case, and it's her that should be locked up in here, not me. Once my dad finds out what she's done, he'll come and get me out of here. He won't let me stay in here when he realises where I am.'

Lizzy felt her eyes go blurry once more, this time from the hot tears that had started to fall down her cheeks. She wasn't sure why she was here, except for her brother being dead. Still, she had no idea why her mum and dad would send her to this horrible place.

The girl on the bed shushed her. 'Look, don't cry: if that nurse hears you she'll be even meaner to you than she already is. I'm sure there must be a good reason why you're here; maybe you're poorly and need a rest to get better. If I were you, I'd keep quiet and eat your food when they bring it, then I'd go to sleep because morning will come faster while you sleep. Then your parents will probably come and get you out of here and take you home.'

Lizzy lifted her sleeve to wipe the tears and snot off her face. 'Do you think so? I don't know why they've sent me here.'

'I'm sure they will. Anyway, there isn't anything you can do tonight, and if you do nothing but snivel and feel sorry for yourself, she'll have a field day with you.' Alice pointed to the nurse, who had her back to them and was talking on the telephone.

'OK, I'll try not to cry.'

'That's a girl; you have to be tough and brave if you don't want to be crying every five minutes because of her.'

* * *

Alice turned away from Lizzy and lay on her side. She knew that whatever the kid had done must have been pretty bad. She probably wasn't going to be getting out of here soon, but Alice didn't have the heart to tell her that. The girl was so young – too young to be in here. Alice was going to have to break her rule of only looking out for herself and help the kid out, at least until she found her feet and could stand up for herself.

CHAPTER NINE

Alice Evans pulled the coffee shop door shut and turned the key. The coffee machine had broken along with the till, and the manager had told her to shut up shop and go home. The security alarm wasn't working and she was glad, because it was such a struggle to remember the right sequence of numbers to set it. Her memory had improved a lot over the years, but it was still not as sharp as it had been before she was taken into hospital. It still amazed her that she'd actually got a job in the coffee shop, although she knew that it was more down to luck than talent – the manager was a friend of her daughter's, and a kind girl. She must have felt sorry for Alice after she'd been fired from her last job. Alice could make the coffee OK, but she'd had to practise a lot to get the lattes and cappuccinos of a drinkable standard. As long as she didn't look at the length of the queue she was all right; when she did, it would send her into mild panic. Today had been quiet, thankfully.

Her daughter was waiting for her in the car, along with her gorgeous granddaughter, Gracie. Alice could drive, but she found it a struggle. Traffic lights and roundabouts confused her, so usually Beth would pick her up. She got into the car now and breathed out a sigh of relief.

'Hi, Mum, busy day?'

Alice nodded. 'Not too bad, how are you?' She began to dig around in her handbag, bringing out a paper bag filled with cakes. 'I got you both a present.'

Beth glanced at the bag. 'Mum, I told you not to bring cakes home. I end up stuffing my face with them all.'

Alice chuckled. 'Sorry, I forgot. I hate to see them go to waste. It's such a shame; they just throw them in the bin.'

'Why don't you ask Charlotte if you can give them to the homeless people that hang around the pier?'

'Oh, I couldn't do that dear. It's not right, all those youngsters sleeping in that abandoned bingo hall. It would break my heart to see them; I hate to think of them living like that.'

'I suppose you're right. You'd end up inviting them all back to your house for tea and a warm bath! You're far too trusting. Are you coming to my house for tea, or do you want to go home and sort yourself out?'

'Well, if you're offering, that would be nice. I can bath Gracie and put her to bed for you.'

Beth reached out and patted her mum's hand. 'That would be great, thank you. She's been a little terror all day.'

They drove past the turning to The Moore and Alice shivered. There were police cars everywhere. A van was parked blocking the turn-off to the hospital. Beth craned her neck to see what was going on as her mum looked the other way. 'Oh dear, that doesn't look good, does it? Look at all the police cars. I wonder what's happened? It must be pretty bad.'

She glanced at her mum, then reached out to pat her hand. 'Sorry, Mum. I know how much you hate that place.'

Alice turned to look at her. 'It's a bad place, Beth; it always has been.'

They drove the rest of the way in silence, until they finally reached Beth's house on the outskirts of Brooklyn Bay. It was one of the new houses on an estate which had been built when they'd knocked the old grammar school down. Alice was very proud of her daughter. Beth was a clever girl, and Alice had done her best to make sure she'd had far more chances than Alice herself had ever been given. Beth had gone to college, then to university in Edinburgh where she'd got a first-class law degree. It was also where she'd met her husband, who was now a barrister. Alice wasn't keen on him. He reminded her of a doctor she'd known a very long time ago.

She shuddered. Just thinking about that man and how he'd ruined her life made her cold to the bone. It wasn't right, how he had justified what he'd done to those poor patients. Even though there had been a scandal a couple of years later, he'd still got off lightly. And it didn't change the fact that those poor kids had been injected with all sorts of drugs. Alice often wondered what they were doing with their lives now. Had they moved on? She hoped that most of them had managed to put it behind them, like she had.

The car door slammed, jolting her away from those awful dirty white walls of the hospital. She still couldn't bring herself to call it by its proper name. The only way she had coped over the years was by trying not to think about it, and when she did, by referring to it as 'the hospital'. She had never forgiven her mother for putting her in there and leaving her to rot. Alice would never have done that to Beth.

Beth, who was cradling her sleepy daughter in her arms, opened Alice's car door. 'Come on, Mum, you can put the kettle on. I'll have a plain old mug of tea please, no more fancy-coffee making for you today.'

Alice smiled; her daughter was such a good girl and Alice would never let anyone hurt her. She never had, even making her husband leave after one argument too many when Beth was a baby. She had decided that she'd rather struggle on her own than put her child in any danger. Getting out of the car now, she followed her daughter up the steps to the shiny oak front door. Walking inside, she kicked off her shoes. The house was full of cream carpets, which if you asked her was a huge mistake with a toddler, but who was she to tell them that? Beth could afford to have them professionally cleaned if they needed to.

Alice walked into the lounge, which still looked like a show home. Nothing was out of place. It was a lot different to the cramped council flat that they'd lived in when Beth was a baby. Walking into the large, open-plan kitchen, Alice filled the kettle. She took some tea bags from the cupboard and put them into the fancy teapot on the worktop, then perched herself on a bar stool. Beth walked in and Alice smiled at her. 'Where's Gracie?'

'I put her to bed, Mum. She fell asleep in the car.'

'Oh, wasn't I going to do that?'

'It's OK, you're making the tea instead. You can go and give her a kiss goodnight if want to.'

Alice nodded. 'That's all right, I don't want to disturb her.' She poured the tea into two matching mugs, adding the milk and passing one to her daughter. She cradled her own mug, forcing herself to watch the television that Beth had switched on. Anything to take her mind off that place where she'd spent the best part of her teenage years. That was the thing with that hospital: once you let it into your head, it was hard to push the memories out. They threatened to take over. It had been a god-forsaken place. It had done nothing except inflict needless pain and suffering onto the innocent souls within it, who had only needed some love and attention.

CHAPTER TEN

Lucy and Mattie arrived back at the station, cardboard coffee cups in hand. Lucy had a paper bag containing a huge slice of lemon cake, which Mattie had declined but was now eyeing up wistfully. Lucy went into her office and shut the door. It was a small room at the back of the open-plan CID office, with floor-to-ceiling glass walls . She set about closing all the blinds, needing five minutes to think to herself about what she wanted before heading up the briefing. As she closed the last blind, she noted that Mattie was perched on the corner of Col's desk, deep in conversation and sipping his hot drink. Browning was sitting at the desk opposite Mattie's. He was doing that awful typing/poking thing he did to input information into the computer. On a good day, people would put up with him, but if they were stressed Browning's typing made them even more so because it echoed around the entire building. The beauty of the old station had been that CID had been made up of an assortment of smaller offices, and usually they would leave Browning in one on his own so that he didn't annoy the fuck out of everyone. This new station was nice, but there were few places to go if you wanted some privacy.

Lucy took out a notepad and wrote down a list of enquiries that needed following up to be dished out at the briefing. A knock on the door made her elbow her latte, almost sending it flying as Tom walked in.

'You're back,' he said. 'Are you ready to do a briefing in five minutes?'

'Yes, sir, as ready as I'll ever be.'

'Did you find any more bodies up there?'

She shook her head. 'The good news is none – well, not on the ground floor anyway. The upper floors aren't really safe enough to search until we've had confirmation from a building inspector that they're not going to collapse.'

'Bollocks; it's never straightforward, is it? How much is that going to cost?'

She shrugged. 'There's no suggestion that there are more bodies up there. And it looks pretty safe to me. I'm quite happy to do a walkthrough of the upper floors; Mattie said the same.'

'Well, that's very good of you, but if they collapse whilst you're up there... Oh, Christ, I can't even contemplate the complications.'

'Apparently the estate agent who is dealing with the sale of it has been up there and said it was OK. Robbo didn't want a mob of coppers up there just in case.'

'Do you really think there won't be any more bodies up there?'

'Who knows? I'd like to say there won't be. I ventured halfway up and couldn't smell anything untoward, but until someone has checked each room it's impossible to say.'

Tom ran his hand over the stubble of his shaved head. 'Can we have a word with the estate agents, see if they know if a building inspector has certified it safe?'

'I've already asked; they're looking into it.'

'Thank you, Lucy. You're good and it's great to have you back.'

For a moment, she thought he was going to ask her if she was OK. He paused for a second and must have read the look on her face before turning around and walking back out. Lucy ate her cake. She needed the sugar rush to give her some energy to carry on, before she had to stand up in front of a room full of coppers and support staff. She'd had no lunch and had skipped breakfast; her stomach had been a churning mass of knots at the thought of having to sit opposite Sara Cross this morning. She was so relieved the session had been cut short – although this was an almighty mess, it was a hundred times better than that.

She brushed the crumbs from her top and realised, horrified, that she was still wearing her casual clothes and smelt bad. The briefing would have to wait a few minutes longer; she wasn't going to stand at the front of that room looking like this. She looked like she was about to go undercover on a drugs bust, not head up her team for a murder investigation.

Dashing out of her office, she went down to the locker room where she kept a spare suit and blouse in case of emergencies. She didn't have a spare pair of shoes, but at least if she stood behind the wooden lectern that all the sergeants leaned on when they briefed the shifts, she could hide her feet. She took the clothes into the ladies and did a quick change, ran a brush through her hair to neaten up her ponytail, then spritzed herself with someone's perfume they'd left on the sink. It wasn't her usual choice, but it didn't smell too bad.

By the time she reached the briefing room it was full: standing room only at the back. She squeezed past the crush to make her way to the front of the room, hoping no one would notice the bright yellow Converse on her feet. Just at this point, Tom came rushing in, managing to knock the mug of coffee he was carrying all over one of the student officers and causing a commotion, which allowed Lucy to take her place without so much as a second glance from anyone. It was a good job, she thought, that Tom's coffee was only lukewarm, or that would have been another bunch of forms for him to fill out.

'Right, are we all here then?' She looked around. Task Force were here, along with everyone from CID. Browning was glaring at her and she smiled at him. If he thought he was going to make her crack he'd have to try a bit harder than that. She'd thought he'd be jealous that she'd got her DI position before him, and it looked as if she might be right.

She coughed, and began her briefing. 'As you know, at eleven forty-five this morning, Cheryl Tate was showing a potential buyer around the old mental asylum. They discovered a body. However, we still have no means of identifying the victim. He was murdered in situ and left there. Dr Maxwell has suggested the cause of death is by lobotomy.'

There was an assortment of gasps and sighs from around the room.

'It's pretty horrific, to be honest,' Lucy said. 'Apart from that, we don't know much else.'

Tom, who had mopped up his coffee with a bunch of paper towels, made his way to stand next to Lucy. 'We agreed a forensic strategy with CSI and cordoned off what we deemed were the appropriate evidential areas. Then Task Force, along with some of yourselves, went in and searched the ground floor. Nobody found anything else, anything suspicious or that you thought was worth looking at?'

Every head in the room shook from side to side.

'The upstairs hasn't been searched,' Tom continued, 'and won't be until we have clarification that it's safe to do so. Lucy, what are our main priorities?'

She looked down at the notes she'd scribbled earlier. 'Obviously we need an ID on the victim. Browning, can you focus on that? Go through the missing persons' reports, locally then countrywide. I have a feeling that the victim is local though. The hospital is not something that's really talked about much, so I have an instinct that there is a personal connection to the hospital – perhaps the patients were treated badly in the months before it closed. Colin, have you made a start with the staff and patient lists?'

'Yes, boss. Well, I've been in touch with the health authority to request the information. From a general search on information about the asylum when it was open, I've discovered that at any one time there were around 2,400 patients and 453 staff.'

There were lots of sighs and murmurs around the room. Lucy felt her heart sink. This was going to be a long job.

'The good news is that because of the phasing out of mental hospitals back in the seventies, there were only children housed inside The Moore when it shut down. So looking at the timescale and taking into account the ages of the patients, we're not looking at thousands – maybe less than a hundred. It had become a sort of a dumping ground for kids with problems; some of them were in there just because they had special needs or couldn't read or write.'

'Wow, thank you for that, Colin,' Lucy said. 'Let's focus on the area the body was left in. Why ward thirteen? There must be some reason for this particular part of the hospital.. So I need to know who worked on it. This might narrow things down significantly. Of course, we might get lucky and get prints from the victim that have a match on the system. Failing that, hopefully someone will realise they're missing a husband, brother, dad, friend – and report him missing. Meanwhile, I want all the builders who are in the process of digging up the cemetery across the road questioned. Seeing as how there are no houses nearby, they are our only potential witnesses at the moment. I want to know if they've seen any vehicles coming to or from the asylum that don't belong to the estate agents, and I want CCTV enquiries done as soon as we finish in here.'

Browning lifted his hand. 'There are no cameras on the outside of the hospital, and the dead people in the cemetery don't have any, either.'

'No, I appreciate that. However, I want the houses checking along the stretch of road that leads to the asylum in both directions. Some of those are big, fancy houses and it's more than likely they have cameras. If we're very lucky, they might have captured a vehicle coming to and from there.'

Browning muttered. 'And we might as well be looking for a needle in a bloody haystack.'

There were a few sniggers that stopped as soon as Lucy stared at the offending officers.

'I think that's it for now. When we get confirmation from the estate agents about the safety of the second floor then the search teams can go back and check the rest of the hospital. Thank you all for your efforts; this is a difficult one and I do appreciate it, but let's do our best to find out who our victim is and get some justice for his family.'

She watched as they began to file out of room, knowing that they were all thinking that this job was going to last forever. She didn't blame them. It didn't look to her like this was going to be case closed any time soon.

CHAPTER ELEVEN

Lucy and Mattie arrived back at the asylum, which was now lit up with portable lights that were being run by the noisiest generator Lucy had ever heard. The dog had done a good job; not only had it found the point of entry into the asylum itself, it had also discovered a smaller rusted gate on the narrow service road that had been used to drive in and out of the grounds. Jack had found traces of tyre tracks and had taken mouldings.

By now, Lucy had swapped her Converse for her old pair of Magnums. They didn't really match the suit she was wearing, but at least they would stop her shoes from getting ruined. She waved at Jack, who had popped his head out of the building to speak to Amanda. He looked knackered. He nodded at Lucy, and she felt terrible for him and Amanda. This was a huge, nightmare of an area to search for clues.

Lucy and Mattie walked across to the main entrance where Amanda was dusting for prints. She looked at Lucy, then stared down at her feet.

'Mattie, did you bring some more shoe covers?'

He nodded, and pulled some out of his pocket, handing them to Lucy. Once they'd both covered their feet he fished in his other pocket and pulled out a handful of blue latex gloves. He passed her a pair and she began to tug them on.

'Amanda, was that side door the point of entry, and the office and foyer the primary scene?'

'Yes. It looks as if the victim walked through the building to that ward of his own free will. Jack said there were no signs of a struggle or any drag marks to indicate he was brought there unconscious. In fact, he said that apart from a couple of prints on the door they used, and the body, there is little other evidence. Of course, the fact that this place is falling to bits and full of debris doesn't help. It's a wreck. Jack has finished inside now, although he said not to release the scene for a while yet.'

Lucy stared up at the huge wooden entrance doors. 'Can I go back in? I want to take another look at the body and the building.'

Amanda nodded. 'You can, but you know what he's like. Don't touch anything at all.'

Lucy stepped inside. It was almost dark outside now and it was even darker in the foyer. She turned the torch on that Mattie passed to her and shone it around. He whistled behind her as he stepped inside.

'This is like some place from your worst nightmare. It's every haunted house and horror film I've ever watched rolled into one. Only you know what makes it a hundred times worse?'

She nodded. 'The fact that it's real, that this even exists. That men, women and poor, bloody children were kept locked up in here is far worse than any horror film.'

It really was awful. Now that the light was fading fast – even with the spotlights Jack had set up – the atmosphere was one of great blackness and despair. Lucy could feel it through every part of her body. She shone the torch towards the ward where the body was. Inside, she could see Jack giving everything the once-over. Then she turned the other way and shone the powerful torch down the nearest corridor. It seemed to go on forever, the torch beam dying out before it reached the end.

'This place is bloody huge,' she said.

'And creepy as fuck,' Mattie added.

It was creepy, but Lucy didn't believe in ghosts or things that went bump in the night. She didn't even feel that scared; well, not as much as Mattie was, judging by his high-pitched voice. What she really felt was sad – for whoever had spent their lives inside here. This building had housed thousands of mentally ill patients and she knew very little about its history, nor had needed to until now. It was one of those things every local knew about, but rarely discussed. When she'd been a response officer they would get called out here quite often, because of kids going ghost hunting or partying in the grounds, but she'd never thought about it beyond that. Now, she wanted to know everything about it.

'Apparently, this place was a state-of-the-art mental hospital at the time. Patients were sent here from all over the country for the radical treatments that they offered.'

'And you know this because?'

'My aunty Alice; told me that she used to work here when she was younger. I think she was a nurse. I tried not to listen to all of her stories, though, because they used to freak me out. She told me that they would lock naughty kids in here and they were never allowed out to see their parents. She was a bugger and would scare the shit out of me whenever I was being bad.'

'What, your cute aunty who is even shorter than me and is always baking apple crumbles?'

'Yep! Only she wasn't so cute when she was telling me and Daryl we were going to end up inside here and they'd make us vegetables.'

'Do you think she knew about the lobotomies then?'

'I suppose she did; she must have if they were as popular as Catherine said. You don't think she did it, do you?'

Lucy began to laugh. 'Don't be stupid, no. I'm thinking that we could probably do with speaking to her, though, to get some background information on the place. She might remember whose office it was that the body was found in. It would save us some time digging around.'

'Well, you know Alice, any excuse to feed someone apple crumble and sit gossiping. She'll be over the moon. She's always had a bit of a soft spot for you, too – just don't let her know about your tattoos. She doesn't like them.'

Lucy began to walk towards the light-filled entrance and the huge, sweeping staircase. 'We might as well go and check the upstairs; no point in keeping everyone hanging on waiting for the building inspector.'

'Really? You want just the two of us to go up there? In the dark, with just torches?'

She looked over her shoulder at his face to see if he was joking. He wasn't.

'Are you scared, Matthew? Because if you are, wait down here and I'll go on my own.'

'Don't be daft; I'm not scared. I just don't know if we should.'

'Well, it's your choice, obviously. I'm not going to make you accompany me somewhere that might be dangerous. You wait down here for me; I'll be as quick as I can.' She began to run up the stairs, not waiting to hear his reply. The sound of his much heavier footsteps began to follow her and she smiled to herself. She reached the first floor and shone her torch around. There were four sets of double doors. Behind them; sheets of darkness.

'I wonder how the killer knew where to find the trolley?' Lucy said. 'Whoever it is definitely must have been in here before, to know where to find it. If you were working on your own, would you really want to start searching this place looking for props with your victim present? I reckon they'd been here before and got it ready.'

'What do you mean, "props"?'

'Well, this is obviously staged. The killer could have just killed the victim anywhere and left his body on the floor. Why go to the trouble of luring him here, getting him on a trolley then stabbing him through the eye socket with that metal instrument? This is personal, not some random stranger killing.'

'You ever thought of becoming a psychological profiler, Lucy? Like that one on the television, what's his name?'

'I have no idea who you are talking about. And no, I can't say that it's ever crossed my mind.'

'Cracker, or that odd one out of *Wire in the Blood*. You'd fit right in, weighing up the loonies.'

Lucy stared at him. 'And what do you mean by that tasteless remark?'

Mattie shrugged. 'Nothing. You're good with the crazies though, aren't you? They all like you.'

'Have some respect, will you? A lot of people have died in here. Probably living the most miserable existence you could imagine. Let's not be disrespectful to their memories by using words like that. It's just not right.'

They carried on searching, going through each set of double doors and looking into all the rooms and empty wards. There were still metal beds everywhere, with wardrobes and drawers. The curtains around the beds were moth-eaten and hanging off the rails. In one side room there was even a set of toiletries laid out on the sink, covered in dust now, the liquid in the bottles a funny green colour.

Satisfied there were no more bodies, they went back downstairs. Jack had gone outside, so Lucy went out to find him. He was busy loading his van up with the equipment.

'So what's the verdict?' he asked as he saw her approach.

'Upstairs was clear and we've done everything that we possibly can; we need to go back and upload the images and book all the evidence in. Task Force can go back in tomorrow and do another search if you need it.'

'Can we get the body moved now?'

'As soon as the boss gives the go-ahead.'

Jack arched his eyebrow at her and it took a moment for it to sink in.

'Oh yes; I suppose that's me, then. I'm not used to being the one making the big decisions. I don't see why it can't be moved, if you're happy? At least it will be there for Catherine, so she can crack on with the PM first thing.'

Lucy took her radio out of her pocket, walking across to the gate where there were two PCSOs on scene guard. 'I'm going to request the duty undertakers come and move the body. If we leave you a car, will you be OK to stay on for a little while?'

They both nodded in unison.

'Thanks, I really do appreciate it. I'll get night shift to come and take over so you'll be back at the station by the end of your shift.'

Lucy walked back to the car, in which Mattie was now sitting with the engine running and the heater on full blast.

'What time do you think we'll get away, boss?'

'Your guess is as good as mine. Have you got somewhere you need to be?'

'No, just wondering. You know how long these things take.'

Lucy leant back in the seat and closed her eyes, signalling for him to be quiet for a while. The sooner they could ID the victim, the better. Currently, he was known as 'John Smith'.

Before they drove away, Mattie took out his phone and sent a quick text to the woman he was supposed to be meeting for a date: *Sorry, working late. Not sure what time I'll get there.* He slipped the phone back into his pocket before Lucy realised. He didn't want her asking any awkward questions or wondering what he was up to.

CHAPTER TWELVE

September 1975

It was night time, but Lizzy couldn't sleep. She had been asleep most of the day, and anyway, it was far too noisy in here. To occupy herself, she counted the beds in the ward. There were ten, containing figures of assorted sizes. The bed opposite her had a small boy tucked into it. He was sitting up and staring at her. He had a scruffy teddy bear clutched to his chest, and there was a line of saliva running down his chin. His tongue, which was huge, was resting on his lips and as yucky as it was, Lizzy couldn't help feel sorry for him. He looked so sad. She smiled at him and he stuck his tongue out at her, making her giggle. She stuck hers out back at him and his sullen face broke into a smile. One of the two night-shift nurses walked out of the medicine cupboard and straight towards him.

'Tommy, why are you not asleep? It's late.'

He stuck his tongue out at the nurse, who slapped his cheek in response. Tommy didn't cry, but held his hand to his cheek. Lizzy was too scared to move. She felt as if her chest were on fire. How dare that nurse hit that little kid? Were they even allowed to do stuff like that? She didn't think they were.

Tommy lay down, closing one eye, and the nurse walked away. As soon as the nurse's back was turned, he pushed himself up on his elbows, sticking his tongue back out at Lizzy. She grinned at him, then tried to settle back down to sleep. She could hear the nurses chattering away to each other in the small back office where they kept the files. They were talking about someone's boyfriend and giggling.

Just as Lizzy's eyes finally began to feel heavy, and she was beginning to drift off, she heard the mean nurse whispering.

'Did you see the latest list for procedures?'

'No, not yet. Are any of ours on it?

'Yes, that brat from bed ten who thinks she knows better than anyone else is down for a lobotomy. It says it's dependent upon her behaviour over the next few weeks. She's to be closely monitored and assessed to see if she's a suitable candidate.'

'I don't know why they don't just do it anyway. Who cares if she's suitable or not? It will make our lives easier if we don't have to argue with her every day. She'd soon change her tune if she knew what was in store for her, wouldn't she?'

'Probably, so it might be best not to tell her.'

The nurses began to giggle again. Lizzy wondered who the kid was in bed ten, and what they were going to do to her, before her eyes closed as she drifted off.

The sound of squealing woke her up. In her dream she had been at home in her own bed and her dad had been sitting on the bed next to her, reading her a story, just like he had done every night until they'd brought the baby home. Then she'd had to start tucking herself into bed. Lizzy looked around, unable to remember where she was – until suddenly her hair was tugged so hard her eyes began to water.

'Ouch! Get off me, you little brat!'

As she struggled to free herself, Lizzy saw two nurses running in her direction. One of them had one of those awful sharp syringes in her hand. For a moment, she wondered what she'd done wrong – and then the grip on her hair loosened as the kid let go and threw himself under her bed to get away from the nurses. She still wasn't sure who it was until she heard the nurse growl, 'Tommy!' He was halfway down the ward by this point, skidding under beds to get away from them. Lizzy found herself hoping that he did, even though he had hurt her.

There was a large crash: the nurse with the needle in her hand had tripped over a wheelchair that Tommy had pushed in her way. It was quite spectacular, the way the woman fell into it and somersaulted over it, landing in a heap on the floor with a loud 'Jesus, fucking Christ! You little bastard; I'll get you!'

The other nurse stopped mid-step, clearly wondering whether she should continue chasing Tommy – who had now run into the shower rooms – or help her colleague up. She decided she'd better help the other woman up and held out her hand; the first nurse grasped it and stood up. She looked as if she'd been in a fight. Her tights were laddered. Her uniform was no longer white, it was smeared in dirt from the wheels of the chair, and her cap wasn't sitting straight on her head. She limped back to the nurses' station with the help of the other nurse, leaving the syringe full of brown liquid where it had rolled on the floor under a nearby bed.

Lizzy wasn't sure why, but she wanted that syringe. She jumped out of bed and ran along to where the wheelchair was toppled over. In case anyone was watching, she made out that she was just picking up the wheelchair – but at the same time, she bent down to grab the syringe and slid it up her sleeve. Then she went into the shower rooms to see where Tommy was.

It was cold in the shower rooms. They smelt of damp and something old inside. Tommy was nowhere to be seen, but there was a door closed at the other end which Lizzy knew he must be hiding behind. Alice came in behind her, and walked straight to the end of the room to whisper at the door.

'Nice one, kid, but you're going to get your arse kicked. You know that, don't you?' There was no noise from the other side and Alice walked away, towards one of the shower cubicles, with her towel slung over her shoulder.

Lizzy waited until the shower was running, then looked around for somewhere to hide the syringe. Before she had found anywhere, a heavy hand slapped the side of her head so hard that she felt her head snap forwards. The syringe was grabbed out of her fingers.

'And what, may I ask, were you going to do with that? This is dangerous medicine, not to be messed around with.'

Lizzy looked up to see the doctor from yesterday standing behind her.

'Get back to your bed; I'll deal with you later. Where's Tommy?'

Lizzy was still shocked by the blow, but she looked at him and shook her head. 'I don't know who Tommy is, and I just found that needle on the floor. The nurse dropped it.'

The doctor stared at her, as if by looking into her eyes he could tell whether or not she was telling the truth. Alice, who had emerged from the shower with her towel wrapped around her, and was standing watching with her arms folded across her chest, had moved in front of the wooden door where Tommy was hiding. The doctor marched down towards her.

'Where is he, Alice? He's been a bad boy and needs to take his medicine.'

'I don't know who you mean. And how has he been a bad boy, exactly? We're all bad kids according to you, Dr Wilkes.'

'I'm not going to argue with you, Alice. Step to one side or you'll be getting some of the same as Tommy is about to.'

She glared at him, but she clearly knew what the stuff was in that glass syringe. Moving out of the way, she grabbed Lizzy's hand and led her out of the shower room. Two male porters came running in past them, both of them out of breath, and Alice shook her head in disgust. 'Three grown men,' she whispered to Lizzy, 'to cope with an eight-year-old handicapped kid.'

CHAPTER THIRTEEN

Mattie and Lucy had finally left the hospital grounds and were on their way back to the station. Mattie, who had been checking his watch every few minutes, looked at it once more.

'It's almost nine o'clock.'

'I know,' Lucy replied. 'I can read the time. Are you sure you don't need to be somewhere? You're getting on my nerves with your sighing and clock-watching.'

'Well, actually, I was supposed to be meeting this bird tonight. I've told her I can't make it, though.'

'Why didn't you say something sooner?' Lucy asked.

'Because I dragged you into work early for this and I would have felt bad leaving you on your first day back.'

Lucy patted his arm. 'You know, you drive me mad, then out of the blue you say something that knocks me for six. I appreciate you hanging around, but as soon as we get back, you get off. I don't want to be responsible for ruining what's left of a hot date.'

Mattie laughed. 'Cheers, Lucy. You know, I'm really glad that you're back. It's been so boring around here without you. This is the first murder we've had in months.'

Lucy stared out of the window, trying to stop the bloody images of the lifeless Natalia and her daughter Isabella from filling her mind. It had been so close, so damn close. Just a few minutes more and she wouldn't have had to be terrified every night of falling asleep and seeing their bodies in all their blood-red glory.

Glassy-eyed, staring at her. Accusing her of letting them down. A cold shiver ran down her spine.

'You're welcome,' she said, trying to get her mind back to the here and now. 'I'm glad that I'm of some use. Although I'm not sure that I'm altogether happy that there's a murder the same day I come back to work.'

The new multimillion-pound police station came into view and she shook her head. 'That is one fucking ugly building.'

'Yep, it is,' Mattie agreed. 'Modern architecture isn't all it's cracked up to be.'

The gates opened to let Lucy drive in. She followed the one-way system, stopping next to Mattie's pickup truck. His car looked like one of those monster trucks compared to her tiny Fiat.

'Go on, get yourself away,' she said. 'I'll update everything and speak to CSI tonight; you just make sure you're in bright and early tomorrow. Don't drink too much, because the post-mortem is scheduled for first thing.'

Mattie grinned at her and got out of her cramped car, relieved to be able to stretch his legs. 'See you in the morning, boss – and thank you.' He slammed the door too hard and Lucy heard him shout 'sorry'.

She drove off to park in a space further up, nearer to the station's rear entrance. She didn't intend on being here too long herself. After all, they had no family or friends to visit because no one had yet come forward to report their John Smith as missing. He wasn't on the system as a missing person because Browning had phoned her a couple of hours ago after he'd done some checks to find out. Tomorrow, before the post-mortem, he would be fingerprinted and his DNA would be taken. Hopefully, they would find some kind of link. She hated it when they had a body and no one to claim them. To die alone was a terrible thing; to be murdered in cold blood and for your loved ones to not even know must be horrific.

This job was awful at times, she thought, but impossible to give up on. For Lucy, there was no greater sense of satisfaction than catching a killer and seeing them brought to justice. She had dreamt about being a detective ever since she'd been a kid, when she'd watched every American crime show on the television and had read as many true crime books as she could find. What she'd really wanted was to be an FBI agent, but she'd realised as she'd got older that the fact that she wasn't American meant that she never could be. So she'd settled on becoming a copper, and working her way up to her current rank. It hadn't been easy and she'd had to sacrifice a lot to get where she was today: mainly her husband and her child. Her chest heaved, full of guilt, as she wondered once more what would have happened if she'd got a normal job or had stayed at home to look after Ellie.

She knew what would have happened, though. She would have gone insane. She liked the challenge of solving clues and tracking down killers. *You are what you are, Lucy, so don't be too hard on yourself.*

The inside of the station still smelt brand new – of paint and fresh carpet. Lucy made her way up to the CSI department on the second floor. There wasn't much more she could do tonight; they had no solid leads. In fact, they had no leads whatsoever. A large glass of wine and a takeaway were on the menu once she got home. She let out a loud yawn. It had been a long day. Last night, she'd tossed and turned, worried about coming back into work – but she needn't have bothered. No one had taken much notice of her. She was old news, which was exactly how she liked it.

As Mattie parked outside the house on the tree-lined street, he wondered if he was doing the right thing. He liked Heidi – in fact, he liked her a lot – and the sex was amazing. But – and this was a big 'but' – he'd forgotten how much he enjoyed working with Lucy, and he hadn't realised until today just how much he'd missed her. And maybe not just as a colleague.

Movement from Heidi's upstairs window broke his trance. She was watching him, and he felt a spark of guilt for thinking about another woman when he was in a relationship. Heidi waved at him, then drew her curtains. Mattie's stomach let out a loud groan. He was starving. He got out of the car, and as Heidi's front door opened, all thoughts of Lucy were pushed to the back of his mind. He tried his best not to whistle at the tight-fitting black lace dress and stilettos she was wearing. Lucy would probably turn up in a pair of Wonder Woman leggings and her trusty Converse if they ever went out on a date. He swore underneath his breath. *Enough with Lucy.*

'Wow. You look amazing, Heidi,' he said. 'Totally amazing.'

She laughed. 'Thank you. I was hoping you'd be here in time to scrub my back. I couldn't wait any longer and had to bathe all on my own.'

'Yeah, I'm really sorry about that. Work was mental. A murder came in that I've had to work on all day, and to be fair I'm lucky I was able to get away now. It's a good job Lucy is back; if she wasn't, I'd probably still be there.'

He followed her inside the house, which smelt of garlic – something Italian cooking. They went into the kitchen, where the table was set for two and a candle was flickering away. There was a bowl of salad, and a bottle of uncorked red wine and two wine glasses: one half-filled, the other empty.

'Do you need me to do anything?' he asked.

'No, thank you; it's all under control.'

Mattie watched as Heidi took a huge dish of creamy chicken pasta out of the oven, along with a tray of home-made garlic bread. He found himself hoping she hadn't gone overboard on the garlic, because he didn't want to stink Lucy out tomorrow. Heidi plated his food up and passed it to him. He took the plate

from her, then piled it high with salad, and waited for her to sit
down with her much smaller plate before he began to tuck in.

'Is it OK for you?' she asked.

Mattie, who had just forked a mouthful of food into his
mouth, stuck his thumb up and Heidi laughed. When he could
talk, he took a sip of the wine she'd poured him and reached out
to stroke her hand.

'This is amazing, thank you. In fact, you're amazing.'

She smiled at him as she played around with her plate of food,
'So, tell me about this murder. It sounds fascinating.'

Mattie looked down at his food, then at her, and she lifted her
hand to her mouth.

'Oh, I'm so sorry. I didn't think; I suppose the last thing you
want to talk about whilst eating is a dead body.'

He laughed. 'It doesn't bother me any more. I mean, it used to,
in the beginning. I'd look at a decomposing body and not be able
to eat for hours – but not now. I guess it's like anything: if you do
something long enough, the horror of it wears off and it's just another day at the office. I wouldn't dream of talking about it to you
whilst you're eating, though. Take it from me, it's not very nice.'

'OK, sorry,' she laughed, flushing. 'I hope you don't think I'm
ghoulish or anything. It's just that your job is so interesting compared to mine – all I do is work with bratty kids all day! I sometimes wish I'd chosen a career in the police instead. You know,
I always used to watch *Quincy* when I was a child and loved it.'

Mattie had no idea what she was talking about, but tried not
to show it. Heidi laughed anyway, picking up on his confusion.
'It was a show about an American pathologist who used to solve
the murders of the bodies he had to autopsy. It was a bit corny,
come to think about it.'

'Ah. It must have been a bit before my time.'

'I would probably say it was a lot before your time, and don't
apologise. Yes, there is a twenty-year age difference between us,

but it doesn't bother me in the least. I have to admit, I think I got the better deal.'

He felt her foot begin to make its way up his trouser leg and he grinned at her. 'I think it was me who got the better deal. Not only can you cook, you're a fantastic...'

Mattie stopped himself from being crude just in time. Sometimes he forgot himself. As if she knew exactly what he'd been about to say, though, Heidi's foot began to massage his crotch. He almost choked on the full slice of garlic bread he'd just shoved into his mouth.

She dropped her foot to the floor. 'Sorry, I can't help myself. Just looking at you turns me into some kind of nymphomaniac.'

'That's fine with me. Don't you know that's every man's fantasy?' He lifted his wine glass, swallowing the rest of it in one gulp.

She stood up, walking around to where he was sitting. She leant right over his shoulder and he felt the soft swell of her breasts brush against his arm. 'Have you finished? Would you like some dessert?'

He shook his head, standing up he pulled her close. 'I'll wait for my dessert. Right now, I want to eat you instead.'

She began to giggle as she took his hand, leading him towards the stairs and her king size bed.

Lucy had opted for pizza as her takeaway of choice. She pulled up outside her favourite Italian, wondering if she should have gone for something a little healthier. Sod it, though; she was starving, and the last thing she wanted to eat was a bowlful of salad. She wanted meatballs, pepperoni and onions, smothered in hot melted cheese.

The huge man behind the counter smiled to see her. 'Lucy, where have you been? It's good to see you.'

He put the huge box in front of her and she nodded in appreciation. 'Busy; you know what it's like. I've also been trying to be good.'

He put his hands on his hips. 'You can afford to eat pizza every night with your figure.'

She laughed. 'I'm not sure about that; I'd end up looking like one.'

She passed her money across to him and he blew her a kiss. 'Enjoy, my lovely lady, I've made it extra special for you.'

She picked up the box and smiled. 'Thank you, Alberto.'

'You're welcome – and don't leave it so long next time, eh?'

As Lucy manoeuvred the huge pizza box into the front passenger seat, she realised it would probably last her all weekend. A wave of sadness washed over her. Before Ellie had turned into the nightmare child from hell, they'd used to have a movie-and-pizza night once a week. She wished that she could turn back the clock to the time when her daughter hadn't hated her so much, and George had still loved her enough to stick around.

Ten minutes later, she parked up outside her semi-detached house and got out. At least she hadn't needed to go to the off-licence – she always had a couple of bottles of wine in the fridge for emergencies. As she let herself into her too-quiet house, she dropped the pizza box and a brown folder containing copies of the case files onto the coffee table in the living room. She went into the kitchen for a plate, then opened the fridge and poured herself a large glass of rosé. If she didn't have some, it would take her ages to get to sleep. Her mind would keep on replaying today's events over and over, chasing away her tiredness, and the last thing she needed tomorrow was to be knackered and not on top form.

Putting the glass next to the pizza box, she ran upstairs and had the quickest shower she could manage. Then, after dressing in her warm fleecy pyjamas and wrapping her wet hair in a towel, she returned downstairs. She opened the pizza box and almost managed to shove an entire slice into her mouth at once. It was divine: just the right amount of grease and carbs to satisfy her craving.

Turning the television on, she flicked through the channels, looking for something that would make her laugh. She smiled to discover *Bridesmaids* had not long started. It was one of her favourite films; she loved Melissa McCarthy and the guy who played the cop, Chris O'Dowd. He was so cute, with that lovely Irish accent. Soon, all thoughts of Ellie and George were pushed to one side as she ate her pizza, sipped her wine, and giggled out loud at the film.

When she couldn't eat any more, she stood up to get the huge corkboard that she kept in the kitchen pinned full of Ellie's school stuff and appointments. Taking them all off, she then placed the board on the sofa next to her and began to re-pin it with the various pictures and pieces of information they had on the case up to now. There wasn't much, but it was a start –

and now she didn't have to worry about Ellie coming home and seeing it, she could leave it out. In fact...

Standing up, she crossed to the wall above the fireplace and took down the huge canvas of herself, George and Ellie when she was a baby. She hung the corkboard there instead. Then she sat back down on the sofa, crossed her legs, pulled the soft woollen throw over her, and stared at the board. Taking a sip of wine, she picked up a notepad and pen off the coffee table, then began to write down the list of actions she wanted carrying out tomorrow. John Smith was her first priority now – until he had a proper name and a family that wanted him, she knew she wouldn't be able to concentrate on anything else.

CHAPTER FOURTEEN

Lucy arrived at work nice and early. She'd slept well, considering she'd spent the night curled up on her sofa. As she got out of her car, she was impressed to see Mattie walking towards her.

'Morning. How did your hot date go?'

She was taken aback to see the normally cool and collected Mattie's cheeks turn crimson. 'That good, eh? It's all right for some. Well, I hope she hasn't worn you out too much; we have a long day ahead of us.'

He yawned and she started to laugh.

'Bugger off, Lucy,' he said. 'I did well over my hours yesterday and I'm in much earlier than I'm down on duties for. Anyone would be tired.'

'Yes, anyone would. Especially someone who smells like a cross between a brothel and Debenhams perfume department. Is that red lipstick on your collar?'

Mattie shook his head and walked on ahead of her. She knew exactly where he was going – straight to the gents to check his collar. She smiled to herself. *Gotcha.*

Lucy went up to her office. She liked that the floor was deserted. She preferred this time of day, when the station was empty and she could think to herself in peace.

Mattie reappeared. 'You're such a liar. I have no lipstick on my collar.'

'I know, but you fell for it. Honestly, I'm not interested in your love life. Good for you that you have one and I hope that whoever it is makes you very happy. I really do.'

'Cheers, want a brew?'

Lucy gave it some serious thought. 'Only if you don't use milk out of the fridge that's gone past its sell-by date. You might be resistant to it, but my delicate taste buds aren't.'

Opening her desk drawer, she passed him her chipped Starbucks mug with her collar number written in black pen on the base. Mugs went missing all the time in the station, and it really annoyed her to see some student officer sipping their tea from her mug. Mattie took it and wandered off in the direction of the brew station at the end of the corridor.

Lucy opened her emails, reading the one from Catherine Maxwell first.

Be here for nine. I want to get started ASAP. I've got a busy day ahead of me.

Catherine.

Lucy picked up the file that she'd put together last night – the same one she'd made copies of and taken home with her – and began to flick through it.

Mattie returned, placing Lucy's mug on her desk. He watched as she peered into it and nodded, clearly relieved to see no specks of flaky milk floating around on top. She put down the file that she was reading and logged into the computer, opening up the folder that was running on the system for their John Smith.

'No one has come forward to report our victim missing then, judging by the lack of entries on it since we left last night?'

Mattie shook his head; he'd already been told this information by Col in the gents.

'Maybe he lived on his own and had no family or friends,' Lucy said. 'It happens.'

'Maybe he did.'

'Well, let's hope that someone comes forward today. And there's a chance we might get lucky with his fingerprints or DNA. For all we know, he could have been a master criminal with a file as long as your left leg.'

'That's very true, boss. Just because he looks like a sweet old man, it doesn't mean that he actually was, does it? As we know all too well. And if we're relying on his DNA coming back for identification then we'll be waiting forever; you know how long that takes.'

'Exactly,' Lucy said. 'Anyway, Catherine wants us at the mortuary by nine, so there's just enough time to read through this lot and drink this wonderful coffee that you made for me.'

Mattie looked at her to see if she was taking the piss, but she wasn't smiling – she was leaning on one elbow, staring at the computer screen, which she only ever did when she was concentrating. He left her to it. His desk was just outside her office. Near enough that he could hear her shout for him, but not so near that he had to sit and stare at her all day.

He should tell her about Heidi, he thought. There was no reason to be so secretive and act like a teenager about it. He supposed he was embarrassed by the whole situation – although really, he had nothing to be embarrassed about. Heidi was a good twenty years older than him, but it didn't matter because she looked better than half of the women in the station who were his own age.

He waited for his computer to log him on, and sipped his coffee, wondering why life had to be so complicated at times. He could hear Lucy frantically tapping on her keyboard inside her office. She was stressed. Whenever she was, her computer bore the brunt of it. Mattie finished his coffee, then went to rinse out his cup. Memories of what Heidi had done to him the previous night filled his mind. He was knackered and knew he would pay for it all day. Still, it had been very good, and he'd never had that kind of sex with any of his younger girlfriends.

Lucy joined him at the sink and began to wash her cup. 'I suppose we should make a move. The sooner it's done, the better.'

As they walked back to the office, they passed the open door to the CSI department. Lucy spotted Jack and Amanda inside, and stuck her head in.

'We're going up to the hospital now. I take it you got Catherine's email?'

Jack and Amanda were both tucking into bacon and egg buns; both of them stuck their thumbs up at Lucy. Jack had a line of yellow egg yolk slowly running down his chin and Lucy felt her stomach turn. She pointed at his chin and he picked up a napkin to wipe it.

Mattie shook his head. 'How can you guys eat that right before a post-mortem?'

Amanda smiled. 'Once you've seen one, you've seen them all. Isn't that right, Jack?'

He nodded in agreement. Lucy smiled. She was hungry this morning, too, despite having consumed most of her pizza last night. As soon as the post-mortem was over and her stomach could take it, she was going to the hospital canteen for a fry-up. She preferred not to eat before one if she could help it, just in case she did throw up. Although, touch wood, she hadn't been sick since her first – but she didn't want to push her luck. Besides, her poor stomach was probably still trying to digest last night's late supper.

As they walked out to the car park, Mattie took out his car keys.

'It's all right, I'll drive,' Lucy said. 'I can squeeze my car in almost any corner of the hospital car park, whereas you'll spend ages trying to park that beast.'

Mattie sighed. She knew he hated being seen in what he described as her 'mint green tin can'.

'You know,' he said now, 'it wouldn't be so bad if it was plain white. It's like driving around in a mint choc chip ice cream cone. Do you have no self-respect, Lucy? You're a DI now. You should be driving around in something which reflects your status – a BMW or a Mercedes.'

'Don't you disrespect my car! It's cute, my favourite colour and cheap to run. Not like yours. Do you have any idea of the damage you're doing to the environment driving that around?'

He shrugged. 'Compared to what, the nuclear power plant up the road that emits green clouds of toxic gas when we're all in bed? Nah, that's rubbish. You're just jealous that you don't have a car like mine.'

'Believe me when I say I'm not jealous. I'm glad I don't have to drive around in that.' Lucy strode towards her car and Mattie had to pick up his pace to keep up with her.

Catherine Maxwell was waiting for them to arrive at the mortuary. She was already dressed in the signature pink scrubs that she insisted on wearing for every post-mortem. It was always a bit of a shock for student officers when they attended their very first PM to be greeted by the ultra-glamorous Dr Maxwell. Her long brown hair was always immaculately pinned up in a chignon, and there was normally a diamante clip securing it to her head. She had told Lucy that the hospital had refused to buy her the pink scrubs so she'd ordered them herself. When Lucy had asked her why she didn't just use the standard blue ones, Catherine had laughed.

'Just because I deal with the dead, it doesn't mean that I shouldn't make an effort for them. I refuse to spend my life wearing those dowdy blue scrubs – and besides, I've never really suited blue.'

Lucy hadn't been able to argue with her. She was the complete opposite to Catherine, much preferring to dress down rather than up. If she could, she'd wear her jeans and Converse all day every day to work. Then again, if she looked as good as Catherine she'd probably make a point of wearing pink scrubs as well.

Mattie smiled at Catherine. Lucy knew that he had a soft spot for the doctor, even though she was tough on him. She always made a point of asking him lots of questions.

When everyone was scrubbed up, and Jack and Amanda had flipped a coin to decide who was going to be the wet CSI and who the dry, Catherine began. Jack, who had won the prime position of dry CSI, was ready with his pen to mark up the exhibits as they were passed to him. Amanda, having lost, would have to do the photography and work closely with Catherine.

The mortuary technician wheeled the trolley over with their John Smith on it, and Catherine read out the information from the tag attached to the zipper on the outside of the bag. It was cut off, and the body bag unzipped to reveal the elderly male inside.

Catherine began by examining his fully dressed body, checking to see if there were any other tears or defects in his clothing. These would be used to correlate with any injuries they might find once his clothes had been removed.

'His clothes are intact,' Catherine said. 'There are no signs of any obvious injuries on his body, apart from the massive trauma to his eye socket.'

She continued doing what she was so very good at, whilst Lucy watched and Mattie took notes. Lucy knew Mattie preferred not to watch every slice and dice, so she'd let him take the notes to keep him busy. Every item of the victim's clothing was removed, examined and sealed into evidence bags for identification. This was fairly straightforward, and before long the body was undressed, lying naked under the glare of the bright lights, ready for the external examination. Catherine began to describe his physical appearance to Mattie, who was trying his best to write fast and keep up. Catherine used a Dictaphone, but Lucy preferred that they had their own set of notes as well.

'We have a male around seventy to eighty years of age, approximately five foot nine inches tall. He's slightly overweight, no visible scars or tattoos. Teeth are all false.' She picked up his arms to examine his wrists. 'There is slight bruising to the wrists where he was restrained by the leather straps on the table.'

She pointed to the wrists, which Amanda photographed, taking close-ups.

'The trauma to the eye is the cause of death.' The sound of the camera clicking filled the room. Catherine took hold of the metal spike and pulled it from the wound. The squelching sound made Lucy grimace. Catherine held the instrument next to the injured eye socket so that Amanda could photograph it.

'And this is an orbitoclast, which is a modified ice pick to me and you. It's the cause of death. Can you see the depth of the injury? Whoever did this definitely meant business. This would have been inserted into the victim's eye socket using a hammer. Ordinarily, for a lobotomy, the surgeon would only insert it far enough to be able to separate the frontal lobes from the thalamus – which is the part of the brain that receives and relays our sensory input. However, the killer has used the hammer – or something similar – to drive the orbitoclast as far into the brain as possible, causing death.'

Lucy shuddered. What a terrible way to die.

Finally, Catherine was ready to make the thoracoabdominal incision, more commonly known as the Y incision. She made a point of puncturing the victim's abdominal wall so that the morbidity gas was released; this made Amanda, Mattie and Lucy all groan in unison. Lucy knew that if Catherine hadn't done that, the gas which had built up would have made the body sit up on the table – which was something she had only ever seen once when she was in her training, and never wanted to see ever again.

When Catherine had finished weighing and measuring all the internal organs, they were placed in a plastic bag, ready to be sewn back into the victim's body cavity. The whole process was so awful, yet necessary. Lucy had noticed that Mattie hadn't looked up from his notepad for the last twenty minutes, and she couldn't blame him. Lucy had felt her own stomach clench a few times and she had to concentrate on taking deep breaths to keep herself calm. When Catherine finally stepped away from the body, the relief in the room was almost tangible.

'Well, in my opinion, "John Smith" died as a result of the catastrophic injury to his brain through his eye socket. The manner of death was definitely homicide. Unless the man was Harry Houdini, there was no way he would have been able to use the orbitoclast to pierce his own eyeball and brain.'

Lucy sighed. They had already established all of this at the actual crime scene. The post-mortem had been necessary, though; official conclusions had to have been reached for when they caught the killer and it went to court.

'Thank you so much, Catherine,' she said, trying not to sound disappointed.

'You're welcome. I'd appreciate it if you didn't bring me any more of these, Lucy. For the first time in forever I actually felt a little bit queasy doing this one – and I thought I was hardened to everything.'

'I'll try my best. Not sure I can promise you, though.'

CHAPTER FIFTEEN

Lucy, who had scrubbed her hands clean more times than she could count, was still outside the changing rooms before Mattie. She leant against the cold painted wall and took some deep breaths. The door to the men's changing room slammed open and she watched as Mattie walked out, his face even paler than hers.

'This is some fucked up shit, boss. I mean, it's serious to do what that killer did.'

'It's serious to do what every killer does.'

'You know what I mean. This is unlike anything I've ever seen. You know yourself – in this town, when a murder happens, well… It's not like this one, is it?'

Lucy shook her head. He had a point.

'I mean, stranger-killings are very rare, aren't they?' Mattie continued. 'It's normally some domestic gone wrong, or something to do with women, drugs or sex. But you can usually guarantee the victim and the killer know each other. I think that in this case, the killer has taken revenge on the victim. So therefore they must have known them.'

'I think you're right, Mattie. It does look like a revenge killing. But revenge for what? Until we can ID the victim, we have nowhere to start looking for a connection. We have no choice: we need to issue a press release with a picture of his face and hope that someone recognises him, otherwise this isn't going anywhere.'

They had been walking towards the bank of lifts at the very end of the hospital corridor and talking in whispers – there were too many normal members of the public around. Lucy spoke in a normal voice now: 'I'm starving. Let's go and get something to eat from the canteen and have a think. I can't work well on an empty stomach.'

'I don't know if I'm hungry, boss.'

'Well I am; you can decide whether or not you are whilst I'm eating.'

They reached the lift and Lucy pressed the call button. The doors opened and they stepped to one side to allow a porter to push out a bed with an elderly woman on it. They took the lift to the floor below, where the huge canteen was situated. As the lift doors opened, the smell of fried bacon hit their nostrils and Mattie decided that he was hungry after all.

They joined the queue of visitors and doctors and nurses on breaks, all of whom were waiting for the full English breakfast that the hospital canteen was famous for. Lucy had everything except for black pudding; Mattie asked for the same. They sat down to eat at a table in the far corner of the restaurant, as far away from anyone else as they could manage. Neither of them spoke as they ate their breakfasts, both of them trying not to think about the post-mortem. When they'd finally finished the food, and were just sipping their coffees, Lucy took out a notebook from her pocket.

'The victim had something to do with the asylum; I'd swear on it. And I think our killer was linked to the asylum, too. We're talking years ago – whatever happened between them must have happened a long time ago because the hospital has been shut since the seventies.'

'So we're looking at a killer who has harboured a grudge for – what? Over forty years?' Mattie frowned. 'I don't know about that, Lucy. Why now? It seems a bit too far-fetched. Maybe we're completely wrong and it's just some sick random killing.'

Lucy's phone began to ring and she picked it up. 'DI Harwin.' She listened to the angry voice on the other end. 'Have you tried phoning my husband George? I mean, Ellie's dad.' She looked at Mattie, her face a mask of anger. 'Right. Well, I'm at work and it's not a very good time for me, to be honest.' A few moments passed as she listened. 'I'll be there as soon as I can.'

She ended the call. 'Bloody kids.'

'Ellie?'

'Yes, Ellie. She's only gone and nicked some expensive make-up from Debenhams and been caught by the security staff. She has more make-up than me; she doesn't need any more and she certainly doesn't need to steal the stuff.'

'Where is she now?'

'Back at Burlington House. There was a meeting about Ellie today, which George promised me he'd attend. I can't believe she'd be so stupid. Did you know that she moved in with her dad the day after I was suspended?'

Mattie shook his head.

'She told George that I was angry and taking everything out on her.'

'Ouch, that's mean. Were you?'

'No, I bloody wasn't. She never bothered to tell him that me being angry wasn't because of what happened at work. She conveniently forgot to mention that it was because she'd been found in a back street by a PCSO lying in a puddle of her own vomit, off her head on cheap vodka.'

'Look, you go and sort Ellie out, and I'll go back to the station and fill Tom in on the post-mortem,' Mattie said. 'There's not much we can do until we get an ID on the victim. If anything comes up I'll let you know.'

'Thank you, Mattie; I really appreciate it. I won't be long, because if George doesn't turn up I'll drive her to his offices and march her in there.'

Lucy stood up and left Mattie to clear away the plates and mugs.

CHAPTER SIXTEEN

By the time Lucy had found a parking space in the busy town centre, and had then walked the short distance to the youth offending support workers' offices, she was even angrier than before. It wasn't fair. She'd done her very best for Ellie. Yes, they argued a lot, but didn't all teenagers hate their parents? Lucy felt as though Ellie held everything against her – the long hours she worked not helping. At least she tried her best to be a good mother, which was more than some women did.

She buzzed to be let into the building and was met at the door by a girl who didn't look much older than Ellie. Lucy felt some of the anger begin to subside when the girl smiled at her. Her daughter was a mess; her whole life was one big, bloody mess, if she was honest. She'd known the teenage years would be tough, but no one had warned her they would be this tough.

The girl led her up a winding staircase to the next floor, where she could hear a commotion. There was a lot of shouting, and she recognised the petulant voice as belonging to her daughter. Inhaling, she stepped into the room to be greeted by Ellie, who was standing behind a chair, both hands gripping the back of it as if she was about to launch it at the woman opposite her.

'Ellie, what are you doing?'

Ellie rolled her eyes at her mum, but let go of the chair.

'What is wrong with you, Ellie?'

'Mrs Younger.'

Lucy turned to the woman, cutting her off. 'It's Ms Harwin, actually.'

'Oh, I'm sorry. Ms Harwin. I'm afraid Ellie is out of control. I believe that she's been drinking in the Kings this morning when she should have been in maths.'

Lucy looked at the large clock on the wall behind her daughter. It was only twenty past eleven. She felt her heart sink. The Kings was the local dive pub where all the hardened alcoholics spent their allowances. What the hell was she supposed to do now, and where was George? He was the calmer, cooler, wiser parent.

Ellie glared at the woman. 'You fucking grass.'

Lucy felt her cheeks flush. 'Ellie, don't you dare speak to anyone like that. I won't have it. What the hell is wrong with you?'

She felt a warm hand touch her arm and she turned to see George. Relief flooded through her. They might have their differences, but George was a good man and a brilliant dad. Ellie burst into tears at the look of disappointment on his face, and Lucy felt a small spark of smugness ignite inside her chest. Good; she wanted Ellie to understand what a disgrace she was.

George took hold of Ellie's arm and pushed her down onto the nearest chair. The woman who was watching nodded her head in approval, which instantly made Lucy feel angry towards her. What did she know about their life and how hard it had been for Lucy, managing on her own?

'Thank you, Mr Younger; I think things were getting a little out of hand. I'm Jane Toppan, Ellie's support worker while she's here at youth offending.' She reached out and shook George's hand, then held out her hand towards Lucy, who took it reluctantly.

'Look,' Jane continued, 'I don't know what's caused Ellie to act like this today. I can say that it's completely out of character for her. She is normally very well-behaved and respectful towards her peers and the staff. Perhaps, Ellie, you could tell us what happened, and then we can try to figure out what to do?'

Lucy looked across at her daughter, who was now sitting with her head bowed, looking as if she was the one who had been hard done by. Ellie shrugged her shoulders as if she couldn't care less. Lucy opened her mouth, but George beat her to it.

'Ellie had some news yesterday that she didn't take too kindly to, and I think this is her way of letting us know exactly how she felt about it. Why, though, Ellie? Your behaving like a spoilt six-year-old child isn't going to make any difference to how things are at all.'

Lucy's mind was frantically trying to work out exactly what it was that George had told their daughter to get this reaction from her. She didn't have to wonder for very long.

'Don't lie. When that blonde-haired bint has her baby, you won't want anything to do with me. You'll just toss me to one side like she did.' Ellie pointed at Lucy, who for once was confused. Had Ellie just said that Rosie was *pregnant*?

It hit her like a lead ball. They must be serious about each other, then. Lucy had been hoping that Rosie, with her youthful looks and childless lifestyle, was going to be a passing phase in George's life. In fact, she'd been praying that she would, because Lucy wanted him to come back to her so they could pick up where they left off.

'See? Even she's shocked.' Ellie was pointing at Lucy, who realised that she should probably close her mouth and attempt to smile.

'No, I'm not. Well, maybe a little bit. That's great news all round; you're going to have a baby brother or sister. Why would that make you angry?'

But Lucy already knew why. Ellie had been George's golden girl. Even though she'd turned into the nightmare teenager from hell, he still doted on her. Now she was going to have to share him.

George took hold of Ellie's hand. 'It doesn't change how I feel about you, Ellie. You'll always be my little girl.'

Ellie's hand lingered in his for a few seconds before she snatched it away. Jane smiled. 'Now that everyone has calmed down a little, we need to discuss the drinking and the stealing.'

Ellie's cheeks turned crimson and Lucy felt a small sliver of hope. Somewhere underneath all that angst and hate was her little girl, who she'd brought up to have good manners and morals. Her little girl, who knew that stealing and underage drinking was wrong.

'Are they pressing charges?' Lucy asked.

Jane shook her head. 'No, because Ellie gave them the stuff back and apologised. They have said that we can deal with it by way of a community resolution.'

Lucy would need to thank the security staff at Debenhams. She knew them well from back in her days as a response officer, when she had spent hours in the cramped security room in the winter, keeping warm and watching their CCTV system for shoplifters.

'Thank god for that,' she said.

'I will need to speak to my supervisor about today's incidents,' Jane added. 'She isn't in until Wednesday, so I'm afraid I'm going to have to ask you to keep Ellie at home until I find out what we're going to do. Is that OK?'

George nodded. 'Yes, thank you. That's fine.'

Lucy had forgotten it was Friday, when Ellie normally came to hers. *Crap.* She couldn't take her; there was too much to do at work. She was pretty much going to be working flat out all weekend. She looked across at George.

'It's only my second day back at work and I've got a major incident going on. I can't have her this weekend.'

Ellie glared at her. 'Since when did you bother anyway? It's always work, work, work.'

George threw his car keys to Ellie. 'You go and get in the car. It's just across the road. And don't speak to your mother like that. I'll be down in a minute.'

Ellie stood up, making her escape. Jane waited until she'd left. 'Lucy, I don't want to upset you further, but I think you should know that she blames everything that happens on you. It's as if she hates the very ground that you walk on. I'll speak to the psychology team on Monday and see if we can hurry her referral up.'

Lucy bit her tongue, wanting to tell the arrogant woman in front of her to fuck off, but then of course she would think it was no wonder Ellie was behaving this way. Her phone began to vibrate in her pocket. 'Look, I'm really sorry, but I'm on duty and up to my neck in it. I have to go.'

Jane smiled at her, which upset Lucy even more.

George nodded. 'Me too. I'll speak with her and try to get this sorted out. Sorry, this episode is all my fault.'

Jane reached out and patted his arm. 'Don't go blaming yourself because you're happy, Ellie is going to have to learn to accept the consequences of life.'

George nodded and turned to leave. Lucy pushed past him, eager to get out of there. The anger was burning so hot inside her chest that she thought she might explode. That smug woman had not shown her one bit of respect.

'Lucy, wait.'

She turned to look at him. Despite being ten years older than her, George still had his good looks – although his dark brown hair was now peppered with silver, and the laughter lines around his hazel eyes were a little deeper than they had once been.

'I'm sorry, Lucy; it wasn't meant to happen like this.'

'What? Ellie finding out, or me?'

'Both of you. I told Rosie that I didn't want any more children, and she swore that she didn't either. We were arguing last night when Ellie walked in and heard us. It's all very early days and I wanted to be the one to tell you. In person.'

'You don't owe me any explanations, George. You have your life and I have mine. It's fine. Congratulations. I hope you'll both be very happy.'

'I'm sorry, Lucy. I always seem to hurt you so much when I never mean to. I'll sort Ellie out this weekend; you go to work. How are you, by the way?'

She nodded. 'I'm good. There's been a murder, so I've been thrown straight in at the deep end.'

'You be careful, Lucy. I'll be in touch.'

She turned and ran down the remaining stairs so that he couldn't see the tears that were welling inside her eyes. She tried so hard not to love him, but she did and always would. The nights after he'd left her she'd lain in their bed, trying her best to hate him, and she hadn't been able to. The guilt was always there in the back of her mind: if she hadn't worked so hard or drunk so much, perhaps things could have worked out a lot differently between them.

As she reached the bottom of the staircase, her phone began vibrating again. She took it out to answer it, glad to have the distraction of work to ease her still-broken heart.

Jane Toppan watched from the window. She was worried about Ellie. She liked the girl's dad, who was rather attractive, and she could see why Ellie was at loggerheads with her mother. The woman was a workaholic, who, according to her daughter, liked to party just as hard in her spare time. That said, she hadn't looked one bit like Jane had imagined – she'd been expecting to meet a frazzled alcoholic, but Lucy had looked anything but frazzled. She was very attractive. A bit stressed, maybe. Although, after thirty years of working with troubled kids, Jane knew that looks could be deceiving.

She was taking early retirement soon and couldn't wait to be able to spend her days stress and tantrum free. She was getting too old for all this bullshit now. Things were a lot different now to when she'd started; back then, they hadn't pandered to the kids like they had to now. They would be given a good shake and told to sort themselves out. The adults had been in charge in those days – now the adults were the ones being told what to do and being run ragged by the kids. Having to bow down to the little shits. It made her sick.

Jane did like Ellie, though, and was determined to do whatever she could to help her. Logging off the computer, she gathered her things together, glad that she only worked a half-day on Fridays. She caught sight of her cropped ash-blonde hair in the window and smiled. Her hairdresser had done a fabulous job this time. And now she was out of here for the weekend. No teenagers or stress, just lots of sleep and sex. There was no better antidote to keep you younger.

She turned off the lights, locking her office door behind her. The rest of the kids had finished for the weekend; the only person left was Mel, who for some reason volunteered here a couple of days a week.

'Mel, come on. We're going now; time to call it a day.'

The quiet girl came running down the stairs with her coat and bag.

'Thanks. Have a nice weekend, Jane.'

'You too, Mel.'

Jane walked the short distance to her car and got in, relieved to be free of work and the nightmare teenagers for a couple of days.

CHAPTER SEVENTEEN

Col squealed to a halt outside the accident and emergency department. Mattie opened the car door to find him in full conversation with someone on his radio.

'That's illegal, using your handset whilst driving. And pretty shit driving at that.'

Col stuck his middle finger up at him and carried on talking into his radio. Mattie wondered what it was that had the normally reserved Col so uptight. Finally, Col ended the conversation and turned to Mattie.

'That was Mason. He's been part of the search team that went through the hospital and grounds this morning. Guess what one of the builders handed to him a couple of minutes ago?'

Mattie shrugged.

'Some builder only went and found a wallet near to where they're excavating across the road. It's a bit muddy, but there's a driving licence with a faded picture and a bank card inside. There's also a train ticket with a reserved seat for the eighteenth of September.'

'Get fucking in. It would probably fit with the timescale of our vic. What does the licence say?'

'Edwin Wilkes. Of course, it might not be our vic. Mason's on his way back to the station with it.'

'And it doesn't belong to one of the builders working on the site?'

'Apparently none of them are over the age of forty. And no one is called Edwin.'

Mattie pulled out his phone, dialling Lucy's number. 'Boss, where are you?'

'On my way back; do you need picking up? I completely forgot that you didn't have a car, sorry about that.'

'No, Col's picked me up. One of the builders found a wallet on the site opposite the hospital.'

'Does it have ID inside?'

'Yes. Not only does it have ID, it also has a reserved train ticket, so I'll get onto that as soon as possible. Mason is on his way back to the station. We'll meet you up at CSI.'

Mattie knew that Lucy would be punching the air in that green tin can she was driving. This was the break they needed; it would change the whole ballgame. Of course, the wallet wasn't definitely their victim's – it might be a huge coincidence. Mattie had a gut feeling though that it was, and that by teatime, their John Smith would be identified and his family informed.

Audrey Stone listened to the patient sitting across from her as he told his tale of why he hadn't followed his diet plan this week. She had to lift her hand to stifle her yawn. *Stop telling me crap; face the truth. You're nothing but a greedy bastard who has no self-control and we both know you're never going to lose any weight.*
'I know it's hard, Brian, but come on. You need to do this for your own sake. Did you fill out a food diary for me?'

He shook his head, the misery and shame radiating from him in waves. Audrey didn't care; if he was going to waste her time, he could wallow in his self-pity. She wanted to go home, make something to eat, then put her feet up with a large glass of wine.

'Right, listen to me,' she said. 'Tomorrow is a new day and I want you to read the diet sheet I gave you six weeks ago and make a start. You could have lost nearly a stone by now if you'd got your act together. It's not rocket science, Brian; all you have to do is stop stuffing everything in your fridge down your throat.'

She watched and felt a glimmer of satisfaction inside her chest when his cheeks flared bright red. He nodded and pushed his bulk off the chair.

'Sorry, nurse, you're right. I'll try my best this week.'

He turned and began to shuffle out of the room. He didn't shut the door behind him, so she marched over and slammed it with a smile on her face. She knew she had been mean; that was how she was and how she always would be. She enjoyed watching people squirm under her scrutiny. If the doctors at the surgery ever heard her, or one of the patients put in a complaint, she'd be in trouble. But that wouldn't matter; she only worked here part-time because it got her out of the house and earned her some pocket money. She'd been nursing since she was twenty-one and enjoyed the power it gave her.

As she put on her coat and grabbed her handbag from under the desk, she wondered if she should go for a drive or go shopping before she went back home. Maybe she should do something different for once. Every day was the same. She had the same routines, depending upon whether or not she went to work.

Audrey closed the door of the consultation room and locked it behind her;. Lauren, a receptionist who lived a few doors up from Audrey, rushed past, her arms full of patient notes.

'Bye, Audrey. Have you heard the news?'

Audrey shook her head, expecting some gossip about which doctor was sleeping with which receptionist or nurse.

'There's been a murder,' Lauren said. 'Something to do with the old hospital. That place has always scared the life out of me; they should have knocked it down years ago. I never have understood why it's just been left there rotting all these years.'

'Who's been murdered, and do you mean the old asylum?'

'Yes, The Moore. That creepy old place. I have no idea who the victim is. It said on the radio that a body had been found inside, and the police were treating it as suspicious.'

Audrey shrugged. It meant nothing to her. It was probably some drug addict or homeless person who was dossing in there. 'See you next week, Lauren.'

As Audrey walked to her car, though, she found that she couldn't help but wonder who had come to such an untimely end in the asylum. She'd only driven past it last week, and had parked for a few moments opposite the main gates, reminiscing about the good old days. The days when she'd been young and carefree, running ward thirteen almost single-handedly – with the help of the doctors, of course.

She had done her training at The Moore and spent all her time on the same ward. It was there that she'd discovered just how much pleasure she got from being mean to the patients. If she was having a bad day she could take it out on the kids in there, and nobody would be any the wiser.

The hospital had housed thousands of adults before they'd decided to turn it into a children's psychiatric hospital. The sheer number of children who had been diagnosed as mentally ill back then was beyond comprehension. The Moore had been a dumping ground for anyone who didn't fit into society. Audrey remembered the face of every single child who'd been in her care; the names were a little harder. All except for that little monster who had killed her own baby brother – Audrey would never forget Lizzy Clements. She had been brought in screaming like a banshee that night, and they'd had to try to sedate her in the ambulance to even get her to the hospital. A defiant little witch, she'd never settled and had caused all sorts of unrest between the other children. Especially that horrible teenage girl, and the little kid who stuck his tongue out at everyone. Audrey had slapped the kid across the face more than a few times, which would be frowned upon now. That was the whole problem with society today: the little bastards who played up never got a good slap like they had back then.

On her way home, she called in at the corner shop for a paper to see if there was anything about the body in it. Then, grumbling that she couldn't get parked outside her own house, she parked in front of Lauren's and walked the short distance, her head bent so she didn't have to speak to any of her neighbours if they passed her. Pulling her door key from her pocket, she fiddled with the lock, which really needed replacing. She put her shoulder against the door, shoved it hard and stepped inside. There was a crisp white envelope on the floor. She bent down, picking it up and placing it on the hall table – she was too intrigued to read the headlines of the paper to take any more notice of it.

CHAPTER EIGHTEEN

Lucy arrived back at the station in a much better mood than when she'd left Mattie. Her anger and disappointment with Ellie had been pushed to the back of her mind for the time being –besides, this mess was George's and not hers for a change. She was buzzing at the thought that they might be on the brink of identifying the victim.

The CSI office was busy. Mattie and Col were standing behind the desk where Jack was sitting. He had his gloves on and was busy spreading the contents of the wallet out onto the desk, ready to photograph and bag up. Lucy leant over Jack's shoulder.

'Can you send me the photos, and has anyone tried ringing the train station?'

Mattie nodded. 'Yep, same as always. Data protection. My mate is working today though, so if we actually go and speak to him he might be able to log onto the system to double-check the booking.'

'Have you done a driving licence check?'

Col rolled his eyes at her. 'Yes, boss, and an address check confirms that Mr Edwin Wilkes is registered as living at one, Bay View Gardens along with his wife, Florence. He's not on our system at all.'

'Excellent news about the address,' Lucy said. 'Come on, Mattie, let's go and see if his wife is home and whether she's noticed her husband is missing.'

* * *

Tanisha, who worked behind the front desk in the police station, was busy chatting on her phone in the small back room. Her friend had just announced on Facebook that she'd thrown her boyfriend out for cheating on her. The loud swoosh as the automatic front entrance doors opened made Tanisha look up at the CCTV monitor, irritated to be disturbed at this crucial point in her conversation. If it was one of the regulars coming in to ask for their seized property back, they could wait until she had the full gossip before she'd go and attend to them.

It wasn't a regular. Standing at the counter was the cutest elderly lady Tanisha had ever seen. She was looking around with a confused expression on her face. Tanisha ended the call, putting her phone down on the desk. She'd always had a bit of a soft spot for the oldies; the woman, who had to be in her seventies, wasn't very steady on her feet and had a walking stick. How on earth had she got here? This new station was very nice, but it was miles from anywhere, and Tanisha knew the reason for that. It was to cut down on the timewasters and foot traffic they'd got whilst at the old station, which had been slap bang in the middle of the town centre.

She walked towards the counter and smiled. 'Can I help you?'

'I hope so, dear.'

'What's the matter?'

'Well, I seem to have lost my husband; he hasn't come home. He went away to visit a friend for a couple of days, and I haven't spoken him to him since I dropped him off in a taxi at the station over a week ago.'

'Have you spoken to his friend to see where he is?'

'Yes, and this is where it gets a bit worrying, because he said that he never turned up in the first place. I'm such a bad person; I feel terrible because we'd had a bit of an argument before he left and I was glad to see the back of him. He's getting a bit forgetful and he's always been a stubborn man, so I assumed when he didn't turn up yesterday he was stopping on at his friend's another day. I should have phoned his friend earlier to double-check that he'd arrived.'

She began to cry and Tanisha let herself out of the security doors to go and help her. Alarm bells were ringing in her head. She needed to find one of the detectives. She led the woman into one of the small interview rooms off the reception area, and sat her down on a chair.

'If you could give me some details, I'll try and find an officer to come and speak to you.'

'Thank you, dear, that would be wonderful. My name is Florence Wilkes and my silly husband is Edwin Wilkes.'

Tanisha took down their dates of birth and address. 'I'm sorry, but it could take a while. They're very busy at the moment.'

'That's fine by me; I have nothing better to do.'

Col looked up as the receptionist crossed the room to his desk.

'Where's the DI?' she asked.

'Gone to do an address check for the dead guy, why?'

'Can you get hold of her? There's a little old lady at the front desk reporting her husband missing.'

Col stood up. 'Shit, yes; she might not have left yet.'

He ran to the spiral staircase, taking the narrow steps two at a time, pushed his way through the double doors at the bottom and ran down the corridor to the steel security door which led out to the rear yard of the station. He saw Lucy's car at the main gates, about to leave, and he ran after her, waving frantically.

Lucy looked into her rear-view mirror and jumped, slamming the brakes on. 'Jesus Christ! What's the matter with Col? He looks as if he's having a heart attack!'

Mattie whipped his head around to see a red-faced Col bent over double, trying to catch his breath. He got out of the car.

'What's up with you?'

Col held up his hand whilst he took deep breaths. 'Argh, I've got a stitch. There's a woman at the front desk.'

'And?'

'Her husband is missing.'

Mattie opened the car door and peered in at Lucy. 'There's a woman at the front desk; her husband is missing.'

Lucy reversed into the nearest parking spot, then jumped out. 'Cheers, Col. Do you need an ambulance?'

He stuck two fingers up at her and she grinned.

She hurried back into the station, Mattie a short distance behind her, and headed in the direction of the front office to speak to Tanisha.

'She's in the first side room,' the receptionist told her.

Lucy walked towards the door. Cupping her hands, she peered through the small pane of glass to see the elderly lady sitting at the table and dabbing at her eyes with a tissue. Her heart ached for her. She knew there was a good chance that what she was about to tell the woman would irrevocably change her life forever.

She walked into the room.

'Hello, Florence. I'm Detective Inspector Lucy Harwin, but you can call me Lucy.' She held out her hand, which Florence took and shook with a much firmer grip than Lucy had expected. 'Florence, we really need a picture of Edwin to circulate to the officers who are going to be out searching for him. Would you have one with you?'

'No, I don't,' Florence said. 'How silly of me; it didn't even occur to me. Of course you need one. I have lots of them at home; I can go back and get you one.'

'Why don't I take you home and I can get a picture from you?'

'Of course, if you don't mind. That's very kind of you. Tell me, do you know if anyone has phoned up to say they've found him yet?'

Florence smiled at her joke and Lucy felt her heart sink even lower for the grief she was about to cause this lovely woman.

'Excuse me for a minute while I sort out a suitable car,' she said. 'Then we can go and get that photograph.'

Lucy left the room to speak to Mattie, who was waiting outside.

'Get me a family liaison officer on standby and a plain car. I can't cram her into mine and she'll do herself an injury trying to climb into yours. Then we'll take her home and see if the photographs match our victim.'

'Shit, poor woman.'

Lucy nodded; it was very shit indeed. She went back into the small room and led Florence into the reception area. A silver Ford Focus pulled up in front of the doors and Lucy took the woman out to it, opening the rear door for her.

'Florence, this is my colleague, Matthew. He's going to be our chauffeur.'

'You know, I've never been to a police station before in my life,' Florence said. 'I was quite worried in the taxi on the way here, but you've all been so very kind.'

Mattie smiled at her. 'You shouldn't believe everything you read in the local paper about us; we're quite a nice bunch.' He winked at her and she laughed, giving them a glimmer of the attractive woman that she must have once been.

Mattie drove them to the outskirts of town, where the really nice houses that overlooked the bay were. As he turned into the street, Florence pointed to a huge white bungalow with the neatest garden Lucy had ever seen.

'Wow,' Lucy said. 'You have a beautiful house and garden.'

'Thank you; that garden is the only thing that keeps us going. We both like to potter around in it. Edwin mows the lawn and does the weeding, I do the nice jobs like planting flowers and watering. It is rather nice, isn't it?'

Lucy smiled at her. 'It's beautiful. Have you lived here long?'

'Oh, around fifty years or so. Our son keeps dropping hints that we should sell up and move into one of those horrid retirement flats at the top end of the promenade. Well, I can tell you now that is never going to happen. They'll be taking the pair of us out of here in our coffins before we let him sell our home from underneath our feet.'

Lucy found herself praying that they were mistaken about the wallet, that Edwin had misplaced it and would come home with his tail between his legs. She didn't want to be the one to tell this lovely lady that her husband was dead and was currently lying in a mortuary fridge with his internal organs stuffed into a plastic bag and sewn back into his body. The familiar butterflies began to flutter inside her stomach. No matter how many times she had to do this, it never got any easier. She found her hands had slipped behind her back with her fingers tightly crossed.

Mattie parked the car. They all got out and followed Florence, who was clutching her front door key tightly in her hand.

'Does your son live locally?' Lucy asked, thinking that they'd need to call him soon to come and take care of his mum.

'He does; no doubt he'll be at the golf course. Paul is a good boy, but he spends all his time playing golf. He drives his poor wife mad with it all.'

'Do you have any other family?'

'Yes, I have a daughter who lives in Manchester. She's a doctor, just like her father was, and we're both incredibly proud of her.'

Lucy glanced at Mattie and mouthed the words, *A doctor?* He nodded.

'Florence,' Lucy said, 'have you told either of them that Edwin hasn't been home?'

'Of course not. They have very busy lives. And I don't make a habit of telling my children every time we have a disagreement because I'd be on the phone to them at least once a day.' Florence laughed a little. 'To be honest with you, officer, I have to admit I'm very worried about him. In forty years he's never not come back home, and we've had some huge arguments in the past.'

They followed her inside the house, which was so light and airy that Lucy couldn't believe that it belonged to an elderly couple. It was much nicer than her house. 'Wow,' she said. 'You really do have a lovely home.'

'I used to daydream about the day my kids would be all grown up and leave home so that I could paint my entire house white,' Florence said. 'Of course, Edwin isn't so keen on having such a white, light-filled house, but he knows it makes me happy.'

Florence winked at Lucy and pointed towards the kitchen. 'You go and take a seat in there and I'll see if I can find you a recent photograph of him. He really doesn't like having his picture taken. He insists they're not allowed to be on show.'

Lucy went and took a seat at the chalky white and grey painted table. Mattie perched himself onto one of the bar stools at the breakfast counter, and spoke in a low voice. 'God, I'm praying that it isn't him – even though I know we need it to be him. I'm hoping he's shacked up in a brothel with some Polish bird, having the time of his life. Anything has to be better than what I think is about to happen.'

Florence walked back in with a photo frame held to her chest. She turned it around and showed it to Lucy, who nodded. She knew that Mattie could tell by the look on her face that they'd just identified their John Smith. He stood up, taking hold of Florence's elbow and guided her to a dining chair. She sat down and her shoulders began to heave. Mattie opened his mouth to speak, but Florence shook her head.

Lucy reached out her hand and clasped hold of Florence's. The picture was face-up on the table and there was no doubt about it. Apart from the fact that he now had a gaping hole where his left eye socket was, their John Smith was identical to the man in the picture. Edwin Wilkes was never coming home.

Florence looked into Lucy's eyes. 'I knew this was going to happen. Well, I knew that something was very wrong. And you've all been so nice. He's not coming home, is he?'

'I'm very sorry, Florence, I'm afraid not.'

Lucy gave Mattie the nod to let the duty sergeant know that they needed the family liaison officer to come and take over. As heartbreaking as this was, they now knew who their victim was, and that meant that they were closer to a possible motive. Dr Edwin Wilkes must have really upset someone for them to drive a metal instrument through his eye socket.

CHAPTER NINETEEN

September 1975

Nurse Stone was blocking the exit from the showers; Dr Wilkes was standing behind the two porters who had come to help catch hold of Tommy. Nurse Stone pointed at the closed cubicle and the two men strode towards it. Billy, who was the bigger and more experienced of the two, pushed the door. It was locked. He leant his ear against it to listen. He could hear noisy breathing coming from the other side. Tommy always sounded as if he had a blocked nose. Billy knocked on the door.

'Tommy? It's Billy. Come on, lad. Let's get you out of there and back into bed.'

There was no reply. Nurse Stone, tired of waiting around, glared at him and pointed to the door.

'Tommy?' Billy said again. 'You need to step away from the door now because I'm going to open it whether you like it or not.'

Without hesitation, he kicked the door until it splintered and flew back, hitting the shower cubicle so hard that the whole room vibrated. Tommy ran at Billy, his head bent, and slammed into his stomach with as much force as he could muster. Billy yelped, then crumpled to the floor clutching his stomach, all the wind knocked out of him.

The other porter, who was younger and faster than Billy, lunged for the boy, managing to grab a handful of his shoulder-length curly brown hair. Tommy let out a yelp and began to scratch and flail at the man's hands. Dr Wilkes ran towards him and sank the syringe full of sedation straight into Tommy's neck. The boy screamed, then fell to his knees. His eyeballs rolled to the back of his eye sockets, leaving just the whites of his eyes showing. He keeled over and hit the floor with a thud.

Billy, who was still gasping for breath, watched in horror. 'Did you… give him… too much?'

Nurse Stone looked at him sharply, then bent down to press two fingers to the boy's neck. He still had a pulse.

'Help me get him into bed,' she said. 'He'll be fine. It might take him a little longer to come around, but he's still breathing.'

The doctor was looking at the syringe he was holding in his hand. Nurse Stone leant over to whisper into his ear. 'Pull yourself together, doctor. He was a danger to us and himself. You did the right thing.'

Dr Wilkes nodded in agreement with her. The younger porter scooped Tommy up into his arms and carried him to the bed.

'If he'd stayed in there and gone to sleep like he should have,' Nurse Stone said, 'none of this would have happened.'

Billy pulled himself to his feet. 'I need a cigarette,' he said.

Nurse Stone covered the boy up to his neck with a sheet. His eyes were still open with the whites showing. Shaking his head, Billy turned his back and walked away.

Nurse Stone looked at her watch. 'It's late, doctor. Why don't you go home and get some sleep? You have a big day tomorrow – isn't it the board of directors' meeting at eleven?'

Dr Wilkes ran his hand through his greying hair, then glanced at the comatose Tommy. 'Yes, yes it is. I'll expect you to ring me if you need me, though. And… the emergency doctor on call doesn't need to know about this. If Tommy gets into any difficulty, I want you to ring me straight away and I will come right back.'

'Of course I will. What do you take me for?'

* * *

Dr Wilkes walked away as briskly as he could without running. He knew full well what Nurse Stone was capable of, and now he'd proved himself as bad, if not worse. He'd just overdosed a child on Haldol – if Tommy woke up tomorrow, it would be a small miracle.

He let himself out of the children's ward and headed straight for the staff entrance without so much as going to his office for his overcoat. His mind was a whirlwind of the consequences of what tonight's actions would bring if Tommy didn't wake up – so much so that he didn't see Billy until they'd collided. He muttered an apology, barely even aware of Billy staring after him.

Pulling his keys out of his trouser pocket, he unlocked his car door and climbed inside. As he drove away, the full moon illuminated the hospital building in his rear-view mirror. It looked like something out of a horror film.

Before he knew it, he'd reached home. The house was in darkness. As he let himself in the front door and kicked his shoes off, a wave of tiredness washed over him. Instead of going for a shower like he normally would, he decided to put his pyjamas on and climb straight into bed.

He crept upstairs, not wanting to disturb Florence or either of their children. He tiptoed into his bedroom, and pulled back the covers as softly as possible. Florence let out a small moan, then turned on her side. She didn't wake, and for that he was thankful. He didn't want to talk tonight.

When Nurse Stone did her hourly checks, she found that Julie, who had no arms or legs, had managed to crap all over the bed. It took her the best part of an hour to clean the little witch up.

She had to strip and remake the bed. If the rest of the ward hadn't been so quiet, she would have made her have a cold shower, but Julie's squeals would have disturbed the other kids so she'd let her have a warm one. Afterwards, she put her back into bed and covered her up.

'Get back to sleep, and if you do that again, you can stay in it until the morning.'

If she'd given Tommy a second glance, she would have discovered that his breathing was very shallow and irregular – but she didn't. Instead, she went to the staff kitchen and made herself a mug of coffee, and helped herself to the biscuit tin, which was full of biscuits brought in by Julie's family. It was the least they could do, Nurse Stone thought. If they weren't too selfish to let Julie live at home with them, then she wouldn't be having to clean the shit off her back in the middle of the night.

Carrying her mug of coffee and a saucer full of biscuits, she went into the staffroom, where she shut the door and sat down. She took her book out of the drawer, put her feet on the desk and began dunking her biscuits into the mug. When she'd finished, she lay the book on her chest. A little nap wouldn't hurt; the bastards were all fast asleep.

Her eyes closed and she began to snore. With every movement of her chest, the book began to slowly slip from her body, until it hit the floor with a bang and jolted her from a nice dream about having an affair with Dr Wilkes. She opened her eyes and blinked a couple of times, wondering where the hell she was. At once, it hit her that she was at work and not supposed to be sleeping.

She stood up and stretched before wandering back out onto the ward. It had never been so quiet. Normally at least one of the brats would be awake, or calling out in their sleep for parents who were never coming back. Not tonight, though. It seemed different tonight.

She began walking towards Tommy's bed to check on him. From a distance, she could see that he hadn't changed position since she'd last looked over at him. Not that she really expected him to: he'd been drugged up with enough antipsychotic medicine to knock an elephant out. As she reached the bed, her footsteps slowed. His mouth was open and his eyes were glazed.

She ran the last few feet, but she already knew that it was too late. The kid was dead. She bent her head, putting her ear to his mouth. There was no sound. Tommy had already breathed his last breath. Reaching out, she touched his forehead with the back of her hand. It was cool to the touch. Panic set in. She pulled her hand back and ran to the staffroom, where she picked up the phone and dialled the number that was written in red marker pen on a piece of paper sellotaped to the wall.

Edwin Wilkes was dreaming about his mother, which was strange, because she'd been dead for ten years. She was sitting at his kitchen table, sipping tea from a cup and watching him. He was sitting opposite her, staring at the blue and white teapot in front of them. She placed her cup back down on the table and began to shake her head at him.

He heard a noise and wondered what it was, then realised it was the telephone and opened his eyes. Relief filled his heart that his mother wasn't really sitting opposite him, berating him. He scrabbled around in the dark to pick up the telephone.

'Hello,' he whispered, his voice dry and groggy with sleep.

'It's Audrey; you need to come back now. He's dead.'

Edwin had no idea who Audrey might be. He tried to clear the fog that was filling his mind. 'Who's dead?'

'Tommy,' the voice hissed at him.

He felt a surge of water and bile rise from his stomach to his mouth. Slamming the receiver down as if it were burning his fingers, he had to hold his hand over his mouth as he ran to the family bathroom. A hot stream of vomit exploded from him as he reached the toilet. His legs were trembling. He wiped his face with some toilet roll, then flushed the toilet.

'Daddy, are you poorly?'

He turned to see his five-year-old daughter standing there, her long hair sticking out in places and her beloved pink teddy tucked under her arm.

'No, not really,' he said, weakly. 'You go back to bed, princess; it's the middle of the night.'

She stared at him for a few seconds, making him feel even worse than he already did, then left the bathroom to go back to bed. He heard Florence's voice.

'What are you doing up, sweetie?'

'Daddy's sick.'

'Well, let's get you back to bed and then I can see if he needs my help.'

Edwin splashed cold water into his cupped hand and drank it down greedily to take away the burning sensation at the back of his throat. Then he splashed more all over his face to wake himself up.

'What's wrong, Edwin?' Florence had appeared behind him in the bathroom door.

He didn't like lying to his wife, but he couldn't tell her the truth, either. 'I have to go back to the hospital; there's been an emergency.'

'If you're ill then you'll do no such thing,' Florence said. 'They'll have to manage without you for once. Get back into bed.'

He shook his head. 'I can't. I have to go.'

She reached out her hand to touch his cheek. 'You're cold and very pale. I really think they can manage without you.'

'No, they bloody well can't. Stop interfering, woman.'

He pushed past her to go and get dressed, unable to look at the hurt expression on her face. Guilt wracked him; this wasn't her fault. He wanted to apologise, but he didn't have time – besides, she'd ask what was wrong and he was terrified that he might tell her. He couldn't burden Florence with what he'd done and then expect her to keep it a secret.

He ran downstairs. Letting himself out of the front door, he got back into his car and began to drive back towards the asylum.

CHAPTER TWENTY

When Lucy finally left Florence's house, she stood on the drive and inhaled the fresh, salty sea air for several seconds, needing to restore some balance to her life. The sky over the bay was filled with orange and pink fire. Not only had Edwin Wilkes had a gorgeous home, he'd also had a perfect view of Brooklyn Bay's golden sandy shoreline. The tide was coming in and it was a beautiful sight. Lucy could imagine sitting in this front garden with a large glass of cold white wine and watching the sunset every evening.

Mattie nudged her. 'Are you OK?'

She nodded. She was as OK as anyone could be in these situations. Florence had been reluctant to let them inform her son; she had taken some persuading. However, she had finally agreed, and he was now inside, taking care of his mum and making the relevant phone calls to the rest of the family. He'd also agreed to attend the hospital first thing to make the formal identification, which was a relief to Lucy. It was a shame that they'd had to go ahead with the post-mortem before the identification, but they'd had no choice. Sometimes bodies were never claimed or identified. It didn't happen very often in this part of the world, though, thank god.

She found that she was glad to let Mattie drive. She felt worn out, emotionally drained –

and this was only her second day back at work.

'So,' she said, as he drove away, 'thanks to Florence, we now know that Edwin was the doctor in charge of the asylum until 1977, when it was shut down. It looks to me as if someone from back then has been bearing a grudge, and has finally taken action. It could be a patient or a colleague. We need a motive. What did Edwin Wilkes do that made someone hold that anger inside of them for all that time, festering away?'

'It seems that way,' Mattie said, 'but why wait until now? I mean, how many years ago did it shut?'

Lucy worked it out. 'About thirty-eight years ago. Crap. That's a very long time to hold a grudge.'

'Where the hell have they been all this time?' Mattie wondered. 'Maybe it was a former patient and they've only just been released from a mental institution. That would make sense.'

'Or prison; it could be someone who'd already been locked up for a serious crime.'

'You mean murder. There aren't many other crimes where you'd serve a thirty-eight-year sentence, are there? Most killers are out well before then – unless they've killed multiple times.'

Lucy rubbed the side of her head. 'I don't know. I can't think straight. I need to go home. I have a stinking headache and I don't know if I'm hungry or need wine – I definitely need painkillers. Why don't we call it a night and start fresh tomorrow? We can have a briefing and discuss our next steps. How does that sound?'

'Bloody amazing. That's the best idea you've had all day.'

'Glad you approve. Tell you what, can you drop me off at home and pick me up in the morning? I don't need my car tonight.'

'Course I will.' He looked at her. 'Are you OK, Lucy?'

'I wish everyone would stop asking me that. Yes, I think I am.'

They drove the rest of the way in silence. Mattie pulled up outside Lucy's house, which was all in darkness.

'Thank you, Mattie. Whatever you're doing, have a good night.'

'See you tomorrow.'

Lucy got out of the car. Mattie drove away and she waved at him. Then she realised that her handbag was in the boot of her car with her house key inside it. *For fuck's sake, what are you like?* Taking a cursory look around the street to make sure no one was watching, she bent down as if tying her shoe lace, retrieving the spare key from under a plant pot. For a second she wondered if Ellie had taken it and not put it back – but it was there, pushed to the side underneath the heavy terracotta pot.

She let herself inside and locked the door behind her. She didn't bother to turn the hall light on, not wanting anyone to know she was in. Her neighbour was lovely and meant well, but he had a habit of knocking on her door for some strange reason whenever he saw that she was home.

As she went into the kitchen, her stomach rumbled. She opened the fridge to see two pasta ready meals and a bag of salad on the shelf. She picked up the salad, saw that it had turned brown and threw it straight into the bin. The meals were out of date, but only by a couple of days. She pulled the cardboard sleeve off the lasagne, peeled back the film and sniffed. It smelt OK. She put it in the microwave for seven minutes, figuring that at least if she nuked it, she'd kill any bacteria that might be growing inside it.

Her bottle of vanilla vodka was on the top shelf of the fridge and she pulled it out, pouring a large measure into a glass. Then she rooted through the kitchen drawer until she found a half-empty packet of paracetamol. She popped two out and swallowed them with a swig of neat vodka.

The microwave beeped, signalling that her feast was ready. Lucy smiled to herself. It was a good job Ellie wasn't here; the poor kid would have starved to death. She topped the vodka up with coke and ice, put the glass and her dinner on a tray and carried it into the living room.

As she ate, she tried not to look at the crime scene pictures that she'd pinned onto the noticeboard above her fireplace, but her eyes kept glancing up. What the hell had happened at that hospital? What had Edwin Wilkes done to make someone kill him in such a horrific way? She needed to know if Edwin Wilkes had a skeleton in his closet.

They would need to go back and question Florence, she thought. If there was some great scandal in his past that had eventually caught up with him, she hoped that his wife would know about it. Although sometimes the spouse was the last to find out about such matters. Hell, she should know: look at George and his affair with the much younger Rosie that had gone on for six months before she had found out.

Leaving a quarter of her food, Lucy picked up her vodka and turned off the living room light. She was going to get into bed, where she could watch Netflix on her laptop until she fell asleep. Most of the coppers she knew didn't watch detective programmes, but she was addicted to them. Her favourite at the moment was *Luther*. She was glad that her job wasn't anything as complicated as his was. He managed to get himself into so many scrapes that it made her feel a little bit better about her fucked-up life. It also helped that she had a bit of a thing for Idris Elba; he was definitely a ten on her male scale.

After thirty minutes of *Luther*, Lucy downed the rest of her vodka and closed the laptop. She pushed it onto her bedside table, upsetting the stack of books that she was trying to make her way through. They clattered to the floor and she left them there, promising herself that tomorrow she would have a tidy round and pick them up.

Lying down, she wondered how poor Florence was. What was the connection between the killer and the elderly couple? Did Florence know why her husband had been murdered? And what if the killer decided to go after Florence?

Lucy felt that the woman was safe enough tonight because her son had told them he was staying with her. She would decide what to do tomorrow. She closed her eyes, willing sleep to come before the tablets wore off and her headache returned.

CHAPTER TWENTY-ONE

Audrey Stone was sitting in front of the television, not really watching it. She glanced at the card on the coffee table. She had no family to send her cards – they'd all fallen out with her years ago because of her outspoken manner. She hadn't yet bothered to open it; it was probably an invite to Lauren's birthday party – which was all the receptionist had talked about for the last month at work. Audrey wouldn't be going to the party. She couldn't think of anything worse, although Lauren was a nice girl compared to the rest of them.

She picked up the paper, reading the story once more. Why had someone been found dead in the asylum after it had stood empty all this time? Memories of the night little Tommy Wright had died flooded back to her. She still thought he'd got what he deserved. He'd been a horrible child.

That night had changed Dr Wilkes, though. From that point on, he'd turned into a quivering wreck whenever any of the kids had needed higher doses of medicine or disciplining. Audrey had once thought that they might have had a thing together – after all, they worked so closely. After that night, though, he'd become distant, and had rarely looked her in the eye. It was a shame. She had spent the best part of five years dreaming about them becoming lovers.

Sighing loudly now, she picked up the envelope and slid her finger under the flap, lifting it up. She pulled the contents out. At first, she didn't understand what she was looking at. It was a photograph of a man lying on a hospital trolley, taken from a distance. Slowly, she recognised the huge, boarded-up windows behind him. It was an office in the asylum.

She brought the photograph up to her face to look closer at the man – and let out a squeal. It had been a long time since she'd seen him, but it looked like Dr Wilkes. Her hands shaking, she turned the photograph over. The words jumped off the page at her. In big, bold letters, it said: **'YOU'RE NEXT'**.

Audrey dropped the card and jumped up. What kind of sick person would send such a horrible thing? She ran to the hallway to check her front door was locked, then to the kitchen, where she could see the heavy-duty bolts fastened across the back door. Picking up the phone, she tried to dial 999, but found that she couldn't. This wasn't actually an emergency, was it? Ever since she'd been a child it had been drummed into her: you only phone the police if you're in dire straits. There was another number, for the life of her she couldn't remember it. It was probably one of those arrogant teenagers who insisted on playing football outside her house whenever the sun shone. She'd told them off on more than one occasion – they probably held it against her.

She went back into the lounge, where the photograph was lying face down on the carpet. She collapsed onto the sofa, her shaky legs unable to hold her upright any longer. *Calm yourself down, woman; it's just some sick joke.* Her elbow pressed the 'on' button on the remote control and the television burst into life, making her jump. Her heart begin to race.

She forced herself to laugh out loud. She was being silly. First thing in the morning, she would take the awful card to the police station and ask them to do something with it. She paid her taxes; they could find out who had sent it, and why.

There was a loud noise in the kitchen. She jumped.

'Hello? Who's there? What are you doing in my house? If you don't leave now, I'm phoning the police.'

She was greeted by a loud miaow as her old tabby cat strolled into the lounge as if there was nothing wrong. Audrey breathed out a sigh of relief, and a nervous giggle escaped her lips.

Moments later, a loud knock on the front door made her gasp. Then: *pizza*, she realised. She'd ordered a pizza for her supper. It was Friday night, and she always ate pizza on a Friday. Standing up and forcing herself to move, she walked to the front door where she could see the outline of the delivery person through the pane of glass. She recognised the bright green baseball cap that they always wore. Her stomach rumbled and she realised just how hungry she was. She opened the door a little and the smell of fresh pizza filled the small hallway.

'Sorry,' she said. 'I'll just get my purse.'

She left the door ajar, and went to get her purse from the hall table. When she turned, she jumped to see the delivery person standing right behind her.

'Sorry,' she said, again. 'I'm a bit jumpy tonight.' She handed over a twenty pound note, and received the pizza box in return. The delivery person walked to the front door and almost stepped back outside, before pausing and turning back.

'Do you remember me?'

I lunged towards you. You dropped the pizza box and ran towards the phone on the table, but you weren't fast enough. I know that you felt my shadow descend over you as you felt the band of tightness wrap around your neck. You will never know how good it felt squeezing the breath out of you. You tried your best to stop me, your weak fingers trying to pull the ligature free. You were no match for me, were you? It was no use; I could feel the pressure filling your head and knew that your eyes would be watering. The tiny blood vessels bursting inside as they felt as if they were about to explode from your sockets. When the room turned black and you fell to your knees, you wondered when the relief would come from the biting material as I pulled even harder.

Do you remember me now? No, I thought, not Nurse Stone. All you ever cared about were your cigarette breaks and laddering your tights. You never gave a fuck about any of those kids in that hospital, did you? Kids who were scared and didn't understand why they were there. You did your best to make their miserable lives even worse. Well consider this your payback, you evil bitch.

When it was done I stepped back, admiring my handiwork; a shameful waste of good pizza if you ask me. It smelt so good, I kicked it to one side and went into the lounge to collect my photograph. Picking it up, I tucked it into my pocket. As I returned to the front door I was shocked to see a young woman, standing there with her mouth wide open, staring at the body on the floor. She drew in a deep breath to let out a scream and I had no choice. Grabbing a handful of her long, blonde hair, I slammed her head into the brick wall so hard it knocked her out cold. I took a quick look around the front street, amazed no neighbours had come out. Then I dragged her to my car which was parked behind the pizza van. It was a struggle; she was such a dead weight for a little thing. The baseball cap fell from my head so I picked it up and threw it back to where the pizza boy was beginning to groan. Then I drove away and never looked back.

CHAPTER TWENTY-TWO

The call for the injured pizza boy came from the next-door neighbour, who had found him on his way out to go to work. The normally quiet street was now alive with a multitude of flashing lights. Paramedics were working on the boy. Police Constable Joe Hull, who had been first on scene, was standing to one side to let them get on with it. A van bearing the words 'LITTLE ITALY PIZZA DELIVERY' screeched to a halt beside them, and a very animated Italian man got out. He took one look at the man on the ground and stopped shouting. Joe took him to one side.

'Sir, can you tell me who that is?'

The man nodded. 'Of course I can; it's Arnie. What happened to him?'

'At the moment it's looking like he's been assaulted. He's in and out of consciousness and the paramedics have found quite a nasty-looking injury on the back of his head. I'm going to need his full details so we can contact his next of kin to meet the ambulance up at the hospital.'

'*Si, si.* Yes, yes. I haven't got them on me; I need to phone the shop. Give me a minute.'

Another police van arrived. Police Constable Leanne Burton got out, crossing over to where Joe was waiting patiently for the man to finish his phone call. She looked at the lad being lifted onto a trolley.

'What happened?'

Joe shrugged. 'GBH, assault.'

'Have you called out CID?'

He rolled his eyes at her. 'Yes.'

'Oh, well done. I suppose we better seal off the area until they get here and assess it then?'

Joe, who hadn't even thought about sealing off the crime scene, nodded. He wasn't going to admit that it hadn't occurred to him. 'Yep, I've got tape in the back of my van. I'll go get it.'

He took out the huge roll of blue and white tape and tied it around a lamp post, before walking to the opposite side of the street and doing the same. He then threw the tape to Leanne, who walked to the far end of the street and tied it off there, too. Joe just hoped that whoever the duty DI was wouldn't take forever to come and look at the scene. It was freezing cold tonight and he was hungry. All this talk of pizza had him craving a huge meat feast covered in extra cheese and he didn't want to have to wait for hours before he got it.

Lucy was about to walk into her favourite restaurant with George. He was holding her hand and telling her something funny. Whatever that vibrating sound was, it was really annoying. She didn't know where it was coming from. It was spoiling the ambience.

It stopped and started again. Her eyes opened. *Bollocks.* The vibrating was close by – in fact, it was underneath her head. Lifting her arm, she felt underneath her pillow and pulled out her phone. She squinted one eye at the bright display. It was an unknown number, which meant only one thing. *Fucking work.*

'DI Harwin.'

'Sorry to bother you, Inspector, but there's been a serious assault on Cottage Lane. You're the on-call DI?'

'OK,' Lucy said. 'Give me the address, I'll be there as soon as I can. Have you phoned DS Jackson?'

'Yes, Inspector, although he didn't answer so I've left him a voicemail. The address is eighteen, Cottage Lane.'

'Thanks. Bye.'

Lucy ended the call and reached over onto her bedside table for a pen to write down the address. She didn't want to get out of bed; she was too comfy. Forcing herself to move, she threw back the duvet and swung her legs out. Thank god she'd only had one drink, otherwise she'd need a car to come and pick her up— *Bugger. I haven't got a car. It's at the station.*

She grabbed her phone off the bed, went into the bathroom, splashed cold water on her face and brushed her teeth. Now she was a little more awake, she rang Mattie. He answered on the third ring, sounding rougher than she did.

'What?'

'Wakey wakey, this is your early morning wake-up call.'

He whispered. 'Fuck off, boss.'

'Oops, I forgot you had a date last night. Well, I'm sorry to break up your party, but we're needed.'

'For what?'

'Did you not answer your phone to the control room when they rang you? You *are* a naughty boy. There's been a serious assault; I've got the address. They want our expert opinion.'

Mattie growled, which made Lucy laugh.

'I love it when you're angry. Now, get your arse into gear and come and pick me up please.' The line went dead. 'How rude,' Lucy muttered. 'Some people are just not morning people.'

She looked at the clock on the wall and saw it was only quarter past eleven at night. This time it was her who let out the groan: she'd thought it was almost morning. No wonder Mattie was pissed off. She'd probably disturbed him and his girlfriend.

Lucy got dressed, then ran downstairs to make herself a quick mug of coffee. Just as she was starting to sip it, there was a loud beep outside her house. She put the mug down and waved at

Mattie from the window. When she got into his truck, she couldn't help smiling at his rather scruffy appearance. His normally immaculately gelled hair was sticking up.

'Do you know it's an offence to beep your horn at this time of night?' she said, smiling sweetly at him. 'I don't want you upsetting my lovely neighbours.'

Mattie looked at her and shook his head. 'I don't care; if I'm up then everyone else can be. Anyway, it's not that late.'

'You're such a grouch. You should be happy you get to spend more time with me.'

He rolled his eyes at her.

'So where were you?' she asked. 'It didn't take you long to get here, so you weren't at home.'

'None of your business. Did anyone ever mention you'd make a great detective?'

'Grouch. I'm going to start calling you Oscar. Right, chauffeur: eighteen, Cottage Lane, please.'

'Who the hell is Oscar?'

'No way! Don't tell me you never watched *Sesame Street* when you were a kid?'

The look on Mattie's face confirmed that not only had he never watched it, he didn't have a clue what she was talking about.

'God, you make me feel old! You must have had a deprived childhood. Oscar was a grumpy green monster that lived in a trash can.'

'What the hell? Are you tripping, Lucy? Did you hit the old wine a bit too hard when I dropped you off?'

She stuck two fingers up at him and began to watch out of the window as they drove in silence the rest of the way. When they finally turned into the street, which was lit up like a fairground with all the flashing lights, Lucy looked at him. 'It looks as if no one in this street is going to get any sleep, either.'

Mattie parked up behind the CSI van, which had just beaten them to it. Jack climbed out, lifting his hand to stifle a yawn. Lucy knew how he felt.

'You drew the short straw?' she asked.

He nodded. 'Amanda did have a good laugh when my phone began ringing.'

Mattie came and stood next to Lucy. 'I don't know how you two manage to work and live together; it would drive me mental.'

'We don't always work the same shifts, and to be honest, we don't see that much of each other at work unless there's a big job on, or you two are on shift. What is it about the pair of you that causes complete chaos in this normally lovely, peaceful town?'

'Blame the boss,' Mattie said. 'It was all quiet until she started back at work two days ago.'

Jack looked at Lucy. 'Technically, I would have to agree with him.'

'Hey,' she protested, 'he was the one that called me in early to come and see that body at the asylum. Don't go blaming me.'

Jack slung his bag over his shoulder and walked towards the front garden that Joe was pointing to. Lucy and Mattie walked over to join Joe. Mattie nodded at him, while Lucy began to ask questions.

'What happened?'

'Pizza guy got whacked on the head delivering pizza. It's a pretty nasty wound.'

'Where's his pizza?'

'What?'

'There's no pizza. Did someone mug him for his pizza, or had he already delivered it?'

Joe shrugged. 'I don't know. I just assumed he'd already delivered it.'

Lucy pointed to the house in front of them. 'Have you spoken to the occupants?'

'No, sorry. I didn't want to mess the scene up for CSI.'

'It's OK, I'll go and speak to them,' Lucy said. 'Although it's a bit strange they've not come out, if you ask me. If this circus was going on outside my house, I'd be out here getting in the way and wanting to know what had happened.'

Mattie nodded in agreement. 'Or you'd be upstairs, curtain-twitching like a professional.'

Lucy stepped into the narrow front garden and walked up the path to the front door, lifting her hand to knock. As her knuckles rapped on the glass, though, the front door opened inwards a touch. She pulled her sleeve down, and used her covered hand to push the door open a little further.

'Hello? It's the police.'

Mattie was now standing behind her. 'Do you want me to go in first?'

'No, thank you, but I could do with a torch.'

He handed one to her. She turned it on, shoving the door wide open, and the torch shone upon the body lying at the foot of the stairs.

'Oh fuck,' Mattie said. 'Is she dead?'

Lucy ran to the body. Bending down, she shone her torch on the woman's face and noticed the tight ligature around her neck. The woman's eyes were wide open and glazed. Lucy touched the woman's neck with her fingers to feel for a pulse, then snatched them back. A flashback to the bodies of Natalia and Isabella lying dead on their living room floor filled her mind. She had to blink a couple of times to clear it away.

'She's a foxtrot, definitely dead,' Lucy said. 'It looks like she's been strangled with a pair of tights. Get one of the paramedics to come and confirm the death, if they're still around.'

Mattie turned around. The first ambulance had already left, but another was about to drive away. He ran towards it, waving his arms.

'Another casualty inside.'

The driver cut the engine. Lucy, who had come outside, whispered into Mattie's ear. 'Naughty.'

'I know,' he hissed back. 'But if we tell them she's dead, they might not want to come inside. They'll faff around and insist on a doctor. At least this way it will be quicker.'

'Nice one, Sherlock.'

The paramedic came running and Mattie stepped to one side to let her past. She took one look at the body on the floor, then turned to arch an eyebrow at him before bending down. Mattie began to whistle to himself, then turned away.

'Have either of you performed CPR in the last ten minutes?' the paramedic asked.

Both of them shook their heads. She felt for a pulse and checked if there was any respiration. Taking a pen light out of her pocket, she lifted one of the half-closed eyelids to see that the pupils were fixed and dilated.

'She's definitely dead, but I'll run a one-minute rhythm strip so I can say that I tried.' She fixed the ECG pads onto the woman's upper body, waited, then stood up again. 'Sorry. I'll go and fill out my forms.'

'Thank you,' Lucy said. She began to relay the situation to the control room. 'I can confirm we have a female fatality inside a property: number eighteen, Cottage Lane. The previously reported assault has taken place in the front garden of the same property. I'm going to need some more officers and an address check to see who the occupant is, please.'

'Roger. On it right now.'

Lucy and Mattie carefully made their way back down the garden path. Lucy pointed to Jack's protective suit, and he nodded.

'Help yourself; there's plenty in the back of my van.'

She stuck her thumb up at him, wondering what the hell had happened. They would need to wait for Jack to do his preliminary investigations before they could go back inside the house to properly assess the scene.

Lucy's radio began to ring. 'Go ahead.'

'Inspector, the only occupant listed for eighteen, Cottage Lane is a Ms Audrey Stone. We're just running checks to see if she's on our system.'

'Thank you.'

Lucy turned to Mattie. 'She was near to the telephone, her feet were facing the kitchen and her head the front door. That suggests she was trying to get away from whoever it was and they got her from behind. It looks as if the pizza guy interrupted the killer, so he then went after him.'

'Oh, you're good,' Mattie said. 'You're very good. That's why you're the inspector.'

'Why did the killer open the door to the delivery guy, though? Wouldn't he just have ignored the knocking? Unless the victim screamed and he panicked.'

'It's too late for this, Lucy. My brain isn't fully functioning yet.'

'Or mine. We need to speak to the pizza guy. Have you got a name for him yet?'

Joe, who was still standing nursing the scene-guard booklet, turned around. 'Yes, he's called Arnie Hope. Nineteen years old. A patrol has gone around to inform his mum that he's been taken to hospital.'

'Thanks. Right then, Mattie, we need to go to the hospital after we've finished here. He could be our star witness, and we need to establish exactly how much he saw. And if the killer finds out he's still alive, what's to stop him coming back to finish the job?'

'This isn't some television show,' Mattie said. 'Do you honestly think they'd bother their arses to go back and finish him off when they might get caught?'

'Mattie, whoever did this showed no qualms about strangling an older woman and seriously assaulting a teenager delivering pizza. I don't think they really care, do you?'

Mattie muttered something and Lucy ignored him. He wasn't good on no sleep. She remembered he used to be a miserable sod when they worked nights back on section.

'I wonder how long it will take Catherine to get here,' Lucy said. 'At least it's not her anniversary tonight.'

Another car turned into the already overcrowded street, and Lucy smiled to herself. It looked as if they weren't going to have to wait long – Catherine was already here. They were lucky in that most of the important people needed to attend serious crime scenes lived no further than fifteen minutes away. Brooklyn Bay was a popular choice for anyone who was tired of living in the city. It was such a lovely, quaint town to live in.

As Catherine got out of the car, Lucy wondered if there was some connection between Edwin Wilkes and Audrey Stone. Both of them were old – too old to die such horrific deaths. Maybe she'd been a patient in the asylum, or maybe they'd worked together.

CHAPTER TWENTY-THREE

When Catherine had finished her preliminary examination of the body, and the initial house-to-house enquiries had been carried out, Lucy waved Mattie over.

'We need to go to the hospital and speak to the pizza guy. Can you take me there please?'

'He has a name, boss. He's called Arnie. Although I think "pizza guy" sounds a lot better, to be fair.'

'Fancy calling a young lad "Arnie",' Lucy said. 'Poor bugger. I used to have a horse called Arnie.'

Mattie began to laugh. 'Poor fucking horse.'

'He kind of suited it,' Lucy said as they got in the car. 'I was obsessed with the man himself during my early teenage years; naming my horse after him was my tribute to his great acting.'

Mattie chuckled. 'I can't imagine you having a crush on Arnold Schwarzenegger. I would have thought you'd have been more of a Tom Cruise kind of girl.'

'No way,' Lucy said. 'He didn't have what Arnie had, and I could never fancy a guy who was shorter than me. I like my men big and stocky. Come on, our pizza guy might be ready to speak to us now. I'm thinking that there has to be some connection between our two victims. Two murders turning up in two days is very unusual.' She felt the strange sensation in her stomach that normally signalled she was onto something. 'I think this is going to turn into a nightmare of a job. Why me, on my first week back?'

'Because you love it, boss,' Mattie said. 'And I know that if anyone can find the killer it will be you. If I was murdered, or someone in my family was, I wouldn't want anyone else in charge of the case. As much as you're a pain in the arse, you are very, very good. You give a shit and you don't leave anything unturned. It's you because this is what you're good at, so don't forget it.'

Lucy turned away from him to look out of the car window so that he couldn't see the tears welling up in her eyes. That was the sweetest thing she'd ever heard him say. He must be going soft in his old age, she thought. But it was nice to know that he still thought she could do her job after the last fuck-up.

It had all gone horribly wrong that dreadful afternoon, and she'd ended up being suspended. All because the powers that be hadn't listened to her. Even though she'd been officially cleared, it was always there in the back of her mind. Lucy had spent three months doubting herself and wondering whether, even if they cleared her, she'd be able to face dealing with serious incidents again. Up to now, though, she was holding her own, and for that she was thankful. She needed to prove to herself that she could do her job. There was no harsher judge than herself.

They reached the hospital. Mattie parked on the double yellow lines, as near to the Accident and Emergency Department as possible. Considering it was the early hours of the morning, Lucy thought, it could still be daytime, the number of people milling around in the waiting area. Some were drunk, some were sober. There was a group of teenagers in a circle at the back, all fussing around a boy with his arm in a sling who looked no older than fifteen. Lucy would bet that their parents didn't know where they were or what they'd been up to. Some sleepover gone wrong, no doubt. As she looked, for a split second she thought one of the girls with her back to her was Ellie. She had the same ice-blonde hair, and a green parka jacket just like Ellie's. Then the girl turned around, and Lucy felt a huge surge of relief to see that it wasn't her daughter.

Mattie was chatting to the receptionist about the weather. Lucy forced her attention away from the teenagers.

'So can you tell us where Arnie Hope is?' she asked the receptionist.

Mattie shook his head. '*Please* could you tell us where Arnie Hope is? She's forgotten her manners; not a night person, are you, boss?'

Lucy looked at him and he pulled a face at the young woman behind the desk. The woman grinned at him, then turned her attention to Lucy.

'Are you family?'

'No, police.'

'I'm afraid I'm going to have to see some ID.'

Mattie pulled out his warrant card, saving Lucy the embarrassment of admitting she'd left hers in her handbag, in her car, which she'd left at the station.

'Thank you,' the receptionist said. 'I'll just be a moment whilst I go and find out for you, detectives.'

Lucy shook her head. 'Jesus.'

'You really need to work on your people skills a bit more,' Mattie said. 'Tonight, you seem to have forgotten that you possess them.'

The woman came back.

'Do you want to wait in the relatives' room? The consultant said he'll come and speak to you as soon as he can.'

Lucy didn't want to go and wait in the bloody relatives' room; she wanted to go and speak to the kid now. 'Yes, thank you,' she snapped. 'We know the way.'

Mattie grabbed her elbow and led her away from the desk. He was clearly scared she was about to lose her temper. She snatched her elbow back from him. 'I know,' she said. 'It's just that I'm tired, and I've had enough of people who get in the way when we are doing our best to solve murders.'

'We all have a job to do; that's all it is, Lucy. It's nothing personal, is it?'

She slumped onto one of the chairs, letting out a sigh.

Ten minutes later, the door opened. Lucy sat up, surprised to see the young doctor standing in front of her looking as flustered as she felt. All of her anger drained away. Mattie was right, she needed to calm down. The doctor looked at Mattie and nodded, then smiled at her, his face completely transforming into a warm, welcoming mask of compassion.

'I'm sorry to keep you waiting. I'm Stephen King, one of the consultants working tonight.'

Mattie sniggered. '*The* Stephen King?'

Lucy glared at him.

'No, unfortunately not,' the doctor replied with good humour. 'I wish I was, though, because then I'd be living it up in Maine writing horror stories, instead of working a night shift and living them instead.'

Lucy stood up and crossed the room, offering him her hand, which he shook firmly. 'I'm sorry; forgive him. He tends to act much younger than he looks. I'm Detective Inspector Lucy Harwin and this is Detective Sergeant Matthew Jackson. We need to speak to Arnie Hope as a matter of urgency; he could be the key witness to a murder earlier tonight.'

'Well, Detective Inspector, I can take you to him, but I don't know if he's regained full consciousness yet. He's been in and out since he was brought in, and I do know the last time I checked he'd been taken down for a CT scan. If you follow me, we'll go and see if he's back.'

'Thank you so much,' she said. 'Please call me Lucy. I'm not really into all the official bullshit.'

He nodded and smiled at her. 'Well, in that case, please call me Steve, because neither am I.'

Lucy nudged Mattie in the side, warning him not to laugh. They followed him through the department until they reached a cubicle at the end, where a nurse was busy checking the young man's blood pressure. The doctor held out his hand for the chart and gave it the once-over.

'Is he up to talking, nurse?'

'Yes, he's awake. Aren't you, Arnie?'

The boy on the bed, who looked much younger than his nineteen years, opened one eye beneath the huge white bandage that was wrapped around his head.

The doctor stepped closer to him. 'How do you feel? I'm glad to see you're awake.'

'I'm OK as long as I don't move my head.'

'Good. These two detectives need to ask you a couple of questions. Is that OK?'

Arnie went to nod his head and groaned. 'Argh… I mean, yes.'

Lucy stepped towards his bed. 'Arnie, my name's Lucy. Can you remember what happened?'

'I don't really know. I got out of the car and took the pizza box out of the bag. I'd only just stepped through the gate when I heard a rustling noise behind me and I got a whiff of strong aftershave. The next thing I knew, I was on the floor with the worst headache ever. It went black, and then I opened my eyes and I was here.'

Mattie, busy scribbling in his notebook, looked up at Lucy.

'Did you not deliver the pizza, then?'

'No, like I said I can't remember anything except hearing a noise behind me. I don't know what happened to the pizza. Is my boss pissed off with me because it didn't get delivered on time?'

Lucy shook her head. 'Of course not; he's worried about you. Have you ever delivered to that address before?'

'Yes, a few times. The woman that lives there is a right miserable cow. She always moans that it's taken too long or it's cold, and she never tips.'

'When you parked up, did you notice anyone hanging around?'

'No.' Arnie shut his eyes and gulped. The nurse grabbed a cardboard sick bowl off the trolley and handed it to him. She looked at Lucy.

'I think that's quite enough for now. You'll have to come back tomorrow.'

Lucy nodded. 'Thank you, Arnie. I'll leave a card for you. If you need me or remember anything, please call me.' She tucked the card under his pillow and he stuck his thumb up at her.

The two detectives walked away with the doctor, who let them out of the exit doors. Mattie walked through without a second glance, but Lucy turned back to him.

'Thank you so much, that was a huge help. I don't think Arnie is in any danger, but until we catch whoever did this I'm going to arrange for a uniformed officer to come and sit outside his room. It's just a precaution.' She reached in her pocket and pulled out the last of her crumpled business cards. 'The same applies to you – if Arnie remembers anything, or if anyone suspicious turns up, please can you ring me?'

'Of course I will. It was very nice to meet you, Lucy.'

She felt her cheeks begin to burn, knowing that Mattie, despite having his back to them, was listening to every word.

'It was nice to meet you too, Steve,' she said. 'Normally doctors aren't as accommodating or as helpful. I really do appreciate it.' She walked off, letting Mattie follow her. He waited until they were outside before he started laughing.

'Of all the places to get picked up, only you could do it questioning an assault victim in the hospital casualty department. You really crack me up, Lucy.'

She glared at him. 'Piss off. I did not get picked up. He was just very nice and helpful. You have to admit he made our lives a lot easier by letting us go in and talk to Arnie straight away. We could have been hanging around there for ages.'

'He did it because he fancied the arse off you,' Mattie said, getting out his car keys.

'Shut up.' She'd never admit it to Mattie, but she had found Stephen King very attractive. She bent down, scooped up a handful of the pure white snow that had now blanketed the floor, and threw it at the back of his head. Mattie, who had seen her from the corner of his eye, ducked and jumped into his pickup.

'Right,' Lucy said. 'So we know that the killer took Arnie out first. Why?'

'So he could pose as the pizza guy and get in the house.'

'I think you're right, that's exactly what he did. He didn't want to lure her outside and kill her where he might get caught, or scare her enough that she'd phone the police. This was a very organised kill. We are looking for someone who has spent some time planning this murder.'

Mattie began to drive in the direction of the station.

'Did he have his baseball cap on when he was attacked?' Lucy continued. 'If not, the killer removed it before he knocked him out, so that he didn't get blood all over it and could dress up as the delivery guy to get the woman to open the door.'

'Where's that hat, then?' Mattie said. 'If the killer wore it, there might be hair inside it, and you know what that means.'

'DNA. I bloody hope so because if there is, our life may just have been made a little bit easier. Let's go and see if Jack's still at the station. He probably is, because he'll be making the most of his call-out. He'll be able to tell us if the hat was found – and then we're going home to try and grab a couple of hours' sleep.'

CHAPTER TWENTY-FOUR

The station was eerily quiet, so Mattie parked in the bay usually reserved for the marked vehicles.

Lucy couldn't stop thinking about what Arnie had said. He'd smelt aftershave. Why would you wear anything perfumed if you were going to kill someone?

Mattie stopped to talk to a couple of uniforms who were coming out of the door, and Lucy carried on to the spiral staircase, taking her up to the first floor and the CSI office. The lights were on and the door was wide open. She knocked and walked inside.

'I bet you're knackered. I know I am. It's been one hell of a long day.'

Jack turned to look at her, nodding. 'Did you speak to the kid?'

'I did, he's going to have one huge headache tomorrow. He said he was attacked as soon as he walked through the gate. He never even made it to the front door with the pizza. Was his baseball cap at the scene?'

'It certainly was.' Jack pointed to the large table, which had an assortment of evidence bags on it.

'Is it covered in blood?'

'Not a drop. However, I did find a hair inside it. I figured it was probably the kid's, but I've got it ready to send off as well.'

'That's bloody brilliant; it's probably Arnie's but there's a slight chance it could also be the killer's. I think he waited to disguise himself with that hat so that the woman would open the door.'

Mattie, who'd paused in the doorway to look at his phone, walked in. 'Or it might have been pure chance that the pizza guy was there. The killer might have been going to kill her regardless.'

'Unless she was a creature of habit and phoned the same pizza takeaway at the same time every week,' Lucy said. 'It's possible, and the killer would have known this if he'd been watching her for some time.'

'I still think it's more likely just chance. Come on, Lucy, is there anything else we can do tonight? I'm knackered and we're going to have to be back here early.'

'No, I don't think there is. Sorry to have had to call you out, Jack.'

He held his hand up. 'I can't complain; it's the first after hours call out I've had for a while and the extra money always comes in handy. I'll get all this booked in and ready to be sent off to the lab first thing.'

'Thank you.'

They left him to it and went back to the car park.

'Do you want a lift?' Mattie asked.

'I'm OK thanks,' Lucy said. 'I'll take my car. You wouldn't believe how many times I could have done with it tonight.'

'Good night, Lucy.'

'Night, Mattie.'

She walked to her car and began brushing snow off the windscreen, wishing she had a pair of gloves. She got in and turned the engine on, blasting the heaters to warm it up and melt the rest of the snow. She wished with all her heart that she wasn't going home to an empty house. Even Ellie being home would be better than being all alone.

As soon as she could see out of the windows, she began the drive home. Her mind was a whirlwind of dead bodies; it was going to be a nightmare trying to switch off again. What was the connection between Audrey Stone and Edwin Wilkes? She wondered if they'd both worked at the asylum. Maybe they'd been lovers, or friends that were hiding some big secret. She didn't know what the connection was yet, but she would. She loved her job. Catching criminals that was what she lived for. The thrill of it all, the satisfaction of putting someone behind bars, was like nothing she'd ever felt in any other part of her life.

As Lucy drove up the hill to reach her house, she noticed the landing light was on. She was sure that she'd turned it off. Then again, after her rude awakening, she couldn't be one hundred per cent positive that she had.

She parked the car and opened the front door to her house, locking it behind her. The photograph on the hall table – the one of her and Ellie, taken at Scarborough on the promenade a couple of years ago – wasn't in its usual position. It was only out by a little bit, but it had definitely been moved.

Lucy felt the hairs on the back of her neck prickle. Someone was in her house. Taking out her phone, she kicked off her shoes and moved as quietly as she could through the downstairs, checking there was no one there. Everything else looked fine. The back door was locked. There were no open windows.

She made her way to the stairs and crept up them. Her heart was pounding so loudly that she couldn't hear herself think. She made it to the top without a sound, and began to check all the rooms, leaving her bedroom until last. When she opened the door to see it was just as she'd left it, she let out a sigh of relief. Everything was secure. And yet she couldn't shake the feeling that something wasn't quite right.

Stop it now, you were fast asleep when the phone call came, she told herself. *You probably didn't even know that you'd left the light on, and you probably knocked the photo on the way out.*

No one could have been in unless they had a key or knew about the spare under the plant pot, and the only people with keys were Ellie and George. Lucy knew that George would never let himself in – that wouldn't be like him. Ellie, on the other hand, would, but it was almost four in the morning. Surely she'd be tucked up in bed and fast asleep? Then Lucy thought about the group of teenagers at the hospital earlier – their parents probably thought that they were tucked up in bed as well. She would ring Ellie tomorrow and ask her if she'd been here, she decided, as she headed for her second shower of the night.

Once she had showered, and with her pyjamas back on, she ran downstairs and poured herself a large vodka. If she didn't have a drink to relax her, she'd toss and turn all night long until dawn broke – which wouldn't be long. She needed some sleep to rest her brain and let it recharge itself. She began to sip at the vodka on the way upstairs, downing the rest as she reached her bedroom door. Not bothering to turn on the light, she climbed into her bed and snuggled under the king size duvet.

CHAPTER TWENTY-FIVE

Lucy walked into the station, stifling a huge yawn. She got her radio out of the locker room and began the climb up to the first floor and her office. She needed coffee before she did anything. As she reached her desk and bent down to retrieve her mug from the drawer, she let out a loud groan. There was a bright yellow post-it note stuck to her computer monitor:

MY OFFICE NOW.

Taking her mug and the tin of expensive coffee she kept locked in her drawer, she considered sneaking back downstairs first to make a brew. She definitely needed some caffeine before the imminent conversation with her superior took place. Standing between Lucy and her coffee, though, was DCI Tom Crowe's office. Just as she was about to make a break for it, she heard his door open. His loud voice filled the air. 'Detective Inspector? A word, if you might.'

Turning to face him, she smiled and waved her mug in his direction. 'Coffee, sir?'

'In a minute. My office now, DI Harwin.'

As the DCI re-entered his office, Lucy caught sight of Mattie's tanned face as he reached the top of the stairs. He looked good – too bloody good, considering how little sleep they'd had last night. When she'd looked in the mirror this morning, her pale face – which looked even paler framed by her blood-red hair – had stared back at her. The dark circles under her eyes made her look tired and awful. Mattie gave her his best sympathetic smile now, and she sighed as she began the short walk towards the DCI's glass-fronted office. As she walked in, he was closing the blinds.

This isn't good, Lucy. It isn't good at all.

'Take a seat, Lucy. Stop hovering around. I'm not going to bite you.'

Lucy didn't know whether she believed him, because right now she felt like Little Red Riding Hood about to confront the wolf. She wasn't sure why. As far as she knew, she hadn't done anything wrong since she'd come back. She sat down on the chair opposite DCI Crowe's desk.

'I've had an email through from Sara Cross,' he said. 'According to her, you're not engaging with her, and left your last session before you'd even taken your coat off. Would you care to tell me why?'

'Sir, technically that wasn't my fault.'

'Really. Then whose fault was it?' He clasped his fingers together and leant forward, across his desk.

Lucy didn't want to get Mattie in trouble. He'd called her in early when he should have let Browning take the case. 'All right, mine,' she said. 'I didn't want to be there.'

'The whole point of having counselling is for your benefit. Not mine, not the force's. It's for you. After that unfortunate incident with that madman, I find it hard to believe that it hasn't affected you.'

Lucy squeezed her eyes shut, desperately trying to block out the images of seven-year-old Isabella and her mother, Natalia. She might not have been able to save them, but she would do her best to save everyone else.

'I'm sorry,' she said. 'You're right. I will make sure I attend the next session.'

'Good, because I had to fight hard to let them bring you back here, Lucy. They wanted to ship you off to headquarters to work in the control room on the bloody help desk. So it's thanks to me that you're still here. Anyway, enough of that. What's happening with this mess you've managed to get entangled in already?'

'As you know, there was a serious assault and another murder last night. A sixty-two-year-old woman in her own home was strangled with what looked like a pair of tights.'

'I do know. It's the first thing I was told the minute I turned my phone on this morning. So, is this murder connected to the other one? Or do you think they're completely separate incidents?'

'I can't say for definite, but yes, I do believe they're connected. I have a hunch that these two knew each other and possibly worked together at some point – their ages would be right for this. I'm waiting for a staff list from when the asylum was a working hospital, which Colin should have for me this morning.'

'So, how are we going to play this? Are we going to announce to the media that we may have a serial killer on the loose, killing respectable elderly members of the community? Or are we keeping a lid on it until we know for definite?'

'Sir, you know we need three killings for a serial. I'm hoping we'll catch whoever it is before it gets that far. Obviously there needs to be some kind of press release, but for now I want the possible connection and the victims' identities keeping out of it – at least until we have proof of a definite connection.'

'OK, I'll let the press office at headquarters know to play it down as much as they can. I want you to be truthful with me, though: can you cope with this? If it's too much for you too soon, I can get someone else to step in and give you a hand. Let them take away some of the pressure.'

'Sir, I'm fine. I'll ring Sara Cross and rebook my appointment. And I think once we do some digging into the history of the patients and staff from the asylum we will know a lot more.'

He nodded. 'Right then, that's sufficient for now. I'll have a builder's tea with two sugars.'

Lucy uncrossed her fingers, which were hidden behind her back, and felt her shoulders relax. That was her bollocking over with for now – although if they didn't have someone in custody soon, things would get a whole lot worse. Today was about finding what the connection was between the victims.

DCI Crowe passed her his mug. She picked her own up off his desk, along with the coffee, and headed towards the brew station, where Mattie was hovering around, pretending to be making himself a coffee. When she smiled, he mimed wiping the sweat from his brow, which made her giggle.

'Aw, you're far too kind,' she said. 'I'll have a coffee, and the boss wants tea with two sugars.' She passed him the mugs and coffee tin, then went to see if Colin was in yet. When she reached the open-plan CID office, she smiled to see him sitting in the corner.

'Colin, I need that staff and patient list for the hospital, like, right now. Please tell me you have it?'

'Boss, I'll have it by dinner time. I've had some trouble getting hold of it with all the data protection. You know how it is.'

'I do know how it is; I can't wait any longer, though. The bodies are starting to stack up. I would suggest you put those extra special talents to use and get it to me as soon as you can.'

'Are you actually giving me permission to go in through the back door?'

'I don't care which door you use, just get me a printout of the patients and staff and I'll buy your lunch.'

Colin grinned, and Lucy grinned back. Sometimes, to do the right thing you had to go about it the wrong way.

CHAPTER TWENTY-SIX

According to Jane's contract, she wasn't supposed to work weekends, but she'd heard about a job vacancy for a weekend assistant for the new coffee shop. It would be the perfect thing for Ellie, to keep her out of trouble and give Jane less stress. Jane had messaged Ellie on Facebook last night to tell her about it, and asked her to meet her outside the coffee shop so that she could take her in and introduce her. Ellie had reluctantly agreed – Jane had known that the thought of earning her own money would tempt her.

Jane came out of the coffee shop now with two takeaway lattes and an application form. Ellie was waiting in her car. Jane opened the car door and offered a coffee to Ellie, who took it from her. 'Thanks. What did they say?'

'Well, luck would have it that I know the manager from when she was your age. I helped her, and she knows what it's like to be a teenager. She said if you fill out this form and take it in, she'll interview you right now.'

'Really?'

Jane smiled. 'Yes, really. The thing with this life most of the time, Ellie, is it's not what you know, but who you know. So fill that out and go in and charm them with your sparkling wit and personality.'

Jane knew she was pushing it a bit, but if the girl had more to think about than her home life, it would make Jane's job a lot easier. Whilst Ellie bent her head and filled out the form, Jane sipped on her latte, thinking about how she couldn't wait to see her lover later. Finally, Ellie lifted her head and passed her the form. Jane scanned it and nodded.

'Yep, that's pretty good. Now go in and do your very best.'

Ellie got out of the car and walked across the car park to the busy café. An older woman reached the door to exit it at the same time as Ellie was going to enter, and Jane was relieved to see the girl hold the door open for the woman to pass through. She watched the woman walk over to the fancy white car that was waiting for her, where she climbed inside and kissed the woman behind the steering wheel on the cheek. Jane nodded – well, you just didn't know these days, did you? The woman looked vaguely familiar to her. She must work in the café, Jane decided, because she had the same uniform on as the manager.

A hand slammed on the windscreen in front of her and she jumped, spilling latte all down the front of her white blouse. She looked up and frowned at Ellie, who was grinning and mouthing 'sorry' at the same time. Angry, Jane forced herself to smile at the teenager, who was hopping around from one foot to the other. She put the window down.

'That was quick. Well?'

'I got the job, can you believe it? Oh, and sorry about the coffee; you were in a world of your own. I couldn't help myself!'

'Congratulations. I knew you would. At least you have something good to tell your parents now. They'll be so proud of you.'

'Do you think so? I know I've been a pain in the arse lately.'

'I do think so.' Jane didn't tell her that she thought her parents were complete fuck-ups, and that it was their own fault Ellie was playing up.

'Thank you for helping me. I can't wait to get my own money. I can buy what I want – it will be so cool!'

'When do you start?'

'I have to go back this afternoon to learn the ropes – oh, and that woman said that you're welcome to go in for coffee anytime.'

Jane smiled at her. 'Good, that's nice. Right, let's get you back home. I've done my good deed for the day. I have a life as well, you know.'

'Ooh, what've you got planned that's so exciting?' Ellie asked. 'Have you got a hot date?'

'I might just have… or I might just want to go back and put my pyjamas on and do nothing all day. You'll never know.'

Jane drove Ellie home. The girl never stopped chattering all the way. It was nice to hear her so happy; since Jane had met her, she'd only ever seen her sullen and miserable. She parked up around the corner from Ellie's dad's, not sure he'd be happy about his daughter spending time with her out of working hours.

'Thanks, Jane,' Ellie said. 'I won't let you down.'

'You'd better not, or I won't get my free coffees.'

Ellie slammed the door and wandered away, plugging her earphones in and staring down at her phone. Jane drove off. She needed to go to the supermarket to get some bits in for tonight. The only downfall with dating her younger man was the fact that he worked so late: it was impossible to make any plans.

CHAPTER TWENTY-SEVEN

Colin stood up for the first time in a couple of hours and stretched his arms out in front of him. He'd been busy, and when he lost himself in his computer, he lost all track of time and place. He looked to Lucy's office, which was empty. Mattie was on the phone, his feet on his desk and a pen in his mouth. Colin needed to pee and to collect his printing. He'd speak to Mattie once he'd relieved himself.

When he finally returned clutching a sheaf of papers, Mattie was standing up, about to go out.

'Mattie, where's the boss?'

'She had to go. The chief ordered her to go for an emergency counselling session.'

Colin didn't think Lucy would appreciate Mattie announcing her whereabouts so freely. Then again, it could happen to any of them. One dead body too many and you had to go and tell your sob story to the latest counsellor that had been shagging a senior officer and got themselves put on the payroll.

He handed the papers to Mattie. 'This is the list she wanted of staff and patients for the asylum. If you look it tells you that ward thirteen was shut down in November 75, Nurse Stone worked that ward. She left around the same time that Tommy Wright vanished from the system. Dr Edwin Wilkes also worked on the same ward. If you ask me, she was sacked. I bet she was either shagging the good doctor and got caught, or she did something really bad.'

'That's bloody brilliant,' Mattie said. 'Well done, Col. Could you not have found out exactly why she left so suddenly?'

'I may be a complete genius, but I'm not doing all your work for you. You're going to have to figure that one out. I'm going to get something to eat; tell the boss she owes me lunch.'

Col walked off, leaving Mattie grinning. This was going to cheer Lucy up no end when she got back from her head-bashing session. Not that she needed counselling – they all had to deal with shit. Pouring your heart out to a complete stranger was never going to make it go away, no matter what the powers that be thought. Everyone knew that Lucy had done what anyone else in that situation would. The Task Force sergeant was well known for his heavy-handed techniques, refusing to do anything unless he'd made the decisions. If Mattie had been there, he'd have smacked him for Lucy – but he'd been on holiday in Greece. When he'd found out what had happened, he'd gone straight around to see if Lucy was OK. They'd sat and drank a full bottle of vodka between them. They were always there for each other; always had been. No one could ever come between their friendship.

Then why won't you tell her about Heidi? the voice inside Mattie's head whispered.

He didn't know why. It just didn't seem right. She'd only just come straight back to work and was already knee-deep in a shit case. He didn't want to risk upsetting her over his love life.

Lucy was sitting opposite Sara in her office, which was far too warm. She could feel her cheeks flushed with the heat of the uncomfortable questions that were being fired her way.

'Why do you blame yourself, Lucy?

Lucy glared at her. Sara only sat up straighter – she didn't wither or back off. Lucy shrugged. 'I don't.'

'Yes, you do. You carry the weight of what happened that day around on your shoulders; it's so heavy, they almost sag. All right, let's go back to what happened when you were talking to him. You had it all under control and then – bam. In the space of a few minutes it was a mess, a complete circus that ended up with a dead woman and child.'

Lucy tried her best not to engage. She didn't want to relive the whole horrible scenario over and over again. What good would it do?

'Do you think it's all your fault?'

'No.'

'Good. Tell me why it isn't?'

'What good will that do?'

'I need to hear your side of the story.'

'Why? It doesn't change anything, does it? Natalia and her daughter are still dead. They died because that prick ignored me and took it upon himself to be the fucking hero. Some hero. I almost had him. And if I had, they would still be here today. They wouldn't be rotting corpses in a corner of a cemetery, with some dead flowers on the grave and no one to tend to it.'

'But someone does take fresh flowers,' Sara said. 'I visited the grave myself and saw there were some pretty pink roses and baby's breath in a vase. You did everything that you could to save them.'

Lucy felt the hot tears begin to form in her eyes. 'It wasn't enough.'

'No, it wasn't. The situation was taken out of your hands and you need to stop blaming yourself. Isn't it enough that you tried?'

Lucy shook her head. She might have tried but they still died.

'Sometimes life is horrible,' Sara said. 'You can't shoulder the blame for everything that goes wrong.'

'No. I have to make sure it never happens again.'

Lucy squeezed her eyes shut, desperately trying to block out the bloodied, lifeless images of the seven-year-old and her mother lying dead on the living room floor, their throats severed, the blood pooling around them so thick and cloying that Lucy could still smell it now. She'd tried so hard to talk Tony Costella around, had almost convinced him to come outside and surrender. And then the stupid, idiotic silver commander had given the order for the Task Force sergeant to go in. Costella had flipped, and within minutes had killed his beautiful family and stabbed himself in the stomach. Lucy had gone inside to survey the carnage and had lost it, running outside to punch the commander. She'd been dragged away from him and restrained.

Taking a deep breath now, she tried to push the memories away, and stared at the woman in front of her.

Sara shook her head. 'And how can you do that?'

'By being in control, by getting justice for the victims I deal with and by not listening to anyone – regardless of their rank – if I think they're wrong.'

'Look, Lucy, I admire you. I really do. You are an honest, hard-working woman. You also need to go easy on yourself, give yourself a break. When was the last time you did something for you? Not for your family or your work colleagues – you?'

Lucy looked down at the expensive wrist watch George had given her as a wedding present. Her time was just about up. She stood up and smiled at Sara. 'Thank you, I really need to go.'

Sara nodded as Lucy grabbed her bag and coat off the floor. Lucy didn't turn around or say goodbye; she needed to get out of that office before she said something she regretted. Outside the house, the feeling that she needed a stiff drink was overpowering. She looked longingly at the pub on the corner. The Black Dog had never looked so appealing. Stopping herself from heading in that direction, she pulled out her phone and dialled Mattie's number.

'Can you pick me up, please? I'll walk down to Costa coffee on the main street and get us both a drink.'

By the time she'd walked there and been served, Mattie was parked outside waiting for her. Lucy was carrying a cup holder with two drinks and a paper bag with cakes inside. Mattie leant across and opened the door for her so that she could climb in without giving herself third-degree burns. He took the coffees from her so she could fasten her seat belt, then passed them back to her.

'How did it go?'

'Bollocks.'

'That good, eh?'

Lucy stared at him. He changed the subject. 'I have something for you that will put a smile on your face. It's your list from Col.'

'Thank Christ for that – and about time.'

'Wilkes and Stone worked together from June until November 1975, when she left for some unknown reason.'

'Yes, I bloody knew there was some connection,' Lucy said. 'We need to go and speak to Florence Wilkes again. What about the rest of these sheets of paper?'

'A list of patient names. There are an awful lot of them.'

She began to flick through the pages. 'There are so many?'

'Yes. Col said that the ones with an asterisk next to them are dead.'

'Thank god for that – at least it narrows it down quite a bit. We're going to need to cross-reference dates of birth – anyone older than our victims can be put to the bottom of the list because Stone worked on a children's ward and had most of her direct contact with those patients.' She ran her finger along the page. Almost all of these were too old. She turned the pages until she came to a list of patients on ward thirteen from 1975. She counted them: thirteen, and there were four with asterisks next to their names. That left nine.

'I think we need to concentrate on these.'

'Who are they?'

'The patients who were children. There are nine of them that are still alive – or were when the hospital shut down. It won't hurt for any younger members of staff to be checked as well if we can find any names.'

'I suppose nine is a lot better than a hundred,' Mattie said. 'Do you reckon there was some funny business going on in that hospital? Maybe they did something to one of the kids and now they're seeking revenge. It's a very long time to wait to get your own back on someone though, isn't it? Why would you wait this long?'

Lucy was studying the names. Anthony Walker, Julie Pouter, Sharon Sykes, Nora Johnson, Lizzy Clements, Alice Evans, Thomas Wright, Rebecca Smith, Rachel Thompson.

'Maybe they've been in a hospital all this time,' Mattie suggested. 'Or maybe something has stirred up memories that were buried before.'

Lucy stared at the names. *Alice Evans.* She knew that name.

'What was your Aunty Alice's maiden name?' she asked Mattie.

'Evans. Why?'

'I think she might be on this list – as a patient, though. Not a staff member. If it is her, she would know if something had happened up there. She might even know why Audrey Stone disappeared from the staff.'

Frowning, Mattie took out his phone and rang his aunt. He ended the conversation with an 'I love you, Aunty Alice,' which made Lucy smile.

'She's just finished work,' Mattie said. 'She'll be home in half an hour; we can go and see her then. I'm finding it hard to believe that she was a patient though She always told me that she worked there. There are probably hundreds of Alice Evanses in this area. You don't think she's our killer, do you?'

'No, I don't,' Lucy said. 'That's stupid. Alice is far too sweet – and I don't want to sound mean, but she always comes across as being so innocent.'

Mattie began to drive. 'Anyway, I need a pee. Can we go to your house? It's nearer than mine.'

'Actually, can we drive by Cottage Lane first?' Lucy asked. 'I want to take another look at the scene.'

The street was still cordoned off, with a PCSO standing on either end of the police tape, restricting access.

'CSI have just left, ma'am. They said they'll probably be back.'

'OK, that's great, thanks.' Lucy held her hand out for the scene-guard booklet so she could sign herself in, then ducked under the tape. As she was standing staring into Audrey Stone's front garden, she heard a voice.

'Hello? I'm wondering if you could help me to find my friend.'

Lucy looked around, surprised to see a woman standing in a garden a few doors down. 'I'm not sure what you mean?'

'Are you the police lady who was in the paper?'

For a moment Lucy thought about lying – saying no and denying all knowledge. The papers had plastered her face all over their front pages with headlines such as: 'HERO COP LOSES IT'. The fact that she was staring at a crime scene now kind of gave her away, though, she supposed. How had this woman got so far through the cordon without anyone stopping her?

Lucy had a feeling she was going to regret this, but she couldn't lie. It wasn't in her nature – even though telling the truth had got her in a whole world of trouble on several occasions. She turned to see the horrified face of the PCSO pointing to one of the houses a couple of doors down and realised that the woman had probably lied about living here to get in. Lucy went over to the woman now, taking in her smart appearance and neatly cut hair. A salon dye job, too, not some home dye from Wilko's. She didn't look as though she was the type to be sending Lucy on a wild goose chase, or attention-seeking because she had nothing better to do.

'I'm Detective Inspector Harwin,' Lucy said, 'and yes, unfortunately I have been in the paper several times.'

'I'm Shannon Knowles,' the woman said. 'I just knew it was you. My friend Lauren lives here, but she's missing. I can't get hold of her and it's not like her at all. I mean, she's my best friend. Even when we don't see each other, we talk on Facebook all the time or text each other, and she hasn't been in touch.'

Lucy did her best not to groan out loud. She would bet Shannon a tenner that Lauren was currently shacked up with some bloke having a great time.

'Have you rung 101 and reported her as missing?'

'Yes, I did. They didn't seem particularly interested.'

'I'm sure they were. Have you spoken to her family and friends?'

The woman actually rolled her eyes at Lucy. 'Yes, detective; do you not think that I would do that before I even bothered the police? I do understand how stretched you all are with the budget cuts, I appreciate that there is a lot of strain on your resources. But I'm telling you now that something is wrong. I've checked, and the last time she posted on Facebook was yesterday morning before she went to work. Even when she's ill, Lauren likes to tell the whole world just how ill she is and what disease it is she's suffering from. The same if she was going away or doing something like going to the corner shop. I've lost count of how many times I've told her to stop telling the whole world her business.'

Lucy nodded. 'Right, I see.'

'No. I don't think that you do. I know that you're very busy and it's terrible what has happened here. But if you could just take a look at it or ask someone else to when you go back to the station, I'd really appreciate it.'

'Boss, can we get going now?' Mattie was standing some distance away. Lucy turned to him and frowned.

'Look, I'm really sorry about your friend,' she said to Shannon. 'What is Lauren's full name?'

'Lauren Coates; her birthday is the thirty-first of October 1990. Do you want the incident number they gave me?'

Lucy patted her pocket for her notebook and a pen, to scribble it down.

'Yes please.'

'It was log 241 of this morning.'

'Thank you,' Lucy said. 'I'll try my best to make some enquiries. I take it your contact details are all on the log?'

Shannon nodded.

'I'm a bit up to my neck in it at the moment, so it might be one of my team who ring you back. Is that OK?'

'I suppose so, but I'd rather it was you,' Shannon said. 'Something is very wrong and I don't want to waste precious time when we could be out looking for her. When we were watching the news about that poor woman and her kid you tried to save, Lauren said that she liked you. She thought that if she ever needed help from the police, she hoped they'd send you because you were "kick-arse and wouldn't take any shit".'

Lucy laughed. 'Did she, now? Well, I like the sound of Lauren. Leave it with me and as soon as I can, I'll take a look into it.'

'Thank you. I'm really scared that something bad has happened to her.'

'Well, I'm pretty sure she's just fine. Most missing persons turn up with their tails between their legs, not realising what a fuss they've caused.'

'Yes, I suppose most of them do and I really hope that's the case with Lauren. Thank you.'

Shannon turned and began to walk back towards the cordon. Lucy watched her go, then turned to speak with Mattie. Despite her reassuring words to the other woman, her stomach was churning. She felt that there may just be something very wrong about Lauren Coates's disappearance.

Mattie raised his eyebrows. 'Who was that? The press?'

She shook her head. 'No. I wish it had been, it wouldn't have been so bad.'

Mattie pulled a face.

'I'll tell you in the car,' she said. 'Come on, let's get back to mine before those coffees are stone cold.'

Lucy walked towards Mattie's car, feeling as if her head was about to explode with all the stuff going on inside it. Two bodies, one serious assault, and now a missing person who just happened to live in the same street as the assault and one of the murders. She would have a read of the missing person's report and speak to the officer in charge, maybe even the sergeant. Then she could speak to Shannon Knowles and tell her that everything was all in hand. The last thing Lucy needed now was to get involved in a case that wasn't even hers. Unless, of course, there was some connection. Then she would have to.

Lucy could feel a migraine beginning that wasn't going to be pushed away with two paracetamol.

CHAPTER TWENTY-EIGHT

Lucy carried the coffees into her kitchen whilst Mattie ran upstairs to use the toilet. She took the huge slices of coffee cake out of the bag, put them onto two plates and got forks out of the drawer. She heard the toilet flush and Mattie come thundering down the stairs.

'Did you wipe the seat?' she asked as he entered the kitchen.

'Of course.'

'You'd better have; I hate it when you piss all over it.'

Mattie choked on the huge forkful of cake he'd just shoved into his mouth. 'Lucy. Ladies don't talk like that, and I've never done that in your house.'

She grinned. 'No, but you do it in yours.'

He shrugged. 'My home is my castle; it's different there.'

'Not when I sit on it.'

They both started to laugh. Lucy managed to finish her mouthful of cake without choking. 'I don't believe you; I'm going to check,' she said. But she winked at him before she left the room.

She was pleased to see the toilet seat was still up. After she'd finished and come out onto the landing, she noticed her bedroom door was shut. She'd left it open. She knew that she had. She walked across and went into the room. Her bedside drawer was slightly open. She had *definitely* shut that. Opening the drawer further, she saw that her diary had been moved.

Fuck, fuck, fuck. Ellie, I'm not having this.

She stormed back downstairs. Mattie looked at her.

'We need to go and call at George's first,' Lucy said. 'I have to speak to Ellie.'

'Whatever you say. You're the boss.'

They drove to George's large, detached house in silence. Lucy felt her heart strings tug when it came into view. She'd loved that house so much, and had cried when she'd left.

Mattie parked on the double drive and Lucy jumped out.

'I'll just wait here then, should I?' Mattie said.

She didn't answer him, but jogged up the steps to the front door and hammered loudly. The door opened and she pushed past George to go inside.

'Where's Ellie? I need to speak to her.'

She was dimly aware of George lifting his hand to wave at Mattie as she shouted up the stairs: 'Ellie? Please can you come down here now? I need to speak to you!'

'Lucy,' George said, 'I don't know what's wrong, but she's only just come home from an induction at work.'

'What do you mean, she's been at work?' Lucy frowned. 'When did she get a job? Or more importantly, where did she get one?'

Ellie appeared at the top of the stairs in a fluffy pink dressing gown, a towel wrapped around her wet hair. 'If you'd bothered to read the messages I sent you, then you'd know all about my new job.'

'I'm at work,' Lucy said, shortly. 'I haven't had the time. Look, Ellie, I don't mind you coming home when I'm not in, but keep out of my bedroom. You know that's the only room that's off-limits. Have you been reading my diary?' She was trying her best to keep calm, but her voice had risen sharply. Ellie was looking at her as if she was insane, which was even more infuriating.

'I haven't been in your stupid fucking house,' Ellie said. 'And why would I want to read your diary? All you do is work and drink; it's not like you have anything exciting to write about. You come home stinking of dead bodies. Why would I want to read all about your sad, shitty life?'

Lucy watched as her daughter ran towards her bedroom, slamming the door shut behind her. All the anger she'd felt moments ago dissipated as her daughter's words sank in. They hurt. Ellie was right: she *did* have a pathetic, sad, shitty life.

George took hold of her arm, leading her into the kitchen. He closed the door behind him and pointed to a chair, which Lucy slumped in.

'Bloody hell, Lucy, what's wrong with you? She's really tried today and wanted to make you proud of her. Do you know how upset she was when you didn't even bother to message her back and congratulate her? Now you come here and pull this crap.'

'I'm so sorry, George; I was called out again last night. There's been another murder. I'm knackered, and then I went home and thought that she'd been rooting through my stuff instead of going to that shitty place for delinquents.'

'Well she hasn't been to "that shitty place for delinquents" because they told her she couldn't go back until Wednesday. And anyway, it's Saturday.'

Lucy stood up. 'Can I go and apologise?'

The front door slammed and George looked even more uncomfortable than he already was.

'Hello, darling,' a voice called from the hallway. 'You're going to love what I've just bought for the baby.'

George began to shake his head, as if he wanted this whole mess to not be true. Rosie walked in. The smile on her face dropped when she saw Lucy standing there.

'Hello, Rosie,' Lucy said. 'Congratulations. I'm leaving; I just popped in to see Ellie.'

Rosie nodded at Lucy, keeping her distance. She'd once got too close to Lucy the first time they'd ever met, and had ended up in a very unpleasant screaming match.

'I'm sorry, George,' Lucy said. 'Please can you tell Ellie how sorry I am? I'll ring her later when she's calmed down a little.'

Lucy walked past them both, feeling like the worst mother in the world once more. Her heart ached to see Rosie standing in what had once been *her* kitchen, with *her* family. It was a shame, Lucy thought, that she wasn't as good a mother as she was a detective. Solving crimes was easy compared to being a parent. Still, at least she could do her job now and find the killer who was currently on the loose. That way she would prove to herself that she wasn't a complete loser.

She went outside and got in the car. Mattie took one look at her face and muttered, 'Oh fuck, Lucy. What have you done now? Do you want to talk about it?'

He was greeted by a deadly silence.

'I guess not. Come on, let's go and see Alice. She's always happy to see you, and she might be able to help with our case.'

CHAPTER TWENTY-NINE

October 1975

Alice was awake, yet she couldn't open her eyes. She was so tired. Had she dreamt last night or had it been real? Poor Tommy, being cornered in the shower room, to start with. Then there had been that single beam of light as someone had dragged something heavy towards the cemetery in the early hours of the morning.

She forced her eyelids to open and stared across at Tommy's empty bed. His beloved scruffy bear was lying at the bottom of it. She decided she ought to grab it and keep it safe for him for when he came back from wherever it was they had sent him. Before she could move, though, she heard the familiar footsteps of Nurse Stone click-clacking down the corridor.

Alice pretended to still be asleep, watching the nurse through a tiny slit in her eyelids. The woman had a rubbish bag in her hand. She scooped up Tommy's bear with one hand and threw it in.

Alice couldn't help herself. She sat up. 'Where's Tommy?'

Nurse Stone turned to glare at her. 'He's unwell. They had to move him to the general in the early hours.'

'What are you doing with his bear?'

'I'm taking it with the rest of his stuff so that he has it when he wakes up.'

'Are you sure you haven't hurt him?'

Nurse Stone gave her a look of quiet fury. 'Don't talk utter rubbish, girl. Why would we want to hurt him? He's only a child.'

Alice didn't push her any further. Instead, she lay back on her arms and watched as Nurse Stone walked towards the ward exit with the rubbish bag in one hand and her handbag in the other. One of the porters was pushing the rubbish cart into the ward, and the nurse handed him the rubbish bag with Tommy's bear inside it. He took it and threw it in with the rest of the crap.

Alice knew then that Tommy was never coming back. Whatever they'd done to him last night had killed him. Poor Tommy was probably lying stone cold dead somewhere. If only she could tell someone. But who would believe her? They would think she was trying to cause trouble. If only she could get out of here.

She heard a loud yawn come from Lizzy's bed, and wondered if she should tell her what had just happened.

'I'm starving,' Lizzy said. 'And what is that horrible screaming?'

Alice had been so absorbed in her thoughts, she hadn't even noticed the screaming coming from the floor above them.

'Oh, it's just the real crazies upstairs,' Alice said. 'They always scream before they get their morning happy pills.'

Lizzy nodded. 'Where's Tommy? His bed is still empty.'

Alice shrugged. 'He never came back.'

'Oh.'

'Look,' Alice said, 'the nurses this morning are nice, so make sure you eat everything they give to you. The witch has gone home, but she'll be back at teatime. Some days she doesn't even dish the food out, depending on what sort of mood she is in. She'll leave it on the trolley so we can smell it, but we can't eat it and no one dares to ask her for it because if you do, she won't feed you the next time either. I don't know why she does that because it tastes awful most of the time anyway, it's not as if it's something to look forward to. I only eat it to keep my strength up, and so should you.'

'OK.'

* * *

Lizzy settled back down in her bed. She decided that she would do what Alice had said, because her mum or dad would surely be coming to get her today anyway. They wouldn't leave her in this cold, smelly hospital with its mean nurses much longer, would they?

She tried to stand up so that she could go to the toilet, but she felt dizzy. She sat back down. She couldn't take her eyes off Tommy's empty bed. The nurses, who were gathered around the station in the middle of the room, were all watching her. She knew that they had been whispering about her – about what she'd done – when they'd thought she wasn't listening. She didn't care. Alice had told her to do what they said, and then she'd be all right, so she would. She didn't want to get into any more trouble before her dad came to collect her. Hopefully it wouldn't be long before he did, because now she wanted to go home more than ever. She wanted to sleep in her own bed and play with her own toys.

CHAPTER THIRTY

They drove to Alice's house in a comfortable silence. Mattie liked that about Lucy. Some women chattered away, feeling the need to fill an empty void, but not her. She was quite happy to sit quietly, which he found refreshing.

He parked outside Alice's small terraced house, which wasn't too far away from the old pier. He inhaled the salty sea air. This part of town was run down. The majority of houses were all rented properties with a fast turnaround of tenants, some of them well known to the police. Alice had always lived here, though, and wouldn't think about moving. Mattie knew for a fact it wasn't for the lack of her daughter Beth trying.

The curtain moved and Alice peered at them through the glass. She waved, and Mattie waved back.

Lucy smiled for the first time since she'd left George's house. 'I like your aunt Alice. She's one of life's nice people. What you see is what you get. A lovely, kind, decent lady.'

'Yeah,' Mattie said. 'Let's just hope she doesn't turn out to be our killer, then, because that will blow your theory right out of the water.' He winked at her and began to laugh.

Lucy shook her head. 'I can't believe you just said that. You know, sometimes you're a complete cock.'

The front door opened and Mattie stepped in first, kissing Alice on the cheek before going through to the kitchen to put the kettle on. He listened to Lucy and Alice talk as they followed him through.

'How are you, Alice?' Lucy was saying. 'It's so lovely to see you.'

'And you, dear. I've been at work. Did Matthew tell you I have a job now?'

Lucy shook her head. 'No, he didn't. Everyone has jobs now, and I have no idea about any of them! That's wonderful news. Are you enjoying it?'

'Well, it's harder work than I thought,' Alice said, 'and at fifty-six I did wonder if I was too old to learn, but the girls I work with are nice and it's a little bit of pocket money for me.'

'Right, the tea's brewing,' Mattie said.

Alice laughed. 'You're doing a cracking job of getting him trained up, Lucy. You two make such a nice couple; I can't wait for the day that you both realise it and stop skirting around each other.'

Mattie felt himself flush as Alice crossed to take the teapot off him.

'You sit down, I'll finish off,' she said. 'You might make me ill if you carry on; I'm not used to it.'

Lucy began to laugh and Mattie stuck his tongue out at the pair of them. He sat down as requested, and waited whilst Alice poured the tea into pretty china teacups and passed them around.

'Now,' Alice said, 'to what do I owe the pleasure of a visit from my favourite nephew?'

'I'm your only nephew.'

'Same thing, dear.'

It was Lucy who took the lead. 'We have a very bad situation on our hands at the moment, Alice. There have been two murders and we think they're connected, but we don't know how. What we do know is that both of the victims worked at The Moore before it closed down.'

Alice crossed herself, then took a sip of her tea. She stared across the kitchen into space, as if she'd just been sent back to another time and place. Mattie wondered if they'd upset her. Finally, she composed herself and looked at them.

'That was a bad place. A very bad place.'

'I know,' Lucy said, 'and I hate to ask you this, but whilst we were trying to find out the names of staff and patients, your name came up. Or someone with the same name as you, on the patient list.'

'Yes,' Alice said. 'That was me.'

Mattie and Lucy exchanged glances. 'If it's too painful and you don't want to talk about any of this,' Mattie said, 'then we completely understand.'

Alice looked at Lucy. 'Will it help you to catch whoever has done this if I do?'

'I think so, yes.'

Alice let out a huge sigh. 'I wasn't a bad girl – although according to my mother I was. She never liked me the way that she liked your mum, Matthew. I was born out of wedlock, and you know what a big deal it was back then. She met another man – your granddad, Matthew – who married her, and then she got pregnant with your mum. I was so angry with her for getting pregnant again when she didn't even bother with me. I thought she wouldn't care for the baby. But she did – she so obviously loved her. She was very different with her to the way she was with me.'

'I had no idea about any of this, Alice, or why it was such a big secret. It wasn't your fault, it was Grandma's, yet she treated you as if it was?'

'The older I got, the angrier I got. In the end, when I was fourteen, my mother took me to the doctor's, telling them I was some kind of evil devil child. Uncontrollable. She cried and begged, she refused to take me home with her, so he sent me straight up to the asylum.

'I suppose, looking back, it was quite common then, especially if you weren't too bright. There were kids on some of the wards who couldn't read or write. They had no place being inside that hellhole; all they needed was some extra help. I had no place there either. I wasn't mental at all, but my mother had told everyone that I was. I remember sitting there crying tears of anger whilst listening to her lies. All she wanted was to be a happy family with your mum and her husband, I was just an embarrassment.'

'Oh no. That's terrible, Alice.' Mattie dragged his chair closer to his aunt and reached out, putting his hand onto hers. She looked up at him with love in her eyes.

'You know,' she said, 'when I see how teenagers carry on these days, it makes me shudder. If they'd been like that in my day, they would have been lobotomised.'

Lucy looked at Mattie. 'One of the murder victims was lobotomised,' she said. 'There was a metal spike protruding from his eye.'

Alice flinched.

'I'm sorry, Alice,' Lucy said. 'We can talk about something else.'

'No, I want to help,' the older lady said. 'I've been keeping this shame inside my heart for years. It might do me some good to finally tell someone and let it all go. I was lobotomised.'

Both Mattie and Lucy gasped.

'But why, Aunt Alice?' Mattie asked. 'I can't believe they would do that to a kid. Why did they do that to you? You were only fourteen!'

Alice nodded, pulling a tissue from her sleeve to dab at her leaking eye. 'I was, but it was what they did. I'll never forget the day it happened. There was a nurse on the children's ward who was a horrible woman – the nastiest I've ever come across. I've never been able to understand why she was allowed to work with children. She was so evil. She didn't like me because I wouldn't do what she told me. So she told the doctor I was uncontrollable, that none of the drugs they were giving to me had worked She suggested that the doctor carried out the radical new treatment that was taking the country by storm. He agreed, and arranged to perform a transorbital lobotomy on me.'

'I know it was a long time ago,' Lucy said, gently, 'but do you remember the nurse's name?'

'My dear, I could never forget it. She was called Nurse Stone. Nurse Audrey Stone.'

Mattie saw that Lucy was trying to keep her face from reacting, not wanting to upset Alice any more than she already had.

'What about the doctor that performed the lobotomy?' Lucy asked.

Mattie knew the name Alice was going to give before she even opened her mouth, and he knew that Lucy did too.

'Dr Wilkes,' Alice said. 'He was a bit of a bully, too. There was this one little boy, Tommy, who they chased into the showers one night – Dr Wilkes and Nurse Stone together. The next morning when I woke up, Tommy had gone. There was no sign of him anywhere, but his teddy was still on his bed where he'd left it – until Nurse Stone came and took it away in a plastic bag, as if it was just a leftover piece of rubbish. She didn't think anyone had noticed, but I had. Tommy wouldn't go to sleep unless he had that bear to cuddle up to. I often wondered what they did to that poor boy that night. I asked them where he'd gone. I would have kept on asking, too. That was another reason they were so keen to lobotomise me, I think. I was a vegetable for months after the procedure – I can't actually remember it, thank god. I slowly began to regain my memory and various other functions that I'd lost, but it took a very long time. The lobotomy stopped me from talking to anyone or saying anything that I shouldn't. After a few weeks the doctor told my mother I was cured and I was sent home.'

Alice caught Mattie and Lucy exchanging a glance. 'I'm not as frail as you might think,' she said. 'Tell me and I promise that I won't breathe a word to anyone. Those bodies you found: it was them, wasn't it? Nurse Stone and Dr Wilkes?'

Lucy nodded, and Mattie was glad. Alice deserved to know the truth. She was a lot tougher than they'd given her credit for. Besides, the victims' names would be all over the newspapers soon enough.

'Yes, it was,' Lucy said.

'Then I think you need to find Lizzy Clements,' Alice told them. 'She was a fiery child and hated them more than any of us. She was the only one of the other patients I ever really bothered with. I felt sorry for her. She was only a child: nine years old when they put her in there. I looked after her until they lobotomised me, and then I was in no fit state to look after anyone. She took it hard.'

'Do you know why they put her in there?' Lucy asked.

'She told me she'd put a pillow over her baby brother's face because she hated his crying all the time. He'd died.'

'Have you ever seen her since?' Lucy pressed. 'Do you know where she might be?'

Alice shook her head.

'Thank you so much, Alice,' Lucy said. 'You've been such a good help. I'm really sorry if I've upset you by bringing it all back.'

'You haven't upset me, Lucy. Believe it or not, I feel a little bit better for speaking about it. It's always been a shameful family secret. The skeleton in the closet, so to speak.'

Mattie pulled her close. 'You, Aunt Alice, are amazing and I love you loads.' He kissed Alice's cheek and she hugged him back.

'I'm so sorry we have to leave so soon,' said Lucy.

'Go. Don't you be worrying about me. I'll be fine; you have a killer to catch. I'm not sad to hear that those two are dead, though, and I suppose that makes me a bad person. I do feel sorry for their families. They'll be grieving for them.'

Mattie knew how she felt. How many times had he sat in a courtroom, watching the families of the accused? He and Lucy had witnessed first-hand the disbelief of family members that their husband, son, mother or daughter could do something so horrific as to take another person's life. It was truly heartbreaking.

Leaving Alice to her memories, they got back into Mattie's truck to return to the station.

CHAPTER THIRTY-ONE

Nurse Stone. Audrey Stone. You were living out your life just as I'd always imagined you would. A bitter, lonely old spinster. It was nothing that you didn't deserve. I would sit outside your house, waiting for you to come home, just to see if you ever deviated from your routines. You didn't.

I have never met a woman crueller than you – except for me, possibly, but we won't get into that. I have my reasons, whereas as far as I know, you were just an evil bitch for the sake of it. You thoroughly deserved what you got, as did the doctor. Live by the sword, die by the sword – or in your case by your American Tan fifteen-denier tights. How many pairs did you go through looking after us all? Snagging them on the metal bed frames, then punishing us terrified kids because of your own mistakes. How many children had to go without their supper because you were in a bad mood? And do you remember Tommy Wright's last night? Because I certainly do. It's ingrained into my mind.

Did you ever come home and feel bad about the way you treated those children? I don't think that you did; I think you loved every minute of being in charge and making their lives as miserable as you possibly could. Did you ever ask yourself why? Did you have a terrible childhood? Were you abused or mistreated when you were a baby or a young child? I've tried to find out if you were, but all I know is that you were born the only child of a couple who doted on you. What would your parents say if they knew how you behaved towards those scared, sad children in The Moore? I don't think they would have approved of your behaviour, Audrey.

Well, it came full circle, didn't it? You ended up dying on your own, afraid, choked to death by a pair of your beloved tights.

It was such a shame that pretty young girl saw the final moments of your life. I only ever meant to kill the people who deserved it, but she got in the way, and now she's dead. That's your fault, too – I wouldn't have had to kill her if I hadn't had to kill you. So, technically, you are the one who's going to have to explain her death to St Peter, if you ever get near to those pearly white gates. Somehow I don't think God would have you. He wouldn't let you in, would he? And you knew that deep down.

When your life flashed before your eyes at the end, did you have any happy memories at all? I don't think that you did. What did you have to smile about? I'll tell you what: nothing. You never deserved to live this long; neither you nor the doctor should have got away with what you did. I'm just glad that I realised before it was too late that I had to make you pay for every mean, spiteful thing you ever did.

No one is going to be crying at your funeral, Audrey Stone. I wonder how that made you feel at the end, when you realised?

What goes around comes around. Sometimes it just takes a little bit longer than it should.

CHAPTER THIRTY-TWO

Lucy didn't speak to Mattie all the way back to the station. She was in shock about what Alice had just told them. How could they have treated children like that? She couldn't get the image of the metal spike out her mind. They had done that to Alice without a moment's hesitation. What sort of people were they? How had it ever been allowed? And what had happened to that little boy, Tommy, who Alice had mentioned?

Lucy felt her heart break for all the children The Moore had housed. So young and innocent, left on their own in a huge hospital without their families. It must have been terrifying. She might not be the best parent in the world, but she loved Ellie and couldn't imagine leaving her in a place like that just because she was hard work. Poor Alice. How she'd ever got over it and managed to lead a relatively normal life was a testament to her strength.

She needed to know what had happened to Tommy. Maybe he had been sent somewhere else and it was him who had come back to get his revenge? With Lizzy Clements, that was two possible suspects already from the nine names on the list.

Lucy walked back into the office to see Col sitting at his desk in his usual position, head bent and fingers furiously flying over the keyboard.

'Thank you for the list,' she said. 'Now can you try and find me as much information on a Lizzy Clements as possible? I need to know if her parents are still alive, if she's still alive – anything at all.'

'Yes, boss. What about Alice Evans? She's the next.'

'There's no need to find out anything about Alice Evans. I've already spoken to her and she's not a suspect at this time.'

Colin looked as if he was about to ask her how she'd managed this, then changed his mind when he saw the don't-piss-me-off face she was wearing.

'According to that list, the others had more serious physical or mental disabilities; I can't see them living independently. It's highly likely they are living in care homes or assisted housing now. So I suppose Lizzy is as good a place to start as any.'

'Thank you Colin, I thought so too.'

Lucy went into her office, where Mattie was waiting for her.

'Can you believe what Alice said?' he said. 'I'm so shocked by it all. I didn't really know my gran, but Alice has always been there for my mum. She looked after me when I was little so my mum could go to work. I wonder if Beth knows about it?'

'I got the impression that until we jumped in with our big feet, it isn't something Alice had ever talked about,' Lucy said. 'Especially not to her own daughter. It's so desperately sad.'

The phone on Lucy's desk began to ring. Mattie left the office and she picked it up – Col was on the line.

'There is a Mr and Mrs Clements at eleven, Brookfield Terrace,' he told her. 'They're the right age to be Lizzy's parents – no mention of an Elizabeth or Lizzy, though.'

'Well, I can't see her still living with her parents, unless she's unable to live alone. I mean, how old would she be now?'

She could see Col at his desk through the glass partition, counting it out on his fingers. 'Fifty-one,' he said.

'Are they the only Clements in Brooklyn Bay?'

'Yes. Don't forget, boss, Lizzy is probably not called Clements now. There's a good chance she's married or changed her name.'

'Thank you, Col. I'll bear that in mind.' She grinned and put the phone down, and looked through the partition for Mattie. He was laughing with Browning about something. She threw her jacket over her arm and crossed the room towards him, wondering if they were laughing about her.

'Come on,' she said. 'We have an address for the Clements. No record of a Lizzy, though.'

Mattie shrugged. 'What about Tommy?'

Lucy turned to Col and asked, 'Did you find me anything on Tommy Wright?'

Col shook his head. 'Nothing. It's as if both he and Lizzy disappeared without a trace.'

'Well, try and find me something on him, please. There has to be something on record. Why was he in the hospital in the first place?'

'Yes, boss.'

As they were driving towards Brookfield Terrace, Lucy lifted her hand to her mouth.

'Oh my god, I've just had a horrible thought. Do you think Alice is in any danger? She was there in the asylum and knew the other kids. If the killer is one of them, and they found out she'd been talking to us...'

'I didn't think of that. We can't risk it; I'd never be able to live with myself if something happened to her.'

'Go back to Alice's,' Lucy said. 'Let's take her to Beth's house for a couple of nights, or at least until we know who the killer is and what's happening.'

Mattie put his foot down on the accelerator. Alice was far too vulnerable to leave her all alone like a sitting duck.

Much later than they'd planned, they finally parked up outside 11, Brookfield Terrace. Alice had been safely deposited at her daughter's house, much to her objection. Lucy pulled down the sun visor to check her eyeliner hadn't smudged. She'd lost count of the number of times she'd almost been in tears today.

'You look fine,' Mattie said. 'Just as good as when you walked into work this morning.'

'Thanks. I feel like a complete emotional wreck today. Not to mention knackered. How come you don't have dark circles under your eyes like I do?'

'Maybe it's your time of the month?'

Lucy turned to stare at him, shaking her head. 'Don't you dare. You know how much I hate all that crap. Blaming everything on it pisses me off.'

Mattie held up his hands. 'Slow down, tiger. I was just trying to get in touch with my feminine side and be sympathetic.'

'Well if you want to continue working with me, don't bother,' Lucy said. 'The last thing I want is you turning into some fanny.'

Mattie smiled. 'I love winding you up. It's like taking candy from a baby. The reason I don't have dark circles under my eyes is because of my masculine good looks and genes.'

He jumped out of the car before she could punch him in the side of the head.

Lucy smiled, and climbed out with a bit more effort. She smoothed down her trousers and pulled her jacket out of the back of the car, shrugging it on. Mattie was already knocking on the door. It was opened by a grey-haired man, who must have been at least in his seventies. Lucy joined them, her warrant card in her hand.

'Mr Clements?'

He nodded.

'I'm Detective Inspector Lucy Harwin; this is Detective Sergeant Matthew Jackson. Could we come in and talk to you?'

The man pulled a pair of thick black-rimmed glassed from his shirt pocket and put them on. He took the card from Lucy and studied it, looking between her and the photograph closely. She knew why: on the card she had platinum blonde hair, not bright red. The man finally nodded and stepped to one side to let them in, indicating a doorway inside. 'Through there,' he said.

They walked in to a sitting room with a fire burning so hot that Lucy thought her make-up might melt from her face. Beside the fire sat an elderly woman, reading a book, which she put down when she realised they were there. Lucy noticed the hearing aids on the table next to her and smiled at her. The woman arched an eyebrow at her husband.

'It's the police, Sandra,' he said. 'They want a word.'

She shook her head at him. 'What?'

Much louder, he shouted: 'They're from the police!'

The woman looked at Lucy, then her husband, and shrugged her shoulders. He tutted and walked across to her, handing her the hearing aids.

'For god's sake, woman, put them in so you know what we're talking about!'

Sandra smiled at Lucy as she fastened in the hearing aids. 'Sorry, I forget to replace them sometimes. I have to take them out because he snores so loudly, and I can't stand it when I'm trying to read. Isn't that right, Ian?'

Mattie was trying his best not to grin. Lucy waited until Sandra had got her hearing aids in, and had turned them down to stop them from whistling.

'Now, that's better,' Sandra said. 'So, who are you?'

'They're from the bloody police, Sandra,' Ian Clements said. 'How many times?'

Lucy stepped forward and offered her hand. 'I'm Lucy, and this is my partner, Matthew. We need to ask you some questions about your daughter Lizzy.'

Ian sat down suddenly, and Sandra's face paled.

'I'm really sorry if I've upset you,' Lucy said, 'but we desperately need to ask you about her. Is that OK?'

Sandra indicated they should take a seat on the sofa. 'Please sit down, both of you. It's been such a long time, that's all. It's such a shock to hear her name after all this time. We don't talk about her any more – in fact, we haven't spoken her name for years.'

'We have a serious incident involving the asylum and some of the staff who worked there,' Lucy explained. 'We're just trying to work our way through a list of patients that were there at the same time as the staff members. We know that Lizzy was on one of the children's wards, and that she was admitted when she was nine years old. Could I ask for some more information about that?'

Neither one of the elderly couple spoke. For a while, they just stared at each other, as if they were afraid to say anything out loud. In the end, it was Sandra who broke the trance and began to talk.

'We didn't know what else to do with her. Where do you take a child after they've done something so horrific? You do know that she suffocated our baby, don't you? Her own brother? You have to understand, we were devastated about John. The doctors had told me there would be no more children after I had Lizzy. It was such a difficult birth. When I fell with John, we'd given up hope, hadn't we, love?'

Ian nodded, still unable to speak.

Lucy reached out, taking hold of Sandra's hand. 'We do understand, and I'm so very sorry for your loss. I can't imagine how devastated you all were. We are hoping to be able to trace Lizzy now, though. We need to speak to her about the incident I mentioned. Only, we haven't had any luck. Where did she go after The Moore was shut down?'

'As far as I know, they put her into another secure hospital. You can't speak to her, I'm afraid,' Sandra said.

'Why not?'

'She's dead.'

Lucy was stunned.

'We didn't have anything to do with her after she was put into that hospital,' Sandra continued. 'We couldn't go and visit her – no matter how much I wanted to, some days. Every time we looked at her we would have been reminded of what she'd done to our baby.'

Lucy felt a cold chill settle over her. How could they have abandoned their own daughter like that? Yes, what that little girl had done was horrific – but she was nine years old at the time. She likely wouldn't have had any concept about the consequences of it.

Mattie took over, drawing the Clements' attention away from Lucy. 'When did she die?'

Ian finally looked at Mattie. 'Nineteen ninety,' he said. 'We weren't told until after she'd been buried. Can you believe it? We'd gone on our very first holiday abroad since having the children. I'd arranged it as a surprise so we just upped and went, nobody knew where we were. They didn't have those phones all you youngsters have now. It wasn't until we came home that we found out that she'd died of a drug overdose.'

'So, I take it that you never officially identified her?' Mattie asked.

They both shook their heads. 'Her next-door neighbour found her, and he was a good friend, apparently, so he did it. We were grateful. Neither of us wanted to see her like that.'

Lucy thought she knew why. They hadn't wanted to face the guilt of abandoning their daughter – a daughter who, without the support of her parents, had become a drug addict and died. It was awful. Lucy couldn't imagine ever doing that to Ellie if she'd found herself in the Clements' position. The guilt of it would weigh so heavy on her shoulders that she'd end up drowning underneath it all.

'Do you know the name of the neighbour?' Lucy asked. 'And I'm sorry to ask, but have you got a copy of the death certificate we could take a look at?'

Ian shook his head. 'He was called David something; I can't remember the surname. And we never collected a death certificate for her. There was no need to; she'd already been dead to us for fifteen years.'

'Thank you for your time,' Lucy said. 'I don't think we need to know anything else. I'm very sorry to have bothered you.' She stood up and held out her hand to shake Ian's and then Sandra's. 'Once again, I'm sorry for your loss.'

She walked out. She couldn't bear to be in that stifling hot room any longer, absorbing the still-raw grief for their murdered baby that both the Clements radiated from every pore in their bodies. It didn't matter how long it had been, when you lost a child it still felt as if it was just yesterday. She felt even worse now about her situation with Ellie than she had earlier. She needed to sort herself out and stop pushing her own daughter away from her.

Mattie broke the silence as they drove away. 'Phew, that was awful,' he said. 'They must have spent their entire lives grieving for their children. I'm surprised that they're still together, to be honest; normally strain like that finishes off relationships.'

Lucy nodded, not trusting herself to speak just yet.

'Well, if she's dead, that blows our theory that she was our killer out of the water, doesn't it?' Mattie continued. 'Now we're going to have to trawl through the rest of the names on Col's list. This could take forever.'

'I'm not happy with the fact that they didn't get to identify her body though, are you?' Lucy said quietly. 'I think she could have found someone who looked similar to her and killed them – then got that neighbour to identify the body as hers. I still think she could be out there. She's a good suspect. For all we know she's carried on killing since she was released from hospital. She could be an expert at it by now – and when you look at the doctor's murder, it didn't look as if it had been done by someone inexperienced. It was too professional, too clean.'

'Yes, but faking her own death, boss? That's going a bit too far, isn't it? Then waiting years to seek her revenge… It sounds like something out of a book.'

'Sod off,' Lucy said. 'Have you got any better ideas?'

She pulled her hair from the tight bun she'd wrapped it in earlier. Her head was banging and she felt like shit.

'How could they abandon her like that?' she asked aloud. 'Never speak to her again… I can't get my head around it at all. Wouldn't they have wanted to ask her why she'd done it? When we get back to the station, I want to see a copy of Lizzy Clements' death certificate. I want to speak to the officer who dealt with her sudden death, and I want to know who identified her body. We need to speak to whoever it was.'

'It was twenty-five years ago. The officer probably retired long ago.'

'They probably did, but there's still a slim chance it was one of the older coppers who are still around, waiting to get their thirty years in. I also want to see if there's anything on record about the death of the baby, John Clements. It was only in 1975 – there should be a record of it somewhere. I don't want to dismiss Lizzy Clements as a suspect just yet. At the minute, Lizzy Clements and Tommy Wright are all we've got.'

CHAPTER THIRTY-THREE

Lucy made herself a mug of coffee and took it to her office, where she shut the door. She'd given Col and Browning the task of searching for every piece of information relating to the sudden death of Lizzy Clements. She needed a bit of time to herself: time to think without listening to the rubbish that they were all chattering about in the office. She felt as if any moment now, everything was going to collide in a spectacular fashion. There was no denying it: she loved her job. Even on the darkest days, when she told herself she hated it, she was still glad that she didn't work in a supermarket or a school.

She logged on to her computer and waited patiently for the homepage to load, blowing on the hot coffee. She took a sip, but too soon – it burnt her tongue and fur began to form on it almost immediately. She put the mug down, vowing to wait until it was definitely much cooler, and began to type the log number that Shannon had given to her into the search bar. She had promised the woman she would look into it, and Lucy never broke her promises.

The blue screen filled with the incident log and a link to the missing person's report, which she clicked on. An image of Lauren Coates began to load. Lucy was taken aback by how stunning she was. Her pale blue eyes stared out from the screen, her face framed by lots of blonde hair. Suddenly, an image of her lying dead and decomposing filled Lucy's mind. She had to shake her head to clear it, trying her best not to think bad thoughts. It was difficult, though. This girl, who didn't look as if she had a care in the world, smiled out of the screen, and Lucy felt her heart fill with sorrow at the idea that something bad could have happened to her.

She read through the notes on the case. There was a long list of actions on the report that the sergeant had put on; most of them had been completed. Lucy noticed that no one had done a full search of Lauren's house. Lauren's parents were out of the country on holiday. Maybe she'd flown out to be with them? It was a very possible likelihood. She decided to ask Shannon to check. If it wasn't there, they could get hold of passport control and ask them to check if it had been used recently. She copied the contact details for Shannon into the phone box on the computer screen, and dialled her number.

'Shannon? It's DI Lucy Harwin. Have you actually been into Lauren's address and checked to see if she was there? No? Have you got a key? Do you know if any of the officers have been inside to have a look?' There was a slight pause. 'No, OK, that's fine. Leave it with me. I'll ring you when we have some information.'

Lucy ended the call. She had a feeling that she needed to go in and check the house herself. Lauren didn't look like the sort of girl to just up and leave without telling anyone. She had a good job at the local doctors' surgery. No criminal record, wasn't on the system for anything. What if, somehow, she'd seen something she shouldn't have on the night Audrey Stone had been killed? It was a long shot, but she only lived a few doors away from the nurse. And they both worked at the same doctors' surgery – they were connected.

Mattie knocked on her office door and walked inside without waiting to be invited. He had two cardboard cups – the smell of fresh coffee filled Lucy's nostrils. He placed one cup in front of Lucy, then sat in the chair opposite her desk and lifted the lid on his own cup to cool it down. Lucy looked at her mug of almost cold coffee and pushed it to one side.

'You know me so well,' she said. 'The way to my heart is fresh coffee, and cakes with lots of buttercream and jam inside.'

'You don't say?' Mattie grinned. 'Well, I'm sorry about the lack of cake, but have you seen my six-pack lately?' He patted his stomach. 'It's not so much of a six-pack any more. So, what's going on?'

'I'm looking into something from this morning. That woman who approached me on Audrey Stone's street. Her friend has gone missing.'

'Pass it on to uniform; they love a good missing person.'

'It's already been dealt with, but there's something not right. I have a bad feeling about this,' Lucy said. 'It all seems a bit too much of a coincidence that this girl, Lauren Coates, has disappeared off the face of the earth on the same night Audrey Stone was murdered.'

'Argh, there you go,' Mattie said. 'Why did you say that out loud? Well, that's it then: she's a definite goner if you have a bad feeling. We all know your bad feelings are the equivalent to the kiss of death.'

'I think that she's involved somehow,' Lucy said. 'She might have witnessed something.'

'Or maybe she's our killer?' Mattie asked. 'What about that?'

'Bugger off; I don't think she's the killer. She's far too young to have been involved with the asylum; I think we're looking for someone much older. We need to go and search her house though, like, now. There's a chance she might be in there and unable to get to the phone.'

Mattie sipped at his coffee. 'If I'd known you were going to spring that on me I wouldn't have brought you a coffee. Honestly, have we got time for this when there are two bodies up at the mortuary, and we're still no nearer to catching who put them there?'

'Trust me, I didn't want to get involved, but we can't just ignore it,' Lucy said. 'Print me off the log whilst I go and find someone who's door-entry trained and not tied up. If we can't find a key, I'm not waiting around: we'll put the door in so we can do a search.'

'Yes, boss.' Mattie left to unlock his computer, while Lucy headed to the parade room.

A few minutes later, he appeared at the doorway. 'Boss, I've had a brilliant idea,' he said, as he handed her a sheaf of paper warm from the printer.

'Well? Don't be shy,' she said.

'You could give this one to Browning,' Mattie said. 'It will keep him busy and not tie us down.'

Lucy shook her head. 'I'm going to pretend that you didn't just say that. If I wanted him involved, I'd have asked him already.'

'You don't even know anything about this Lauren, though. In fact, do you know Shannon? I could understand if this was some kind of favour you were doing for a friend.'

'No. I've never seen either of them before in my life.'

Mattie rolled his eyes in the most exaggerated fashion Lucy had ever seen.

'I've told you,' she said. 'It might all be connected. So now I feel responsible for her. If I were you, I'd just shut up and follow me. The quicker we get on with it, the quicker we can move on to the next thing.'

Mattie sighed, following Lucy and the two uniformed officers she had found out to the police van that would take them to Lauren Coates's house.

CHAPTER THIRTY-FOUR

November 1975

Lizzy and Alice were in the playroom – well, that was the name that was hand-painted on the door in big blue swirls. It was actually just a spare room that contained a couple of broken dolls and toy cars, a knackered old easel with a wonky set of legs and some dried-up paint pots. They liked it here, though. They could pretty much stay in here all day and be left alone. The nurses knew there was nothing in there to damage, and it meant the pair of them were out of the way, making the nurses' jobs much easier.

Lizzy had done a grand job of picking the peeling paint off the lower part of the playroom wall. She would sit picking at it for ages, until her nail beds began to bleed. It was one of her favourite things to do – that and draw, but Nurse Stone had taken it upon herself to hide all the decent pencils and the sharpener. All that were left were a few crayon stumps.

Alice was busy writing in her diary. She kept it hidden in here, along with the one pencil that still worked. Lizzy had begged and begged her to let her use the pencil, but Alice wouldn't hand it over to her.

'Alice?' Lizzy asked now. 'When are you going home?'

Alice looked up from her writing. 'I don't know. Why?'

'Because you said if we were good, we'd go home, and that was ages ago. I think we've been pretty good, and no one has been to see us or to say we can go home.'

'Lizzy,' Alice said, 'you won't be going home, so stop asking. It's annoying. Let's face it: your parents have never even come to visit you. You're as dead to them as that baby.'

As Lizzy listened to Alice's words and tried to comprehend the meaning of them, the playroom door opened and Nurse Stone stepped inside.

Lizzy felt a red-hot rage fill her chest. She began to scream, which made Nurse Stone jump back. Lizzy didn't stop screaming. She ran at the woman, knocking her to the ground and pummelling her small fists against her chest. With some effort, Nurse Stone managed to throw Lizzy off her. While the girl was recovering on the floor, the nurse stood up, drew her foot back, and kicked Lizzy as hard as she could on the leg.

All of a sudden, Alice leaped forward and attacked the woman, tearing out large handfuls of her hair. The nurse fell back and slammed her hand against the red emergency button, bringing a flurry of nurses running to her aid. The nurses tried to drag Alice off, but she was far too strong. The doors banged open and in ran Dr Wilkes with two male porters.

Lizzy, who was still lying on the floor, watched as the men dragged Alice away from the stunned nurse. They managed to manhandle her onto a metal trolley and strap her down, although she was still fighting against them. The doctor was passed a syringe full of liquid, which he jammed into her arm. The ward went silent as Alice lost control of her voice and the rest of her body.

The doctor, who looked frightened, turned around. 'Nurse? What just happened?'

Nurse Stone, looking more than a little bedraggled, pointed her finger at Lizzy.

'That little bitch started it. She attacked me for no reason, and when I pushed her away the other one came at me.'

The doctor's cheeks were flushed. He ran his hand through his thinning hair. 'I can't have any more carry-ons like this. We're already under scrutiny. The board have being asking all sorts of questions.'

'Well, if you want my opinion you should take her and lobotomise her now,' Nurse Stone said. 'What's the point in waiting any longer for the inevitable? We've tried all the medication you've prescribed, and none of it is having any effect. You have no idea how hard it is working with these vile children. They look so innocent, yet we know full well that they're monsters. She could do this again; it isn't the first time. And she keeps asking where Tommy is. Do you want her asking the wrong person?'

The whole time she was talking, she was pointing her finger at Alice. Lizzy wanted to run and kick the horrible woman. It wasn't true. She'd never seen Alice behave like that before. It was all Lizzy's fault.

'I think you're right,' Dr Wilkes said. 'I'll go and get prepped, then we'll have her brought down to theatre. It will only take half an hour. I can't afford any more of these incidents; the board are already talking about closing this place down. We're hanging on by a very fine thread, which could snap at any moment.'

He left. Lizzy had no idea what they'd been talking about, but she kept quiet. She looked down at her thigh, which had a big blue bruise forming where the nurse had kicked her.

Another nurse came over to help her up. As she bent down, she whispered: 'You keep quiet now, Lizzy. No fuss, or they'll take you away after Alice and do the same to you.'

Lizzy was terrified. She didn't want it, whatever 'it' was, so she nodded. Taking the nurse's hand, she went and sat on the chair next to Alice's trolley so she could be near to her.

Alice was no longer awake. Lizzy didn't know what they were going to do to her. She was terrified. All of this was her fault, because she'd lost her temper again. It wasn't fair.

Thirty minutes later, when they came and wheeled Alice away, Lizzy felt so bad she had to run to the toilet to be sick. It hadn't bothered her much when she'd killed that baby – she hadn't felt sick when he'd stopped breathing. He'd been horrible, and she hadn't liked him. But she liked Alice.

As she knelt on the cold tiled floor, Lizzy realised how much she hated Nurse Stone and the doctor. She knew that she wouldn't feel bad when she got her revenge on either of them. She didn't know how or when she would do it, but she knew that she would. It didn't matter how long she had to wait. She was a patient child and she didn't care if she had to wait until she was grown up. She would take pleasure from seeing to it that both of them paid for what they had done: to her, to Alice and to poor Tommy. And she wouldn't get caught this time, like she had after John.

She pulled herself from the floor, feeling a little better. She went to sit by Alice's bed and stared out of the window, down at the cemetery below and the rows of wooden crosses. She wondered how long it would take for them to bring Alice back. She felt lost without the older girl there to look after her. Whatever it was they were doing to her, it was taking forever. The only good thing was that Nurse Stone was nowhere to be seen.

It was a bright, sunny autumn day, and there were patients being led around outside in the grounds. Some of them even looked as if they had their family with them. Lizzy hadn't seen her mum or dad for such a long time. She felt a tear trickle down her cheek. Did they even care that she wasn't at home with them? It made her sad not to see them. She wondered if they were sad not to see her.

The double doors to the ward swung open with a loud clatter as they hit the wall. A trolley was wheeled in by two porters, with Nurse Stone following behind. She had a smirk on her face that she was trying to hide behind the clipboard in her hands. Lizzy stared at the girl who they were wheeling to Alice's bed. It no longer looked like her friend. This girl had a bandage over her left eye which continued all the way around her head. Her other eye was glazed, and there was a large glob of spittle running down her chin.

Lizzy felt sick. What had they done to her? Scared to go over in case they took her away and did the same to her, she watched in horror as they put Alice's back into bed and pressed the brakes down so it wouldn't move. The two porters left and Nurse Stone bent down to check Alice's breathing and blood pressure. When she had finished, she took the chart and walked back to the nurses' station, turning her back on Lizzy.

Lizzy ran across to the bed, where her friend was lying immobile, staring at the wall. She shook Alice's arm. It was cold and clammy. Frantically, she whispered: 'Alice? Alice, look at me. What's the matter with you? What have they done?'

Alice never moved, blinked or acknowledged that she was there. Lizzy felt as if someone had taken out her heart and replaced it with a block of freezing cold ice. She waved her hand in front of Alice's eye and it didn't even blink. She whispered her name again, but got no reaction. Turning around to make sure that none of the nurses were watching, she began to gently shake Alice's shoulder. The only thing that happened was that a sliver of saliva began to run from the side of Alice's mouth down her chin.

Lizzy stepped away. What was wrong with her? She couldn't even speak. Her heart was racing. What if they came for her next?

CHAPTER THIRTY-FIVE

As Lucy sat in the back of the police van, holding on for dear life, her phone began to vibrate in her pocket. She pulled it out to see Col's number flashing across the display.

'What have you got?' she said as she answered the call.

'Well, there is nothing on Tommy Wright. I've just double-checked. There's a date in October where it says he was transferred to the general hospital; it also mentions he was a mongol, whatever that means. But I've just had an email back from the general hospital records office saying they have no knowledge of a Tommy Wright being admitted in October 1975. So there may be something dodgy going on there. Of course, they did stress that because of the time frame they couldn't be one hundred per cent positive. I've done all the relevant searches to see if there's any record of him anywhere later on, as an adult. But there is nothing to suggest that Tommy Wright lived to be an adult.'

Lucy sighed. 'Poor Tommy. He had Down's Syndrome – back then they were called mongols. I doubt very much he would be responsible for these two murders, even if he is still alive. It all sounds very cloak and dagger, though. I wish I could question Edwin Wilkes and Audrey Stone to find out exactly what happened to him.'

Colin started to cough and splutter on the other end of the phone. Lucy held it away from her ear, until he muttered, 'Sorry, boss; swallowed my tea the wrong way. I've also traced the person who identified Lizzy Clements. It was a David Oldham. Unfortunately for us, he's dead. Died of a heart attack in 2014.'

'Bloody hell, Col, have you not got any good news for me? These are all dead ends.'

'Sorry, Lucy. I'll keep trying.'

Lucy instantly regretted being so sharp with him. It wasn't his fault. 'No, I'm sorry. I'm not having a go at you. It's just annoying that we keep hitting brick walls. It's not your fault. Thanks.'

Cottage Lane had never seen so much police activity. The van parked up just outside the cordoned-off area. Lucy had been considering having the scene released, but had changed her mind, deciding they would wait until they'd searched Lauren's house to make sure there was nothing out of the ordinary there. It was far better to be safe than sorry – even if that did mean the poor PCSOs were on scene guard for days.

She put on a pair of gloves and walked across to Lauren Coates' small terraced house. It was painted white and mint green with a quaint wicker love heart on the front door. The curtains of the front room were open and Lucy cupped her hands to peer inside. There was no sign of life.

Mattie left them to stroll around to the back street. He came back around moments later to where Lucy was knocking on the front door.

'Alley gates,' he said.

'And they're shut?'

He nodded.

'Jesus, this must be the only street in the entire town that bother to close the gates,' Lucy said. 'Typical.'

She had searched in all the usual places that people left spare door keys, and had come up with nothing. It wasn't like her front garden, with its pots of lavender and roses. She turned around to the officers, who were leaning against the van, arms folded, discussing the menu from the latest Indian takeaway that had opened locally.

'Could you please open the door?'

The taller of the two nodded and slid the van door open. He began to drag the heavy red battering ram out. Lucy motioned for Mattie to knock next door, to check the neighbours hadn't seen Lauren lately. She took the other side. Neither door opened, leaving them very little choice.

Lucy nodded at the man with the whammer in his hands and he began to swing it backwards and forwards against the lock. Three loud bangs, and the door gave away. The noise was enough to wake the dead – the whole time, Lucy watched to see if either of the neighbours' curtains were twitching. They weren't, so she let them off.

She stepped inside Lauren's house – the door opened straight into the front room – and inhaled. It didn't smell of anything bad. The air was a little stale, and there was the faint smell of lemon lingering in the air.

'Hello?' she called. 'Lauren? This is the police.'

There was no response. It seemed Lauren was not here. Even if she had been lying in bed poorly, the noise of the door breaking in would surely have disturbed her. Lucy motioned for the two coppers to go and search upstairs, whilst she and Mattie searched downstairs.

There were a few letters on the floor by the front door, which Lucy picked up and placed on the small table next to the sofa. Also on the table was a vase of flowers and a black and white photograph of Lauren with Shannon, the friend who'd spoken to Lucy. She went into the neat kitchen and opened the fridge door. There wasn't much food inside apart from a block of cheese, a packet of chicken slices and a full carton of milk. *Blimey.* Lucy felt a wave of sadness wash over her. This was practically her own life – she had a slightly bigger house, but the contents of her fridge weren't even this grand.

On the kitchen worktop was a half-empty bottle of wine left uncorked. Alarm bells began to ring inside Lucy's head. If Lauren had been drinking wine and hadn't finished the bottle, why not put the cork back? It didn't look as if she had so much money that she could afford to waste a decent amount of alcohol. Or was it just Lucy who would worry about wasting wine? Was she confusing her own, sad, shitty life with that of this woman, who she'd never heard of until a few hours ago?

Mattie came into the kitchen, waving a passport at her. 'She hasn't jetted off abroad to join her parents.'

Lucy took it from him, opening it to see a much harsher photograph than the one on the incident log.

The two officers came downstairs shaking their heads. 'Nothing upstairs, boss. The bed is made and her toothbrush is dry. There's no mobile phone lying around and there were a couple of empty handbags. She's not here. Lucy had to agree there was no evidence to suggest otherwise. Nothing was out of place; there were no signs of a struggle.

Mattie came in from the back yard where he'd popped out to check the small shed.

'Back's all secure. There's only that shed, which is full of crap, and that's it.'

'Right, come on then,' Lucy said. 'We can't do anything else. I'll ask the PCSOs to keep an eye on the place while they wait for a joiner to come and secure the door.' She tucked the passport into her trouser pocket. When Lauren turned up, she would give it back to her. For now, she was going to hang on to it.

As they got back into the van, Mattie looked at her. 'Happy now?'

'Not really. Where is she? If it's out of character for her to do this, and there's no sign of a struggle inside the house, she has to be with someone.'

'I'm not being funny, Lucy, but did you tell your best friend every time you shacked up with a man for a shagfest?'

Lucy felt her cheeks turn crimson. 'Mattie!'

'Come on. You know what I mean. For all we know, this Shannon could be a bit of a jealous friend, so Lauren might have decided not to tell her about her latest conquest.'

'I suppose you could actually be right.'

'Of course I am. You should listen to me a little bit more.'

Lucy began to laugh. 'I'm sorry, you're right. I should.'

'What's so funny?'

'Nothing. I'm just being daft. It's been a long couple of days. I suppose there's not much more we can do. We're a bit limited at the moment.'

'Unless her body turns up before they do.'

'I hope not; I'd kind of feel responsible.'

'And how do you work that one out?' Mattie asked. 'Look, for whatever reason, Lauren's friend sought you out and asked you to look into this. You've done the best that you can. How do we not know that her friend isn't a crazy who's jealous of her?'

Lucy shrugged. 'We don't. Well, I kind of do… I checked her out; she isn't known to us. If she was some kind of psycho we'd probably have some prior knowledge of her, wouldn't we?'

'I suppose we would. Come on, let's get back so you can update her friend.'

Back at the station, Lucy went into her office to call Shannon Knowles. The phone rang out and there was no facility to leave a voicemail. Lucy swore to herself.

Mattie waved at her as he left, and she waved back, wondering where he was so keen to get off to. She felt a twinge of regret. Perhaps it was because he was so happy, while she was so bloody miserable and feeling sorry for herself. Everyone was happy except for her, it seemed. Even Browning, despite being a pain in the arse, was married, and had been for years.

Lucy typed an update onto the missing person's report for Lauren, and decided it was time to go home. She could call at Shannon's house on her way – even though it wasn't technically on her way – or she could wait until tomorrow.

As she left, she passed Browning, who was leaning on his desk. It looked as if he was reading something interesting on the computer. Lucy doubted it was anything to do with work, because if it was, he wouldn't be so enthralled. Browning caught her looking and nodded his head. She waved at him, another wave of guilt washing over her. She didn't really know the man that well, so she should stop being so judgemental about him. Today had turned into one of revelation for her. She decided that tomorrow she would do her best to be a better, kinder person. To everyone: including Browning, and everyone else who normally pissed her off.

Getting into the car, she wondered if Ellie would want to come over for tea. Then she looked at the clock on the dashboard – 19.49, definitely far too late for tea. *Shit.* How had that happened? Where had the day gone? She'd spent three hours looking into Lauren Coates' missing person's case, and now she was going to add on another twenty minutes by speaking to Shannon Knowles.

She sighed and turned the key in the ignition. Prince began to scream at the top of his voice – 'Let's go crazy, let's get nuts' – and she smiled, because at this rate, going crazy was a real possibility for her.

A van behind her turned its sirens on, making her almost jump through the roof of her tiny Fiat. She pulled over to let the van pass as the electronic gate began to slide backwards. It never ended. This job was one incident after another. Lucy certainly didn't miss the days of getting sent from job to job, never having time to clear up the mess before having to move on to the next. She waited to see if a second van would follow. It didn't, so she began to drive through before the gate shut.

As tempting as it was to go straight home, she knew that if she didn't visit Shannon tonight she'd never settle. Before even realising it, she'd turned into the street where Audrey Stone's house was still taped off with blue and white police tape. There was a PCSO sitting in a van outside the front gate, and Lucy knew there would be another one out the back. They had to make sure that they'd collected every single piece of forensic evidence that they could find before they released the crime scene. There was also the fact that Lauren had disappeared to take into consideration, what if she'd got caught up in some foul play?

Lucy waved at the van and smiled to see Rachel, the PCSO, waving back. She stared at Audrey Stone's house, then at Lauren's, which was still in darkness and now had a sheet of plywood securing the door. She needed answers. The more she thought about it, the more she was convinced that Lauren might have inadvertently stumbled onto Audrey Stone's murder.

She picked up the log she'd printed out with Shannon Knowles's address on, and began to drive away in the direction of her house. She parked and went to knock on the door. It was opened by a much different version of the woman who had spoken to her earlier. Gone was the suit, high heels and immaculately made-up face. Instead, Lucy was greeted by a woman in work-out clothes, a high ponytail and a freshly cleansed face.

'Evening, Shannon,' Lucy said. 'I know it's late but I wanted to give you an update.'

'I can't believe it,' Shannon said. 'I didn't expect to hear from you again! Well, I hoped that I would, but I didn't actually think I would, if you get what I mean.'

Lucy smiled at her. 'Well, I told you I'd make some enquiries and I like to keep my word.'

Shannon stepped back and opened the door. 'Would you like to come in?'

Lucy wondered if she should just tell her now, on the door-step, so she could get home. She found herself walking inside, though. What did she have to get home to?

Shannon led her into the living room, where John Luther was paused in his full glory on a sixty-inch television above the fire-place.

Lucy smiled. 'I've just started watching this too; it's really good.'

Shannon smiled back. 'Really? I wouldn't have thought you would want to watch anything like this when you already do the same job.'

'But he's so nice to look at, and his world is a lot more exciting than mine,' laughed Lucy. Although I'm sure the last few days could give him a run for his money.'

'I heard about what happened to that old woman,' Shannon said. 'It's so scary to think that could happen right near to where Lauren lives. Have you caught her killer yet?'

'Ah, the perils of watching detective shows. I'm afraid that in the real world it rarely works so fast, especially if it's a stranger-killing.' Lucy could have kicked herself even as the words came out of her mouth. She'd said far too much. She had no idea what Shannon did for a living. Knowing Lucy's luck, she was probably a journalist for the *Daily Mirror*.

'It's OK,' Shannon said, catching the look on Lucy's face. 'I wouldn't say a word to anyone. You don't need to look so wor-ried. So. What did you come to tell me?'

'We searched Lauren's house, and it was empty. It didn't look as if anyone had been in it for a while, but there were no signs of a disturbance. We also found her passport, so she hasn't left the country.'

'So where is she?' asked Shannon.

'I'm afraid I don't know. There was nothing to suggest that she'd gone away, but it doesn't mean that she hasn't. Maybe it was a last-minute thing, and she forgot to tell you.'

Shannon shook her head.

'Well, I'm stumped,' Lucy said. 'I'd like to say that she's probably stopping at someone's house. Does she have a boyfriend?'

'No, she split up with him last year when he cheated on her.'

'Maybe she met someone on a night out. We've left a message for her parents and until they make contact, there isn't a lot more we can do.'

'Oh, right. It's just I have this horrible churning in my stomach every time I think about her,' Shannon said. 'I'm scared something bad has happened. What if the person who killed that woman has taken her somewhere?'

The more Lucy thought about it, the more she thought that was in fact a possibility. But she couldn't say anything to Shannon about it. 'I think that would be unlikely. Was Lauren particularly friendly with her neighbour?'

'Not that I know of, although they worked together,' Shannon said. 'Lauren is a bit of a do-gooder though; it wouldn't surprise me if she visited her now and again.'

Alarm bells were ringing in Lucy's head. First thing tomorrow, she would get a forensic team to go through Lauren's house, just in case. She just hoped they hadn't trampled on any possible evidence when they had searched it earlier.

'Hopefully she will turn up and not even realise what a fuss she's caused,' Lucy said. 'If she does, can you let us know straight away?'

'What if she doesn't?'

Shannon looked as if she was about to cry and Lucy felt terrible. 'Hopefully she will. I'll see myself out, make sure you lock up and keep everything secure.'

She turned to leave, needing to get out of there before she cried, too. Today had been a roller coaster of emotion for her. She wasn't used to it.

'Thank you,' Shannon said.

'It's what I'm here for.'

She walked out of the front door, closing it gently behind her. She was glad to be outside in the fresh air, even if it was beginning to rain.

CHAPTER THIRTY-SIX

Heidi was waiting at Mattie's house for him. She'd been into work to collect her diary and had then done some shopping before returning to his house. She had steaks on the griddle and a huge bowl of salad prepared: such the perfect girlfriend. She'd even changed his bedding. She looked at the clock, hoping he wasn't going to be too late. He'd left her on her own for most of last night, then had come home before dashing off again in the middle of the night. She was well aware that this wasn't going to be a lasting relationship – partly because of his job, but mainly because it was so blatantly obvious that he had a huge crush on his boss, Lucy.

Heidi logged onto Mattie's computer now, which he never kept locked, and began to flick through his photos. There were an awful lot of him standing close to a very attractive woman. Lucy. His arm around her waist, or draped across her shoulders on what looked like work nights out.

The front door slammed and Heidi clicked off the computer, not wanting to be caught snooping. Mattie came into the open-plan living room/kitchen and grinned to see her lying on his sofa in just her dressing gown, one of her toned, tanned thighs peering at him through the gap at the front.

'I didn't realise you were here,' he said. 'You should have rung. I'd have tried to get away earlier to see you.'

'I haven't been here long – well, only long enough to have a quick tidy around and make tea. I hope you don't mind?'

'Not at all,' Mattie said. 'It's bloody amazing. I'm starving. I was going to order a takeaway, so thank you.'

He took off his suit jacket and loosened his tie and top button, then sat down, kicking off his shoes. Heidi prickled at the untidiness, but she ignored it, reminding herself that this wasn't her house. She sat close to him, laying her hand on his thigh.

'You look tired. Why don't you have a shower while I finish the tea?'

'Would you mind? That would be great.'

He didn't wait for her reply as he jumped up and went upstairs. He hadn't even kissed her, which needled her more than the mess he'd come in and made. She heard the shower turn on and began to put the steaks onto plates. As long as he didn't start talking about bloody Lucy, they'd be OK. If he did, she might just end up walking out and going home.

Lucy had gone straight to the fridge and opened the door, letting her fingers trail over the ice-cold bottle of wine. She was about to pull it out, but then stopped, went to the shelf below and took out a bottle of water instead. She twisted off the cap, took a few long gulps, then grabbed a packet of bacon. Her stomach was groaning so loudly it was embarrassing; she definitely needed to go shopping tomorrow. The fridge currently contained more alcohol than food. If she couldn't sleep, she might even nip to the twenty-four-hour Tesco later.

Her headache hadn't eased so she rifled through the drawer for a packet of migraine tablets. She swallowed two, hoping they'd kick in soon. She made a bacon sandwich, smothered it in tomato sauce, and carried it upstairs to her bedroom.

As she set the plate down on the bedside table, she remembered the diary. It wasn't that she didn't believe Ellie, but she hadn't been burgled, either. She would have known if she had.

And they would have left a mess, not put everything back. She'd checked her jewellery box and everything was still there. The house had been secure, with no open doors or windows, so everything pointed to Ellie having sneaked around whilst Lucy was out at work.

She would move the diary to a better hiding place and forget about the incident, she decided. As luck would have it, even if her daughter had been reading it, all Lucy had written about lately was how much she missed George and her perfect life before it had all gone tits up. At least she wasn't in the middle of a raunchy love affair that had left her writing pages of lusty porn. She began to giggle: the chance would be a fine thing.

Stripping off, she hung her jacket and trousers up and dropped the rest of her clothes into the washing basket. Turning the shower in the en suite as hot as she could stand it, she stepped under and had the quickest wash possible. She didn't want her hair dye to run too much – it was amazing how fast it faded.

She wrapped herself in a huge bath sheet, fastened another towel around her head, and went back into the bedroom. She took her iPad off the dresser. There was no point in trying to ring Ellie now: she wouldn't answer. Lucy logged into Facebook to check her messages, and read the one from her daughter. Ellie sounded full of enthusiasm, telling her how excited she was to have a job in the new café on the retail park. Lucy hadn't bothered looking on Facebook for days. She'd been too consumed with work to even think about it. Too consumed with it all to even bother to check in with her own daughter.

She typed a message back, telling Ellie how proud she was of her and how very sorry she was about today. Ending it with *I love you so much xxx*, she then logged out and put the iPad back, vowing to check it in the morning before she left for work. She hated computers and had needed Ellie to set the iPad up for her in the first place.

Lucy finished her cold sandwich and then lay back, tugging the duvet over her and snuggling down into the pillows. She tried her best to clear her mind of today's events so that she could fall asleep. She pulled the tattered pink teddy that had once been Ellie's favourite off the bedside table and held it close.

Mattie was sound asleep when he felt a sharp nudge to his ribcage. He tried to ignore it, but then it happened again. He stirred. 'Ugh, what?'

'Your bloody phone keeps ringing,' Heidi said.

Mattie groaned and opened his eyes. Stumbling out of bed, he went to the chair where he dug in his trouser pocket to retrieve it. 'Yeah?'

The phone slipped from his hands and tumbled to the floor, knocking on to loudspeaker. Lucy's voice filled the bedroom. 'We should have asked the Clements for DNA samples.'

Mattie bent down and picked up the phone, mouthing 'sorry' to Heidi. Then he left the room to go to the bathroom.

'Yep, we should have. Good shout, Lucy. Why didn't we think of that hours ago – and why couldn't you have told me in the morning?'

'Oh yes, I'm sorry. I've been awake for ages thinking about the case. It came to me that if we get the Clements' DNA, we could cross-match it with the hair from the baseball cap. Then we would know whether Lizzy Clements was our killer, wouldn't we?'

'Yes, we would. It's a great idea,' Mattie said. 'We can go and visit them after briefing and ask them. There is one problem, though.'

'What's that?'

'Even if the hair does turn out to belong to Lizzy Clements, we still have no idea what she looks like, or what name she's using.'

'It's better than nothing,' Lucy said. 'We could get a picture of her from when she was a kid, then get a forensic artist to draw up what she would look like as an adult. It's worth a shot.'

'Yes, it is.'

'Night. Sorry I woke you.'

Mattie ended the call and wandered back into the bedroom, where a fully dressed Heidi was putting on her shoes.

'What's up?' he asked.

'I can't sleep,' Heidi said, 'and your bloody boss needs to realise that you have your own life outside of that job. Does she really think it's acceptable to phone you in the middle of the night to tell you something that could have waited until morning? It's not right. You want to tell her to fuck off once in a while and stop running every time she clicks her fingers. I'll see you later on – *if* you grow a pair of balls and stop following her around like a lap dog.'

Mattie was shocked by Heidi's outburst, yet couldn't really blame her. He could kill Lucy. He grabbed Heidi's hand.

'You're right. I'm sorry. I should have turned my phone on silent.'

Heidi rolled her eyes at him and walked out of the bedroom. Moments later, Mattie heard the front door slam and he got back into bed. He wasn't chasing after her in his boxers. It was too bloody cold; he wouldn't go out in his underwear for anyone. Burying his head under his pillow, he closed his eyes and within seconds was asleep. He could sleep anywhere, at any time.

CHAPTER THIRTY-SEVEN

By seven, Lucy had done a full shop, stocking up on food, wine that was on offer, and a load of Ellie's favourite crap. That included tortilla chips, dips and family-sized bags of chocolates. She hoped she could talk Ellie into coming around. They could have a girly night – stick on *Bridesmaids* or *Bridget Jones' Diary* and chill like they used to, whilst stuffing slices of piping hot cheesy pizza into their mouths.

If she'd checked the damn iPad once in the night, she'd checked it a hundred times. Of course, Ellie would have been fast asleep. Thankfully, she was too young to endure the kind of sleepless nights that Lucy had. Hours spent worrying whether she'd done everything right at work: had she followed all the lines of enquiry, had she asked for the right samples to be tested and so on. Then there was Mattie: it was obvious she'd disturbed him when he had company, and pissed him off as well.

Lucy finished unpacking the food and popped two crumpets into the toaster. As soon as she'd eaten them she might as well go to work and get an early start. Her phone beeped and she saw a message from an unfamiliar number.

Morning, I hope you don't mind me messaging you. I got your number off the card you gave me. I've finished work now for three days and wondered if you fancied meeting up for a bite to eat and a drink. Whenever it's convenient for you? Stephen King.

Lucy didn't know whether to be flattered or shocked, but it put a huge smile on her face. Before she even had a chance to consider the implications, she texted him back: *I'd love to. How about tonight? 8 at The Black Dog?*

Brilliant, see you then.

Lucy let out a squeal, although from excitement or nerves she wasn't sure. What the hell: maybe it was time to start living again. Now all she needed was for Ellie to stop sulking and to agree to spend some time with her tomorrow, and things would be almost perfect. Today was going to be a good day.

Lucy had prepared herself for the briefing. Although she was tired, she wouldn't let it show. She took her place at the front of the room, waiting for the DCI to stop fiddling around with the camera that hooked up to the television and was currently zooming in and out on the left-hand side of the room, making all the officers who were sitting there laugh and yelp with horror. Eager to begin, Lucy turned to stare at Tom, who swore under his breath and switched the thing off at the mains. The television went black, much to everyone's relief. It was too early to have to sit and watch yourself magnified on a television screen.

Lucy looked around for Mattie, wondering where he was. She couldn't wait any longer for him, so she began.

'So, up to now we had two possible suspects: Tommy Wright and Lizzy Clements. Thanks to Colin's hard work, we have managed to rule out Tommy Wright because he seems to have disappeared in October 1975 and I suspect he may have come to some harm. Unless some new information comes to light to suggest that he's alive and well, we are going to focus on Lizzy Clements. I spoke to her parents yesterday, who informed me that she died in 1990 of a drug overdose. However, they were out of the country at the time and never identified her body. Until we have concrete proof that Lizzy Clements is dead, I believe we are looking for a female killer who will be in her early fifties.'

Lucy looked at the faces of her audience. They were sitting there in stunned silence –probably wondering if she'd lost the plot. It certainly sounded that way. A hand raised in the corner and Lucy nodded over at the young officer.

'What makes you so sure it's Lizzy Clements?'

'We have a witness who was in the asylum with Lizzy who thinks she would be capable of these horrific crimes. Lizzy Clements killed her baby brother when she was just nine years old – we know she isn't fazed by murder. We have no actual proof that the body that was identified as Lizzy Clements really was her. It's possible that she faked her own death. I know it seems a bit far-fetched, but we can't rule her out at this moment in time.

'Moving on, there is also a possible link between Audrey Stone's murder and the disappearance of her neighbour – a Lauren Coates. Both women worked together and lived a couple of doors away from each other. Lauren's friend hasn't heard from her since the night of Audrey's murder. I want two of you concentrating on finding Lauren for me.' Lucy pointed at Mac and his student officer, who both nodded.

Tom stepped forward to take over and give Lucy some breathing space.

'As you all know, Lucy and her team have come up with enough of a plausible link to connect both murders. Edwin Wilkes and Audrey Stone worked together in '75 at The Moore – better known to you and me as the asylum. Col is doing his best to find out what happened on that ward between Wilkes and Stone but we all know it's better to get it from the horse's mouth. So I need a volunteer from you lovely lot to go and speak to Florence Wilkes and see if she can shed some light on it.'

Browning stuck his hand up, and for that, Lucy was grateful. She didn't have the heart to upset the lovely Florence any more than she already had. She noticed Mattie slip into the back of the room and take a seat next to the row of PCSOs. She looked at him and he looked away. He was either avoiding her or he was mad at her.

'As Lucy has just stated,' Tom continued, 'this is a complicated case because of the huge lapse in time since the two victims were last connected. We can't afford to not follow up on every possible link. At this stage, I don't want to rule anyone out. Thank you for your patience and keep up the good work.'

Lucy asked the PCSOs to hold back after the briefing so she could give them their house-to-house questions. Everyone else stood up. Mattie was the first to leave. The rest of them filed out of the door, mumbling between themselves.

Lucy briefed the PCSOs, then was about to look for Mattie when the DCI caught her arm, tugging her back and closing the door.

'How are you, Lucy?'

'Fine, thanks.'

'Good, that's good. Sara Cross emailed to say you'd attended your session as promised. I have to say that's a big relief. How did it go?'

Lucy felt the blood begin to rush up her neck. That sneaky woman was driving her insane. Why was she so bothered about what Lucy did?

'Yes, I did,' she said, 'and I can't say that it helped any. Do you seriously think that telling your problems to a complete stranger – who has no idea how hard this job is – helps? I'm sorry, Tom, but it's about as painful as pulling your own teeth out. I could shout it from the rooftops and tell the whole world my problems, but when I'm on my own in bed at two in the morning, those images are always there. So don't patronise me by asking me how the session went. I'll continue to go because I'm expected to, and that's all.'

The DCI let go of her arm and stepped away from her. 'I'm sorry to hear you feel that way. I found her very helpful.'

Lucy nodded. 'Each to their own. Now, is there anything else?'

He shook his head.

She walked out in search of Mattie. He wasn't in the office, so she wandered down to the brew station, where she found him chatting to two of the PCSOs. He passed her a mug of coffee and winked.

'Peace offering. Sorry I was late. I slept in.'

Lucy took the mug from him and sniffed to make sure the milk wasn't out of date. 'Thanks. I guess that's partly my fault – although I'm not taking all the blame.'

'So, boss, what are we doing first?'

'The DCI has agreed to send the CSIs in to search Lauren's house. He thinks her disappearance could be connected to our case, and would rather rule it out than ignore it. Browning is going to visit Florence Wilkes to see if she knew about any scandals involving her husband and Stone. And we, my friend, are going back to visit the Clements to see if they'll come back to the station with us to get some comparison DNA samples. So drink up. I don't want to waste a single minute; I need to finish by seven tonight.'

'Any particular reason?' Mattie asked.

She smiled. 'Erm... Whatever I'm doing when I finish work has nothing to do with you, so keep your nose out.'

She walked back to the office, where she finished her coffee and locked her computer before going in search of whoever was working in CSI this morning. She needed to know that if she and Mattie brought the Clements in, someone would be available to take the swabs.

The door to the CSI office was open. Lucy knocked and walked in. Jack was busy checking his heavy kitbag.

'Is there just you in?' she asked.

'Until twelve, why?'

'I know you're on your way out to visit fourteen, Cottage Lane at my request, but I also have a theory that our possible suspect who is supposed to be dead is actually still alive. I was going to bring her parents here for swabs, so that you could send them off on fast-track to cross-reference them with the hair sample you got from the baseball cap and see if it's a match.'

Jack turned to look at her, pushing his glasses onto the top of his head. 'Well I'm busy, but you know I'll try my best for you, Lucy.'

'Good, thanks. After you've finished at Lauren Coates's house, can you try not to get called out then?'

'I'll do my best, but you know what a shithole this town can be. I can't guarantee I'll be here. If you arrange it for twelve then Amanda will be here, though.'

'Right, I'll see what I can do. Thank you.'

Lucy turned and left. If she could only find Mattie, who was no doubt faffing around in the locker room, things would be hunky-dory.

He wasn't in the locker room, but one of the officers in there told her he'd just gone to the toilet. She shoved the men's toilet door open and heard Mattie let out a groan when her voice began to echo around the room: 'Stop pissing around, we need to go. We have work to do. I want to get Mr and Mrs Clements back here for twelve. I've already cleared it with Tom, and he's agreed that we can fast-track the samples. Come on, I'm driving today. I haven't got the energy to keep climbing in and out of your monster truck. I've got us a brand new plain car – and guess what?'

'What, boss?'

'I'm bloody spoiling you because it actually has a working radio. We can listen to The Bay whilst we work. How civilised is that?'

'Fucking amazeballs.'

She glared at him and he shrugged.

'I mean: yeah, that's great.'

They got into the car and Lucy tried not to grin as she thought about her date later. It was so long since she'd been on one she wasn't sure what to expect. She didn't know what dating etiquette was like these days. Good job she'd shaved her legs a couple of days ago – not that she was expecting him to see her legs on a first date. She didn't get her legs out for many people; he'd have to be incredibly special for that.

As they reached the street where the Clements lived, the hairs on the back of Lucy's neck prickled and she felt her stomach flip. Something was wrong. She didn't know what yet, but in her experience, when her gut feeling kicked in, there was normally a very good reason for it.

Mattie looked across at her. She was sitting forward in the driver's seat, with both hands gripping the steering wheel as if she were holding on to it for dear life.

'What's wrong?'

'I don't know,' she said. 'Something is, though. Can you not feel it?'

'Lucy, I can't feel anything except the need for caffeine running through my veins.'

She parked the car outside number eleven and got out. 'Have you got anything with you?'

'Like what? Could you be a bit more specific? I have my phone, wallet and half a packet of chewing gum.'

'You know what I mean. Handcuffs; CS gas.'

'No, I haven't got anything except for my radio. Why?'

'I don't know,' she said. 'I just don't feel right.' She stared at the Clements' garden gate. It was blowing open with the wind. Yesterday it had been shut tight.

CHAPTER THIRTY-EIGHT

From the impression she'd got of Ian Clements yesterday, Lucy didn't think that he would be the sort of man who would leave his gate wide open. As they walked up the short path, Lucy caught sight of vivid red splatters of blood on the white plastic double-glazed front door.

'Oh shit. What have we done?'

Mattie pushed past her and ran to the door, which was ajar. Putting on a pair of latex gloves from his pocket, he pushed the door further open, calling out: 'Police!'

There was no reply. The house was silent.

Lucy tugged her radio from her pocket and called for uniformed patrols to attend, urgent assistance needed. Then she too slipped on a pair of gloves, her heart racing. She already knew what they were going to find inside.

As they walked into the hallway, the tangy, coppery smell of blood hit their nostrils. In the doorway to the living room, where they'd been less than twenty-four hours ago, two feet were protruding into the hallway. One tartan slipper was still on; the other was lying next to the hairy white foot.

Mattie went first. As they got nearer, Lucy couldn't help the gasp that escaped her lips. The man they'd been talking to only yesterday was lying on the floor with his head partially severed. There was blood everywhere.

Lucy looked around. There was no sign of Sandra Clements. Lucy hoped the woman was OK – she was so deaf there was a chance she wouldn't have heard any of the disturbance down-stairs.

She left Mattie and ran upstairs. All three doors were closed. She pushed open the first door to see a pristine white bathroom. She moved onto the next. This one was empty – she guessed it had once been Lizzy's room. The pastel pink paint had faded and now had a yellow tinge to it. It looked as if it hadn't been touched for a very long time. For a moment, Lucy felt her heart tug for the child who the room had once belonged to.

That left one door. Lucy pushed it open and her nostrils flared once more at the strong metallic smell. She could make out a dark lifeless shape on the bed. She switched on the light. There were blood splatters everywhere: the ceiling, walls and a huge puddle of it on the bed, surrounding Sandra Clements.

Lucy heard the sirens of an approaching ambulance. At least the paramedics would be able to pronounce death – because both of the Clements' injuries were incompatible with life. Sandra's head was also almost completely severed. Lucy noticed the hearing aids on the small bedside table, covered in specks of blood. She hoped that without the hearing aids in, Sandra wouldn't have known about Ian, or heard her killer coming to get her. It would have been terrible if she'd listened to him being attacked and dying whilst she was waiting up here, too scared to move.

Damn it, Lizzy. Why now? After all this time, all these years? Did you wait until they were too old and frail to fight back?

Pounding footsteps echoed throughout the silent house and Lucy stepped aside to let the paramedic into the room.

He whistled. 'What a mess. Who would do such a terrible thing?' He stepped towards the bed, careful not to stand in any-thing, and turned to Lucy. 'She's a confirmed DOA, but you didn't need me to tell you that, did you?'

Lucy shook her head. No, she didn't; it was just all part of the protocol.

The paramedic backed out of the room. 'I'll go and start the paperwork. Your mate downstairs said to come up and see if you were OK. Are you OK?'

She nodded. 'I'm fine, thanks. I take it Mr Clements is the same?'

'Laura is with him, but yes.'

He turned and went back downstairs to where Mattie and the other paramedic were having a conversation, their voices filtering up and filling the silence. Lucy was so angry that she wanted to punch something. Had their visit yesterday sealed the Clements' fate? Or was it pure coincidence, and their killer had already planned this? She wouldn't know until the killer was caught. At the moment, all fingers were pointing to the ghost of bloody Lizzy Clements. Whoever had cut the throats of this couple must have been very angry with them – and Lizzy had forty years of pent-up anger bubbling away inside her.

Lucy was no stranger to violent murders, and she knew that with this much mess and evidence it was likely that the killer would have left some trace of themselves behind. She hoped they had. They needed to figure out who the hell Lizzy Clements was pretending to be, and soon. She was out of control, and god knows who was next on her list.

The DCI was going to have a heart attack, Lucy realised: four murders in four days, and a missing person. Catherine Maxwell wasn't going to be much happier either.

She felt a warm hand on her elbow. Mattie.

'Come on, boss, there's nothing else we can do in here now. We need to let Forensics take over.'

She turned to face Mattie and saw him flinch at the look on her face. She knew he'd be wondering if this was all far too much for her. She nodded, and turned to follow him down the stairs and straight out of the front door, where a PCSO was standing in front of some crime scene tape with the scene log. A uniformed officer was further down the street, taping it off.

Lucy signed herself out of the scene, then walked towards the car on legs that felt as if they couldn't hold her weight. She got inside and leant her head back against the cool leather seat, closing her eyes. From a distance, she heard Mattie begin to give out orders to the arriving officers until the DCI got here to take over.

DCI Tom Crowe was currently in Sara Cross's office, almost naked, having just had sex with her on the huge leather couch. She'd sent him a text message, and he'd come straight over, switching his phone to silent on his way in through her door.

He pulled his trousers back on now, and as he did so his phone fell out of his pocket. He picked it up to see that he had six missed calls from an unknown number, two more from Lucy and one from Mattie. Something was wrong.

'I've got to go,' he said, kissing Sara on the cheek. She pulled him close and raked her long nails along the back of his neck, drawing blood.

'Ouch! What the fuck are you doing? I can't go home covered in scratches. Alison will know there's something going on.'

'Sorry,' Sara said. 'I couldn't help myself. I like it rough; you know that. Why don't you come around to mine later and I can show you exactly how rough I like it?'

'I can't tonight,' Tom said. 'I waited for you last night and you never turned up. You didn't even ring. I sat outside your house in my car like a prick for ages before I went home. There's no way I'll be able to escape again tonight; the boys have football practice and Alison has yoga.'

Sara shrugged her shoulders. 'I'm your lover. You should be making me your priority. And besides, I don't have to answer to you, do I? If you don't come over, it's your loss.'

Tom shrugged his shirt on and fastened it up. He dialled Lucy's number and put the phone to his ear as he turned to leave. As he reached the door, he blew Sara a kiss, and she waved her hand in the air, dismissing him.

He knew this was wrong. So bloody wrong. But his wife would rather spend her time getting sweaty in the gym than getting sweaty with him – and a man has his needs. Sara wasn't the easiest of women to be having an affair with, though: she had a wicked temper. The one time he'd had to stand her up because of work, she'd gone mental and had refused to speak to him for almost a week. That had nearly killed him off. He knew that he should sort himself out. If Alison found out, this was all going to end in tears, and he doubted Sara was the sort of woman who would take him in should he get kicked out of the family home. She wanted wild sex and a good time, not responsibilities.

'Lucy,' he said as she picked up. 'It's Tom. What's wrong?' He got into his shiny new Audi and shut the door, his tanned facing losing all of its colour as Lucy relayed the mess they'd found inside the Clements' house. 'I'm on my way.'

He put his foot down. Of all the bloody days to decide a quick leg-over was more important than his family and his job.

CHAPTER THIRTY-NINE

She sat at her desk, chewing her pen and staring into space. She wasn't sure how she felt now that she'd actually done it. All the years she'd spent plotting and planning her revenge against her parents – and now it was done. She'd expected to feel better, had expected the black, empty void inside her chest to feel full. Only it didn't.

She wouldn't say that she regretted what she'd done – no, it wasn't that. It would have been nice if, when her father had opened the door and she'd introduced herself, he'd broken down and hugged her. Begged for her forgiveness, perhaps. But he hadn't. Instead, he'd looked at her resigned, as if he'd been waiting all his life for this moment.

Had they actually grieved for her when they'd thought she was dead, or had they wiped all memories of her from their minds, as if she'd never existed in the first place? Perhaps they had been glad: it must have eased their pain and guilt so much. If she'd thought about that more at the time, she wouldn't have done it. They deserved to feel guilty. They'd abandoned her without a second thought, left her in that hellhole full of mad, crazy kids and scary staff. He'd been hesitant to open the door when she'd knocked. It had been late at night. When he asked who it was, she answered, 'Police.' He actually asked for her warrant card then, and she laughed. Had he spent his entire life in fear of his crazy kid coming back for revenge?

She told him she'd left her ID in the car and would go and get it, and then she swung the huge butcher's knife, kicking the door out of his frail hand. When he saw the blade glinting in the moonlight, he turned to run. But of course he had nowhere to run to, and he wouldn't have been able to outrun her even if he tried.

She caught up with him as he entered the living room. He didn't even shout for help. Pulling him around, she slit his throat in one swift swoop. It was much easier than she'd anticipated. As he fell to the floor, the horror in his eyes made her smile.

She looked around the room. It didn't seem any different from the last time she'd been in there, just before she'd been carted off to The Moore as a child. The sofa was new and the walls were a different colour, but very little else had changed.

She was covered in blood, and was relieved she'd had the hindsight to put on a protective paper suit. She wondered where her mother was. She hoped she was cowering in the corner of the bedroom, praying for her life.

She took her time climbing the stairs. She hadn't expected the memories she'd repressed to come flooding back so freely. This had been her home, her safe place. She'd loved it until the day they'd brought that horrible baby home. Then he'd become the centre of attention, and she'd been pushed to one side like a discarded sweet wrapper.

Lizzy walked into her parents' bedroom and saw her mum fast asleep in bed. She lifted her bloodied hand and turned on the light, leaving a bright red smear along the wall. She waited until the woman began to stir, then crossed the room and stood over her until she opened her eyes.

The look of fear on her mum's face was even greater than the look that had been on her dad's. She recognised the blood-soaked woman standing in front of her straight away. Her mouth opened, and for a moment, Lizzy thought her mum was going to say how sorry she was for leaving her. If she apologised, then perhaps…

But what came out was one word: 'You.'

Lizzy lost it then. She attacked the frail woman until there was blood everywhere and her anger had been satiated. She didn't care any longer if they found evidence that belonged to her. She knew it was only a matter of time before that copper figured out who she really was. It didn't matter anyway; there were only a couple of loose ends to tie up now. Then she'd be out of here. Out of this ghost town. She would drive to the other end of the country and find a cheap bed and breakfast to stay in until she could sort out something more permanent.

Lucy Harwin might be good at her job, but she was no match for Lizzy Clements. And if she proved that she was, then Lizzy would take care of her. Permanently.

CHAPTER FORTY

Mattie watched as DCI Tom Crowe and Dr Catherine Maxwell arrived at the scene at the same time. Mattie was standing at the gate of the semi-detached house, which was cordoned off.

'Morning, boss,' Mattie said. 'It's a bit of a bloodbath in there. I hope you haven't had much breakfast – although Lucy said no one was to go in except for Catherine and the CSI.'

'I haven't had anything actually,' Tom said. 'And where is DI Harwin?'

Mattie straightened himself up. If the DCI was using titles, he was in a very bad mood. He pointed to the car. 'She's just having a breather. I think it was a bit of a shock for her. She doesn't look well. You know, four murders in as many days is tough on anyone – and I think that her daughter has been playing up. So, you know, she's doing really well. All things considered.'

Even as the words came out of his mouth, Mattie was furious with himself. Although he was genuinely worried about her, Lucy would go mental if she thought he was giving the DCI any hint of an idea that she might not be able to cope.

Tom led him away from the various officers, paramedics and onlookers who had started to gather. 'I need to know she's OK with this, because between you and me, I'm worried that it's all too soon and that we're pushing her too hard.'

Mattie nodded. 'Well, why don't you ask her yourself? Because she's going to have a shit fit if she thinks we've been talking about her.'

'I would if I thought for one minute that she was going to give me a truthful answer,' Tom replied. 'We can't keep this case under wraps any longer; the press are all over it, members of the public are already well aware. Tomorrow it's going to break, and you know what the headlines are going to be, don't you?'

'I can hazard a guess,' Mattie said. 'Something about incompetent cops letting a killer strike again?'

'I'm going to call Browning out to help you and Lucy. He can shoulder some of the burden.'

Mattie thought that he might as well hand his badge in right now, because Lucy was going to kill him. And the idea of working on a big case with Browning… That was the thing he woke up in the middle of the night with cold sweats about.

He didn't realise Lucy had got out of the car until she stepped in front of Tom.

'Forgive me if I'm wrong,' she said, 'but did I just hear you say you were bringing Browning in to take over?'

'Not to take over,' Tom corrected her. 'I just think you could do with a hand. It's a big enough case running a single murder – but four? Well, anyone would struggle. I'm going to assemble a task force, and it will be run by both you and Browning. He will take some of the pressure off.'

Lucy twisted around to stare at Mattie and he knew she was fuming with him. Bloody Tom, he thought. Sticking his nose in, pretending he gave a shit about Lucy, when really all he cared about was how big an impact the whole thing was going to have on the force.

'Well that's nice,' Lucy said, 'and I do appreciate your concern, I really do. Now, if you'll excuse me, I have a murderer to catch – and that's not going to happen if we stand around pretending to be nice to each other, is it?'

* * *

Lucy walked over to where Catherine was signing herself into the scene. Catherine pulled her mask down.

'Lucy, I think we need a little talk. Can you meet me at my office when I've finished here please?'

'Yes, I can,' she said, bitterly. 'Seeing as how I won't be needed here much longer.'

Catherine tilted her head. 'And why is that?'

'They're calling Browning in to assist me.'

Catherine groaned. 'Well, it's you I want to speak to, so make sure you come alone.'

Lucy felt a little better. Catherine wouldn't let her be pushed out of the loop – which was exactly what would happen if Tom got his way.

Mattie came over to her and whispered, 'Sorry.'

She ignored him, deciding she was going to head back to the station to try and get hold of a forensic artist who could draw up an image of what they thought Lizzy would look like now. Then she stopped: there was a problem with that. She didn't have a photograph of Lizzy Clements. She hadn't noticed any in the Clements' house, either – although it was unlikely they would have kept a photograph of her on display, under the circumstances. Perhaps they had some hidden away.

She went to the CSI van and began to dress herself to go back into the crime scene. She hoped she wouldn't need to go where the bodies were. She wanted to try looking in Lizzy's room first, because it looked as if nothing had been touched in there since the day she'd been taken away.

She signed herself back into the scene and was greeted by Jack, who was coming out with his camera. He took one look at Lucy and put his hands on his hips.

'I told you, this town was lovely and peaceful until you came back to work. And I'd rather you didn't go back in the house until I've finished.'

'I need to,' Lucy said. 'It's really important. I don't need to go near the bodies, I just need to check out the spare bedroom. I know where to step, Jack; it was me who called it in.'

Jack looked over to where the DCI was leaning on his car bonnet, talking on his phone.

'Be quick, then,' he said. 'He's not coming in and trampling everything like he usually does. I still haven't forgotten the time he was SIO and ordered me to wait outside until he'd finished having a stroll around the fucking crime scene.'

'Thanks, Jack. I promise I'll be quick.'

Mattie watched Lucy slip back inside the house; he didn't have a clue what she was doing, but he was keeping out of it. Christ, could this day get any shittier?

Another car pulled up, and Mattie saw the familiar bulk that was Browning, hauling himself out. Relief washed over him: the chief must have already told him to come here before the conversation they'd had about Lucy, or how else would he have got here so fast? Now he didn't feel so bad.

Jack, who was getting some more evidence bags out of his van, looked up.

'You lot are seriously having a laugh. What the fuck is he doing here now? Have you never heard the saying "too many cooks spoil the broth"?'

'Anyone would think that you didn't like the guy.'

'I don't. He's a lazy bastard who comes in last minute and takes all the credit. Poor Lucy.'

Mattie saw Lucy appear at the front door now, and did his best to distract Browning so he didn't know that she'd been back inside. She waited until Browning had moved off, then came to the side of the CSI van. Jack handed her a large brown paper sack to put her protective clothing in. She pulled a clear plastic evidence bag out from inside her suit and passed it to Mattie. It was a grainy coloured photograph of what was presumably the young Lizzy Clements. She had a huge cheesy grin and no front teeth. He passed it back to Lucy, who sealed the bag and wrote her name and rank on it.

'I need this photograph to take some copies,' Lucy said. 'Then you can have it, even though it isn't really part of the scene. I had to search through a built-in cupboard in the spare bedroom to find that.'

'Did you make a mess?'

'As if I would. You can't even tell that I've been inside.'

'Good girl.'

Jack went back to the house, where he was approached by Browning, who was grinning at Mattie and Lucy as if it was all some huge joke. Mattie ignored him, but he noticed that Lucy gave him the finger. She just couldn't help herself.

CHAPTER FORTY-ONE

As they drove away, Mattie asked, 'What was that about?'

'Nothing,' Lucy said. 'I can't believe you grassed me up to Tom – and now look what's happened.'

'Firstly, Browning got here far too quickly. Tom must have already decided to bring him on board. Secondly, I didn't grass you up. He asked me if you were OK, and to be honest, I'm worried about you. It's not a crime to care about someone.'

She glared at him. 'Oh please; you'll have me crying with gratitude next. Look, Mattie, I don't care what it takes, I'm going to prove to them that Lizzy Clements is the killer and I'm going to be the one to find her and arrest her. Every piece of evidence points towards her. The fact that she was dumped in the hospital for killing her baby brother is a big start. Then she either suffered some kind of abuse, or something happened whilst she was in that hospital that made her plan out her revenge on Edwin Wilkes and Audrey Stone. She must have hated her parents for leaving her in there, and they are now dead. The only thing I can't understand is where Lauren Coates comes into it, but I will.'

Her phone began to ring in her pocket and she handed it to Mattie, who clicked it on to speakerphone and answered it.

'Hi, Ellie, your mum is driving at the minute. Can I pass on a message or get her to ring you back?'

'Hi, Mattie! When you say driving, do you mean driving you mad?'

'Well, yes. I suppose you could say that.'

Lucy glared at him as Ellie laughed. 'It's OK, I just wanted to ask her if she wanted to come into my work after so I could make her a coffee. You as well, if you like.'

Lucy felt one of the tight knots in her stomach release and she let out a sigh. At least one of her problems had eased a little.

'Well, that's an offer we can't refuse,' Mattie said. 'What time?'

'Any time after three; it's quieter then. Oh, and your aunt Alice said to tell you hello. She was telling me all about her wonderful nephew who was a policeman and I realised it was you.'

Mattie laughed. 'Well I never, it's a small world. See you after three, then.' Ellie ended the call and Mattie looked at Lucy. 'So Ellie's working at the new café on the retail park?'

'Yep,' Lucy said.

'That's the one Alice is working at; Ellie'll be all right with her. Maybe Alice has already taken her to one side and given her a bit of a talking-to.'

Lucy felt another knot untie. It would be brilliant if she was. Alice would look after Ellie and maybe give her some of the grandmotherly advice that she was so good at dishing out. Now if only Mattie hadn't gone and told Tom she wasn't coping, things would be much better all round.

All the way back to the station, she wondered whether Tom might remove her from the case, or make her stay in the office. It would be even worse if he made her go for extra counselling sessions with that bloody awful Sara Cross.

Still angry with Mattie, she got out of the car as soon as he'd parked and strode off before he'd even had time to grab his jacket from the back seat. She had to get an artist's impression made up of Lizzy Clements so they had something solid to work from. She needed to find out who they used for things like this, though, because it was something they rarely requested. Browning would know – Lucy remembered him using a forensic artist years ago. If she hadn't found one by the time he came back, she would have to ask him.

She went straight to Jack's office, which was empty. *They're all at the scene, Lucy.* Taking herself off to the toilets, she typed Jack's collar number into her radio, hoping to catch him on a point-to-point – a private call, which meant the whole station couldn't hear their conversation. Unless it dropped out, which it frequently did – normally right at the point where you were in the middle of slating someone.

Her radio began to ring and she crossed her fingers, hoping Jack was in a position to answer the call. It rang out and the call ended. *Stupid bloody thing.* She felt like launching it across the room at the wall.

She went back to her office. Mattie was nowhere to be seen, so she slammed the door shut and hoped he had the common sense to stay out of her way, at least until she'd calmed down enough to talk to him in a civilised manner. What would Ms Cross say about this sudden, impending anger that was frothing away inside her chest? That made her smile: she didn't give a fuck what Ms Cross would think. She didn't trust her; there was just something about her…

She picked up the phone and rang the forensic department at headquarters, hoping someone there would be able to answer her query about the forensic artist. She wanted to have either emailed the photo or sent it off by express delivery within the next hour.

Mattie was in the gents. Heidi had been ringing him on and off all morning and he needed to check that she was OK, but he didn't want Lucy to overhear. Now was not a good time for her to find out about their relationship when he hadn't had the courtesy to tell her outright.

'Sorry,' he said when she picked up. 'It's been mad.'

'What, again?'

'Yes.'

'Bloody hell. I was ringing to say I'd booked us a table for two at the Belmont tonight for eight. I booked a room, too, so we could both have a drink and enjoy ourselves.'

Mattie grimaced. The Belmont was Brooklyn Bay's equivalent of the Ritz – it was so bloody expensive. 'Oh, that's nice,' he said. 'But what if I'm tied up here and can't get away?'

'Well, then I'll eat my meal and sleep on my own,' Heidi said, frostily. 'I suggest that if you seriously want to keep this relationship alive, Matthew, then you tell your boss to go and fuck herself and put me first for a change.'

'Don't be like that. She works hard and is under an extreme amount of pressure. We both are, Heidi. There have been two more murders. It's neither of our fault that some maniac is going around killing people. Look, I'll be there tonight.'

'You better had,' Heidi said. 'Because if you're not, don't bother phoning to apologise, because I won't be interested. I've decided against my better nature to give you a second chance. If you blow tonight, then we're through. As much as I like you, I am not spending my life being second-best to your boss.' She ended the call.

Mattie was so angry he didn't know whether to punch the wall or smash his phone. Instead, he slammed open a cubicle door. Sitting down on the toilet lid, he leant back and shut his eyes. This case was getting to them all.

Lucy put the phone down. *Bollocks.* So, she needed to get permission from the DCI to enlist the help of a forensic artist, and they weren't cheap. She'd been hoping that there might be one who worked within the force somewhere, but there wasn't. There wasn't enough call for one to be on the payroll. She'd been given the contact details of an independent forensic artist who was based at the University of Lancaster and was also a lecturer there.

Drumming her fingers on the desk, Lucy knew anything would be worth it to have a clear picture of what Lizzy Clements looked like now. She felt responsible for Mr and Mrs Clements' deaths. She couldn't shake the feeling that her visit to the Clements yesterday had sealed their fate. The killer had to be Lizzy. Why else would the person who killed Edwin Wilkes and Audrey Stone go after the elderly couple? Although if Lizzy had thought that killing her parents would stall things, she was very mistaken.

Lucy knew it was all circumstantial until they got some DNA comparisons back. They now had all the blood and DNA samples they could wish for to cross-match against that hair. However, getting the results could take days and they didn't have the time. They needed that artist's impression, and fast. How many more might die if Lucy didn't try her best to stop the killer?

Lucy picked up the evidence bag and stared at the picture of the toothless, happy kid.

Are you starting to lose control, Lizzy Clements? Are you unravelling at the seams? I bloody well hope so, because you can't carry on killing. I won't let you.

Her phone began to ring. Ellie. She didn't answer it, and instead sent her a text message: *I'm on my way, won't be long.* Jumping up, she grabbed the evidence bag and the piece of paper she'd scribbled the forensic artist's contact details on. She would go and see her daughter, drink some coffee, then decide what to do.

CHAPTER FORTY-TWO

She could stand it no longer. She loved returning to the scene of the crime. There were always so many other nosy bystanders that no one ever looked at her twice. No doubt the police would be running around there like headless chickens, which suited her just fine. They would be too busy to notice her.

The only people who really worried her were Lucy and Mattie. As much as Lizzy wanted to hate the woman, she had to admit she did have a grudging respect for her. She imagined that if Lucy played chess, she would be a very worthy adversary. She had much better vision than anyone else, and Lizzy wouldn't be surprised if one day she didn't make it all the way to the top. In fact, there was only one thing standing in the way of Lucy's brilliant career, and that was Lizzy. She wouldn't think twice about killing her should Lucy get too close to finding out her real identity.

She wouldn't get as much pleasure from killing Lucy as she had from the others – except for the young woman, that had just been a necessity. She'd had very personal grudges against the doctor, the nurse, and of course her disgraceful parents. She'd not regretted any of their deaths – she'd spent her entire life waiting for the right moment for them. She'd wanted them to pay for what they'd done; she hadn't wanted any of them to die peacefully in their sleep.

Dr Wilkes had killed Tommy – Lizzy was sure about that. And he might as well have murdered Alice: what he'd done to her was horrific. Nurse Stone had been nothing but a bully; she had made those children's already miserable lives even worse. She had shown not one of them any compassion whatsoever – instead, she had stood and watched, grinning, while they were drugged up and left drooling like dogs.

It was the story on the news last month that had made up her mind. A developer had finally won the right to dig up the graves in the asylum cemetery and rehome them elsewhere, in order to build a housing project. Lizzy had spent years wondering if they would ever find the body of Tommy Wright, and when she'd seen the news story, she'd thought now maybe they would. Maybe they'd find a grave with only one marker and two bodies inside. She was convinced that Dr Wilkes and Nurse Stone had buried Tommy in one of those graves that night and left him there all alone. The news story had brought it all back so vividly. It had played on her mind for days, until finally she'd decided to take action against every single one of the people who had ruined her and countless others' lives. The time had come for them all to pay the price for what they'd done.

Lizzy got into her car now, driving as near as she dared to the street that held her childhood home. She'd considered changing out of her dress and shoes into a pair of jeans and trainers so that she'd mingle in better, but had decided against it. She wasn't a snob, but she did have her standards. Besides, she was hardly going to look like a serial killer in her Vivienne Westwood suit and matching heels.

She parked a couple of streets away, and took the overgrown cut-through where she'd spent so much time playing as a kid. She emerged at the end into quite a large crowd of people, all standing around and muttering about what the world was coming to, wondering what had happened in this nice, quiet street. Lizzy heard one man mumbling about the state of the town these days, and how it was bound to have something to do with the refugees or those foreigners who had bought the corner shop.

She strained to get closer, trying to spot Lucy's car. Why was she not here? Still, it was a good thing she wasn't. She didn't want to get recognised.

Suddenly realising she was almost at the front of the crowd, Lizzy began to move back. What was she doing? There were already too many people here who might recognise her.

Do you want to get caught? Have you had enough, is your façade finally cracking? Is this why you're here? But your job is finally done. You should go now: leave and never look back.

But she couldn't. Not just yet.

CHAPTER FORTY-THREE

The coffee shop was busy when Lucy arrived. Alice was clearing tables and Ellie was behind the counter, serving. Lucy didn't know why, but she felt nervous about walking in there on her own. She wished she'd brought Mattie with her, but she hadn't calmed down enough yet to sit and pretend they were OK in front of Ellie. The last thing she wanted to do was to make things awkward for her. It must have taken a lot of guts for her to ask her mum to come here.

Ellie caught Lucy's eye and smiled, mouthing 'sit down' to her. Lucy picked a table in the corner furthest away from the front doors, where the other customers were congregating around the comfy sofas. Alice waved at her, then went back behind the counter and whispered something into Ellie's ear. Lucy pretended she wasn't looking. She picked up a magazine that someone had left on the chair, and began to leaf through it until she heard Ellie's voice and looked up to see her placing a large mug on the table in front of her. 'I'm surprised that you came.'

Lucy bit her lip. It wasn't a dig. It was a simple statement, a fact: quite often she didn't make it to appointments, school plays or parents' evenings.

'I wouldn't miss this for the world,' Lucy told her. 'You know how much I love my skinny vanilla lattes and my daughter. So to have both of you in the same room at the same time is amazing. It's like Christmas and my birthday rolled into one.' She gave her the biggest smile she could muster, and Ellie laughed.

'Enough of the flattery, Mother; I get it. You were lured here by the offer of a free coffee and I don't mind. Alice has been explaining to me how busy you've been and that you're trying to help her. So it made me realise I shouldn't be mad at you any more. Alice is pretty cool. Do you think my gran would have been as cool as her?'

Lucy felt her heart break. She had no doubt that her mum would have been an excellent gran. She looked at her daughter's happy face and couldn't help wondering if this was the real Ellie, or if the coffee shop had somehow managed to clone her. Whatever it was, this was nice, and she liked it. It would be so good for the two of them to be friends again instead of arch enemies.

'I really did want to see you,' Lucy said. 'Of course, the coffee is a nice bonus, but you are far more important. I'm so sorry about the other day. I shouldn't have shouted at you like that.'

'Yeah, well, it's OK. How come Mattie didn't come? Is he too busy snogging Jane? Of all the women he could go out with, what's he doing with her? I mean, she's OK, but she's miles older than him. She could be his mother.'

Lucy felt as if she'd just been stabbed through the heart. She desperately tried to keep her cool with Ellie: it wasn't her fault that she'd just dropped a bombshell on her for the second time that week.

'Jane?'

'Jane Toppan from YOT: the one who summoned you to her office after my little "episode", as she calls it.'

Lucy picked up her latte and blew it before taking a sip, taking time to compose herself before she spoke. 'How do you know he's seeing her? He's never mentioned it to me.' That said, she had wondered who he'd been sneaking around with the last week. If it did turn out to be Jane, this would explain a lot. He would have known exactly how she would feel about him seeing her.

'Because that day you forgot to pick me up and Dad had to come, we were sitting in the car with Dad on his phone when

Mattie pulled up in that monster truck. Jane climbed inside and kissed him on the cheek. I was nearly sick there and then. The thought of him and her: well, it's just plain wrong. I mean, Mattie's pretty fit, isn't he? I think he looks like Tom Hardy when he played Reggie Kray in *Legend.*'

Lucy was trying her best to keep calm. It was bad enough that Mattie was seeing Jane. Now her daughter had just as good as admitted that she had a crush on him as well. *Shit.* What was she supposed to do? None of this was right.

The voice of reason inside her head told her to play it cool. *Don't let her see how flustered you are. It's not about you, it's about Ellie.*

'I can't say that I've noticed, to be honest. Does he?' But her cheeks betrayed her. She felt them beginning to heat up.

'Mum, you do think he looks like him, and you fancy him. You've gone bright red.'

'I do not fancy him, Ellie,' Lucy said, firmly. 'I work with him. I like him very much as a friend, but not like that. Besides he's a few years younger than me and he drives me mad most of the time.'

Ellie sat back and giggled, making Lucy laugh as well.

'All right,' Lucy admitted, 'he's not bad to look at; I'll give him that. There are much uglier blokes I could be stuck with for hours on end.'

'You should ask him out. On a date.'

'I couldn't do that! I have to work with him.'

'Why not?' Ellie asked. 'You could always work with someone else. You definitely should ask him out; I think you and him would make a good couple. Like you said, there are uglier blokes I could have as a stepdad.'

'Jesus Christ, Ellie! I'm not marrying him.'

Ellie winked at her. 'Never say never – and why not? It would make Alice happy: she keeps telling me what a lovely couple you two make. Anyway, I'd better get back to work. It's not fair to leave Alice for too long. She's such a lovely lady.'

Lucy smiled as she felt her chest swell with pride for her daughter. Maybe Ellie was finally growing out of that horrible, teenage attitude she seemed to have been wearing like a suit of armour since she was twelve years old.

'You do know that I'm proud of you, don't you? Well – when you don't make daft suggestions about me going out with Mattie, I am.' She winked at Ellie, who actually bent down to give her a quick hug, then pecked her on the cheek.

'Enjoy your coffee,' Ellie said, 'and at least think about it. You're much prettier than Jane, and more Mattie's age. Tell him he's going to be stuck with her in a couple of years when she's incontinent. That should put him off.'

Lucy laughed, almost spitting coffee all over herself. Ellie went back to work, and Lucy sipped her latte and watched Ellie and Alice work and chat. When she'd finished, she took her empty mug over to the counter.

'Thank you. That was the best coffee I've ever tasted.'

Ellie, who was serving another customer, stuck her thumb up at her. Lucy turned to leave, mouthing 'thank you' to Alice, who nodded her head and winked at her. Once she was outside in the fresh air, the pride she'd felt moments ago began to disappear as a gnawing worry filled her chest. What if Mattie had been talking about her to Jane? She could see them now, laughing at her expense. So, not only had Jane probably been poisoning her own daughter against her, she could very well be turning her best friend against her as well.

She hoped that Ellie had got it wrong. Maybe Mattie and Jane were just friends. But... *Does he kiss you on the cheek every time he gets into your car? No.*

Throwing her handbag onto the passenger seat, she noticed the evidence bag containing Lizzy's childhood photograph. She peeled off the post-it note with the number of the forensic artist on it, and typed the number into her phone. As it rang, she crossed her fingers that there was someone at the university to answer her.

'Dr Chris Corkill speaking.'

Lucy almost let out a whoop of delight. She explained to him exactly what she needed.

'Well, you're in luck,' he said, 'because it's my day off. I was just leaving. I can hang on, though, if you want to bring the photograph down, so I can discuss it with you?'

Lucy looked at the dashboard clock. It was a twenty-minute drive if she didn't get stuck behind some Sunday driver, crawling along.. *Sod it.* She wasn't doing anything constructive, and if he hassled her about being paid upfront, she'd give him her credit card.

'That would be brilliant,' she said. 'I'll be there as soon as I can. Thank you so much.'

She hoped that by the time she had spoken to Chris – who had sounded lovely – and had driven back to the station, she might have calmed down enough to confront Mattie about Jane.

CHAPTER FORTY-FOUR

When Lucy finally arrived at the university, she parked outside the main building and rang Dr Corkill. He directed her to the main entrance and told her to wait for him there. She slipped the evidence bag into her handbag, then pulled out her perfume, spritzed herself, and applied a quick smudge of lipstick – just in case Dr Corkill was drop-dead gorgeous, single and available.

At the main entrance, Lucy sat down on a bench. She couldn't help feeling like a naughty school kid because she had come here before obtaining Tom's permission. However, she knew they couldn't afford to wait any longer. She had no idea who the next victim was, but she was sure there would be one. Lizzy had waited a long time for this, and Lucy didn't doubt that she wouldn't stop until she'd finished what she started.

Lucy wondered if Lizzy was tired. Lucy supposed it would have made her feel younger: after all, so many murderers had said that killing another person was the ultimate power trip. Being able to decide whether someone should live or die was apparently a huge thrill. How on earth they got a thrill from it, Lucy would never understand – and didn't want to, either. She couldn't imagine wanting to actually end another person's life. Although Mattie was walking a fine line at the moment…

A warm hand touched her shoulder and she jumped so high off the chair that the man jumped as well.

'DCI Harwin?'

'Yes, oh god. I'm so sorry, I was miles away.'

He held out his hand. 'You certainly were. I'm Chris Corkill, we spoke on the phone earlier.'

He was a pleasant-looking man, about in his forties. Lucy took his hand, shaking it firmly. 'We did, and thank you so much for seeing me at such short notice. I really do appreciate it.'

'It isn't often I have the honour of a DCI come to visit me,' Dr Corkill said. 'Actually, I've never had the pleasure. I'll show you to my office and you can tell me what you need.'

He led the way through a maze of corridors until he reached his very clean – almost too orderly – office. Lucy wasn't sure if she should sit down in case she messed the room up.

Dr Corkill grinned at her, noticing her discomfort. 'Ah, this is not me. I have a lovely cleaner called Bertha who I think has OCD. I'm almost afraid to come in here myself some days.'

'I think I could do with a Bertha in my life,' Lucy said. 'I wonder if she lives far away from me?' She handed him the bag, deciding honesty was the best policy. 'Look, I'm sorry, I may have misled you on the phone. I'm not a DCI at all.'

'You are the very well-respected Detective Inspector Lucinda Harwin. Forgive me, but I Googled you. It's a force of habit. I thought perhaps you might have been recently promoted to DCI, but don't worry – I understand. If you're worried about the expenses side of things, then don't. We can sort that out later.'

'Thank you so much. We – the police – have a huge problem and I'm hoping you can help. This has to be between us for now, though. It's about to break in the press anyway, but I'd really ap-preciate it if we could keep this confidential.'

'Of course,' Dr Corkill said. 'It will be one hundred per cent confidential. Although, in a couple of months when it's all blown over, would you allow me to use this as an assignment for my next course?'

'If you can do what I'm hoping you can, then yes, you can do what the bloody hell you want with it,' Lucy said. 'Once we've caught the killer and the trial is over, that is.'

Dr Corkill smiled. 'Go on.'

Lucy really hoped she could trust the man sitting in front of her, because she was about to disclose delicate information pertaining to a high-profile murder investigation that she hadn't even discussed with her DCI. If it all went wrong, she would lose her job, her livelihood… everything.

'There have been four brutal murders in as many days,' she said. 'I believe the girl on that photograph is the killer. The only problem is that she disappeared years ago. We believe that she has grown up and changed her identity. She is supposed to have died in 1990 – only I don't believe she did; I think she is very much alive. We have no idea what she might look like now, but obviously if we had some idea it would make identifying her a whole lot easier. We can't exactly do a "most wanted" appeal with a picture of a nine-year-old girl from 1975. She's going to be in her early fifties now.'

'Wow, this is amazing,' Dr Corkill said. 'I've never heard anything like it. In fact, it's absolutely brilliant – well, obviously not for you and your colleagues, but it is for me. I've been waiting to work on something like this for years. I get asked to do a lot of facial imaging and the odd facial reconstruction – but this would be great, to be involved in an actual case.'

Lucy couldn't help smiling at his infectious enthusiasm. 'I don't know what to say. Thank you, doctor.'

'Please call me Chris; the title is just for my students. I suppose you'll want a timeframe?'

'Yes,' Lucy said. 'It's really urgent, although I'm sorry to have to rush you. I don't think this woman will stop killing, so we need to uncover her identity as soon as we can. I have a feeling

that she already has her next victim lined up, and I'd like to get
to her before she makes her move.'

He nodded. 'Well, realistically it could take a couple of days.
I have nothing pressing on at the moment though, so if I start
working on it now, I should be able to come up with a hand-
drawn composite by the morning – maybe even later on tonight.
The computer programme would normally be quicker, but we've
had a few glitches with it so it could take a little longer.'

'That would be amazing,' Lucy said. 'I can't thank you enough.'

He laughed. 'I'm going to enjoy this. Write down your contact details and I'll email you a copy as soon as it's done.'

Lucy wrote them down on a scrap of paper that he handed to
her. He folded it and tucked it into the pocket of his faded jeans.
'I'll be in touch soon.'

Lucy shook his hand once more. 'Thank you so much, Chris.'

She turned to leave. With a bit of luck, she thought, this
might just give them the break they needed.

CHAPTER FORTY-FIVE

As Lucy walked back into the office, debating whether or not to tell Tom where she'd been, she spotted Mattie sitting at his desk. His was head bent and he was typing away on his keyboard. As much as Lucy wanted to confront him about Jane, she couldn't do it in an office full of colleagues. Instead, she made herself a coffee and took it into her office, closing the door behind her. At least, thank god, there was no sign of either Tom or Browning.

She checked her emails, knowing it was far too soon to expect one from Chris, but still hoping it wouldn't be long. Just as she was logging off again, her phone began to ring. She answered it to a breathless Catherine.

'Bloody hell, Lucy, I've had to run back to my office so I could phone you and let you know the results before that idiot Browning gets back. I hope you appreciate this.'

Lucy laughed. 'Thank you. I sincerely do, from the bottom of my heart.'

'Yeah, I hope you do. What the hell is Browning doing with your case, anyway?'

'He's assisting me, according to Tom.'

'Pfft. So where've you been? I wanted you to be present at the PMs, not him. I prioritised them and rescheduled everything else I had on.'

'I couldn't do it,' Lucy said. 'I'm sorry; I hadn't realised that you'd gone to so much bother. I was so mad when Browning turned up at the scene that I stormed off like a true professional.'

'You know that Tom's only thinking about his own back, don't you?' Catherine said. 'He'll be worrying about the backlash from the press, with four murders and no one in custody. It's damage control, that's all it is. It doesn't mean that he doesn't think you can't do the job, because you bloody well can – and I told him that earlier.'

'Aw, you are such a sweetheart underneath that cool, tough exterior.'

'I know, but don't you dare tell anyone. So anyway, I've sent the DNA off to cross-match with the hair sample and fast-tracked it. These last two murders were brutal. No hesitation at all. Sometimes you get a couple of wounds where the killer made an attempt on the victim's life, but didn't have the balls to do it right the first time. Not the case with our killer: they knew what they were doing and went for it. Both of these recent victims were killed by the same person; the wounds are almost identical. There's nothing to confirm it's the same killer for all four victims though.'

'Why?'

'Well, the mechanism of death has been different for each one: transorbital lobotomy, manual strangulation and the cut-throat injuries.'

'They are the same killer, though,' Lucy said, 'because of the connections.'

'I'm afraid that's not for me to say,' Catherine said. 'Although between you and me, I'd say it most definitely is. Come on, how many murders do we get around here? A couple a year? Four in four days is an awful lot of killing. The chances of it being two or three different killers – well, it's not unheard of, but it's very un-likely. Anyway, I have to go; I'll let you know if I find out anything else. Take care, Lucy. Don't let the bastards grind you down.'

'Thanks, I'll try not to.'

As Lucy hung up, she looked up to see Mattie standing up and tugging on his coat. It was now or never. She walked across to his desk.

'Can I have a word?'

He nodded.

'Not here.'

He followed her to the ladies' toilet – seeing as how she was the only woman upstairs, it was the best she could do for privacy.

'What's the matter, Lucy?' Mattie asked. 'I don't get why you're so pissed off with me.'

'Have you been seeing Jane Toppan?'

'Who?'

'Ellie's youth offending support worker. There's no point denying it. Ellie saw you together.'

Mattie's face turned crimson. 'What are you talking about? And even if I have, it's not really any of your business who I see outside of work.'

'Well, I think that it is,' Lucy said, struggling to keep her anger under control. 'You know how I feel about that woman. For fuck's sake, all the time you've sat in the car listening to me slag off your latest lover, and you've never said one word. What's wrong with you?'

'I've been seeing a woman called Heidi, not Jane,' Mattie said. 'And she's only my girlfriend – it's not as if we're planning on getting married or anything.'

'Heidi who?'

'Heidi Toppan,' Mattie admitted, reluctantly. He looked a little baffled.

'I bet she talks about me all the time, doesn't she?' Lucy pressed. 'What do the pair of you do? Sit getting all cosy, while you're slagging me off for what a shit parent I am, and how terrible it is to work with me?'

'Don't be daft. I didn't know she was Ellie's support worker, and she probably hasn't realised that you're Ellie's mum. Even if we had, we'd never do that. But if the cap fits…'

Lucy stared at him. It felt as if he'd just ripped her heart in two. So he thought she was a useless mother as well, did he? She turned away from him – he reached out to grab her arm, but she shrugged him away – and rushed out of the door. She didn't stop, heading straight for the exit and her car.

Mattie stood there for several long moments, shocked by Lucy's reaction. God, what had he said? And was Heidi really Ellie's support worker? There must be some mistake. He ran after her, down to the car park, but it was too late – she was already driving out through the automatic gates.

'Fuck, fuck, fuck.'

Browning, who had just got out of his car, began to laugh. 'Aw, what's up? You two had a lovers' tiff? And in public as well! Is super-cool Lucy losing her cool, I wonder?'

Mattie turned to look at him. 'Why don't you fuck off and do something useful for a change?'

Browning grabbed his chest. 'Ouch, that really hurt, Matthew. No need to be like that. Send her a bunch of flowers and she'll forgive you.' He went inside, chuckling away to himself at his own joke.

Mattie decided he'd had enough for one day. Let Browning do some work for a change. He was going home for a shower and to pack an overnight bag. Lucy could sulk all she wanted until tomorrow. He would sort things out with her then, when hopefully she would have calmed down enough to talk about it rationally and realise she was being stupid. He'd never once talked about her to Heidi – not in the way that she'd accused him of, anyway.

He took out his phone and sent Lucy a text: *Sorry x*

CHAPTER FORTY-SIX

As much as Lucy felt like drowning her sorrows in a bottle of wine or two, she surprised herself by not even opening the fridge door. Instead, she went upstairs and stripped off her suit, putting on some joggers, a T-shirt and her trainers instead. She was going to go for a power walk. She didn't run – mainly because she was too unfit and she hated to get that hot and sweaty. Walking, though, she did do – knowing it wouldn't result in requiring the aid of a paramedic to restart her heart. Although she did keep to the main roads where there were emergency defibrillators dotted around, just in case.

She opened the playlist that Ellie had painstakingly added to her phone when she'd been in a rare good mood, and plugged in her earphones. She knew that if she didn't do something to work off the anger that was bubbling away like a spring inside her chest, she would explode. And the explosion would probably be over something trivial, which would make everything a hundred times worse.

As she marched out of her front door and down the path, her neighbour, Sam, waved his hand at her. Even he didn't pause to speak to her like he always did – she must be giving off some awful don't-fuck-with-me vibe. She would walk it out of her system. She was angry with herself for the way she'd reacted to the news of Mattie seeing Jane – or Heidi, or whatever it was she called herself. Technically, it had nothing at all to do with her, so she should have kept her nose out and her opinions to herself. What did it matter who he was sleeping with? They were friends, and deep down Lucy knew he'd never betray her by bitching about her. So why had she felt so cross with him?

For the first time, it struck her that maybe the cause of all this anger was jealousy. Maybe Ellie was right. *Do you like him, Lucy?* She shook her head. The idea was ridiculous. She had to get a grip. Maybe she had this Jane all wrong; maybe they just rubbed each other up the wrong way. Mattie was normally a really good judge of character, so if he liked this woman, she must be OK. Lucy should apologise to him. And she would have to try to make more of an effort with Jane, even if it killed her.

Lucy put her head down so that she wouldn't have to look at anyone or stop and speak to them. She marched on to the soothing sound of Ella Fitzgerald's voice, and began to feel the tension and stress of the last few days melt away. At least she'd put things right with Ellie, who was her main priority.

She passed houses, shops and run-down amusement arcades, before crossing the road to walk along the promenade. She stopped to look at the view. She'd been so busy working that she'd forgotten what a beautiful part of England this was to live in. She gazed along the ramshackle pier stretching out into the sea, thinking it was such a shame the council had let it go to rack and ruin. When she'd been a teenager, she'd spent most of her spare time hanging around on there with her friends. They'd used to congregate in the brightly lit, warm amusement arcade, playing the penny slots, looking around on the floor for loose change the tourists would drop. Lucy's best friend's mum had worked in the arcade, and let them shelter in there for hours. Then, when they'd got bored, they would head into the run-down café next door where they'd share a milkshake.

The pier was a magnificent Victorian structure. Lucy thought that the fact that it was still standing, despite having been shut for the last ten years, was a testament to the builders who'd constructed it. It was silhouetted against the sky, which had filled with fire as the sun began to set over the sea. Lucy sighed. It was a beautiful view. She could stand watching it forever... Except that she had a date.

She checked the time. *Crap.* If she didn't want to be ridiculously late, she was going to have to run back home whether it was good for her health or not. She sent Stephen a quick text, apologising for the fact that she would now be a little later than eight. Then she began to run, cursing herself, because now she was going to be all hot and sweaty.

When she reached her house, she headed straight upstairs for a shower, then blasted her hair dry as best as she could. It was still damp as she tried to run the straighteners through it, and she cringed at the hissing noise her hair made between the heated pads. She got dressed, doing the quickest make-up job ever and hoping for the best. At least Stephen had seen her when she'd looked cool and collected at the hospital the other night. She just hoped the shock of seeing her looking like a fried mess tonight wouldn't put him off for life.

By the time she reached the pub and parked in the last available space, it was almost eight thirty. As she had no idea what car Stephen drove, she had no way of knowing whether or not he was here. Inhaling deeply, she applied another coat of lipstick before getting out of the car. Her stomach was in knots – but she wasn't sure whether it was because she was nervous at the prospect of an actual date with an actual man, or whether it was just hunger. This was the first time she'd thought about dating since George had left her. Until now, she'd been too devastated by their break-up.

God, she was late. She was so late that she wouldn't be surprised if Stephen hadn't already left. Forcing herself to walk through the doors into the chic, newly refurbished pub, she looked around. She couldn't see him. Not that she could quite remember what he looked like – she'd been so busy at the hospital that she hadn't taken that much notice.

'Lucy!' The voice came from behind her. She turned around to see Stephen walking through the pub doors, looking even more flustered than she felt. 'I'm so sorry,' he said. 'There was an emergency and I got called back in to help out. I didn't think I'd ever get away. I completely understand if you've been hanging around and don't want to stay.'

Lucy laughed. 'Don't be daft, I've only just got here myself. I thought that you'd left because you were fed up with waiting for me.'

He grinned at her. 'No, absolutely not. I can honestly, hand on my heart, say that I'd quite happily wait all night for you.'

Lucy felt the slow burn of her cheeks beginning to blush. She nodded towards the bar. 'What are we waiting for, then? I'm starving, and now we've decided that we're both worth waiting for, let's get a drink.'

'What do you fancy?' Stephen asked. 'Red, white, Prosecco?'

'Would you mind if I just had a lime and soda?' Lucy asked. 'I'm trying to cut down – oh dear, that sounds terrible. It's not that I'm a raging alcoholic or anything, but I do need to drive back; I'll need my car if I get a call-out in the night. Work is crazy at the moment.'

'That sounds good to me,' Stephen said. 'I'll have the same. It's probably a good idea –

I've not eaten much today so I don't want to be drunk after a glass. Whatever would you think of me?'

Lucy went and sat at a table in the corner whilst Stephen waited at the bar. He came back with the drinks and a menu, which he tried to pass to her – but she shook her head.

'I already know what I want: steak, chips and salad. The steak well-done, please.'

'Good choice,' Stephen said. 'I'll have the same. Gosh, we're easily pleased, aren't we?' He winked at her and went back to the bar. Lucy smiled to herself. He was so nice and easy-going, she would bet all his patients fell in love with him. She watched as he leant over the bar to give his order to the barman, and she couldn't help but admire the view. He turned around and she looked away, hoping he didn't have some secret psychic ability that meant he could tell what a pervert she was.

He sat opposite her, took out his phone and turned it off. 'I've done my good deeds for the day. I hope you don't mind, but I prefer the art of conversation. I hate it when you see couples and families out for a meal and all they do is stare down at their phones. They should be talking to each other, I think. But then, I'm a little old-fashioned. My colleagues all laugh at me.'

Lucy took out her phone, checking it first to make sure she had no missed calls, then followed suit. 'You know what? I think you're right. We rely on our phones far too much. Do you go on Facebook or Twitter?'

Stephen laughed. 'I barely have time to answer my mother's text messages when she's checking up on me – usually asking if I've eaten anything in the last twenty-four hours. I wouldn't know where to start with Twitter.'

Lucy smiled. 'So, do you ever get any spare time?'

He laughed even louder. 'Sorry, I'm being daft. I do get some spare time, just not a lot. When I have time off, I like to go back and visit my parents and my younger sister, although it's not always possible, with the distance.'

'Why? How far away do they live? Florida?'

'Close! New York. Well, Lower East Side, to be exact. I love England, though, and Brooklyn Bay is the closest to NYC that I'll get over here. Even if it is only by name.'

'New York!' Lucy said. 'Wow, that's amazing. It's been on my bucket list for years. I've always wanted to go there. You don't sound American though.'

'No, I don't. That's because I was born and bred in England. My dad came over here for work and met my mum. Then they had me, and I went to school here until I was a teenager. Then, when he got transferred back, we all moved over there – I came back for university. So that's how I got to keep my terribly British accent.'

Lucy laughed. 'I'm impressed. My life isn't anything like so glamorous. My parents were both born in Brooklyn Bay – they met working on the fairground on the pier. The furthest we ever went on holiday was to Scarborough. They're both dead now, though – they died in a car crash when I was twenty-one.'

'Lucy, I'm so sorry to hear that,' Stephen said. 'It must have been tough for you. Do you have any brothers or sisters?'

'I have an older sister, but we're not close.'

They continued to chat away. Stephen promised that if Lucy ever wanted to go to New York, he would take her – even if they only went as friends. He said that he would show her the sights like a native New Yorker. Lucy felt herself liking him all the more. The thought of going to her dream destination with such a good-looking guy made her forget all about what a shitty day she'd had. The murders, Mattie and Jane were pushed to the back of her mind.

They ate their meals and shared a gigantic dessert, finishing with coffee. Stephen insisted on paying the bill. Lucy wanted to split it, but he wouldn't hear of it. As they walked out to their cars, Lucy found that she didn't want the date to end. She'd had a lovely, civilised evening, and she desperately wanted to ask him back to hers for coffee. As they reached her car, Stephen leant down to kiss her cheek just as she turned to say goodbye. Their lips met. Both of them pulled away, a little embarrassed, and laughed.

Lucy plucked up her courage. 'Would you like to come back to mine for coffee? I've had such a nice time and I don't want it to end just yet. But it would be just coffee, mind.'

He grinned. 'Coffee would be great. If I'm honest with you I couldn't do anything more energetic if I wanted to. My last set of shifts were horrendous, so if I fall asleep on your sofa, I won't be at all insulted if you poke me and tell me it's time to leave.'

Throwing all caution to the wind, Lucy gave him her address and told him to follow her home. There was something about him that made her feel safe. He actually reminded her of Mattie: easy-going and fun to be with.

She beat him to her house and, while she was waiting, quickly turned on her phone to check she had no missed calls. God forbid that work had needed her – if there'd been another murder, she'd be so mad with herself for not having been available. She needed to prove to Tom that she could cope with it all.

Stephen's car parked behind her just as she saw that she had two missed calls and three text messages from Mattie, all telling her to ring him. That was OK – if it had been work-related and serious, Tom would have called as well. As it was, it was late and she had no intention of calling Mattie back. He could wait until the morning. She'd apologise to him then.

There was a fourth text message from an unknown number. She felt her heart miss a beat to see it was from Chris Corkill, telling her to ring him. She got out of her car and looked over at Stephen, who was smiling at her as he got out of his own car. She lifted her phone to her ear and mouthed 'sorry' to him. He never even flinched, which she took as a good sign. Taking her door key out of her purse, she walked towards the house.

'Hello?'

'Sorry it's so late, Chris. It's DI Harwin, here. Lucy.' She unlocked the door and walked into the hallway.

'Lucy! Good of you to get back to me. I've not stopped since you left, and I thought that you might want to see the finished results. I was just calling to let you know I've emailed them to the address you left me. I hope that's OK?'

'It's amazing,' Lucy said. 'Thank you so much, Chris. I'll nip to work now to take a look. I can't believe that you've done it already.'

'Like I said, I was excited to have the chance to work on it,' Chris said. 'My motive is entirely selfish; it's a two-way street. I think the images are pretty good, but I'm biased and would say that.'

He laughed and she smiled. 'Well, I'm praying they're clear enough for us to put out an appeal tomorrow, so if they are, you're very good.'

'I'll let you be the judge of that,' Chris said. 'But I think you'll be pleased with them. Hopefully you'll have a much better chance of identifying your suspect now. Let me know. I'm at home now and going to bed.'

'Yes, of course,' Lucy said. 'I'll speak to you tomorrow. Thanks again.'

As she ended the call, she realised that Stephen was standing next to her, having come into the hallway behind her. She'd momentarily forgotten about him in all the excitement. She wished that she'd given Chris her personal email to send them to, but she might get in trouble. It wasn't secure and this was top-secret work stuff. Besides it wouldn't have looked very professional to send them to her Hotmail account.

'I'm so sorry,' Lucy said, 'but I have to go to work for a short time. I don't think I'll be long. I wouldn't go if it wasn't very important.'

Stephen bent down and she felt his lips brush against her cheek. 'Thank you for a lovely evening, Lucy. I understand. I really do. I think we both have pretty crazy, all-consuming jobs that we wouldn't change for the world. I'm knackered anyway, so I think I'll go home, drink my coffee and have sweet dreams about you, if that's OK?'

'Of course it is,' Lucy said, feeling herself blush again. 'And thank you for being so understanding. Not many people get it.'

'I'll ring you tomorrow and see if you're busy. Don't worry if you are. I'm back in work tomorrow afternoon – I've ended up agreeing to cover a shift for my colleague, who has had a last-minute completion date for moving house.'

He turned, walking back to his car. As Lucy watched him go, she realised that she liked Dr Stephen King a whole lot more than she'd ever imagined possible.

She locked her door, returned the key to her purse and hurried back to her car. She was buzzing to see the artist's impression of what Lizzy Clements would look like now. The case was finally coming together. She had a feeling that she was on to something. Some people called it a copper's instinct – and Lucy thought that was a pretty accurate description. Her dad had always told her to trust in her gut instinct and so she had. It had never let her down.

She drove to work much faster than the thirty-mile speed limit dictated. The roads were deserted this time of night, anyway.

CHAPTER FORTY-SEVEN

Mattie made it in time to meet Heidi at the bar of the Belmont, which resulted in her giving him the biggest smile ever. She leant over and kissed him on the lips. Her finger trailed down his chin and neck until she stopped, placing her hand on his heart.

'I'm so glad you could make it,' she said. 'I didn't really not want to ever see you again.'

Mattie thought about telling her that Lucy had gone off on one about them, but then decided against it. If he was here and having to pay for the bloody place, the least he could do was to try to make the most of it. He couldn't relax, though. The conversation with Lucy kept replaying in his mind. For a start, why hadn't Heidi told him that her real name was Jane? And then there was the fact that he felt bad that he'd upset Lucy with his sneaking around. He should have had the balls to tell her from the beginning about his relationship, and then it wouldn't have been so bad. Even though his personal life had nothing to do with Lucy as a colleague, she was his closest friend. He ought to be able to share things with her. God knows, there had been plenty of times when he'd had to tell her to wind her neck in, or had given her advice about her problems at home.

He felt his cheek sting. Heidi had just slapped him. He rubbed at his face, bewildered. 'What the hell?'

'You're thinking about her, Matthew,' Heidi said. 'Don't deny it. Jesus Christ, every single time you think about her, you get that sad little puppy-dog look in your eyes. Well, let me tell you a home truth: she doesn't give a shit about you. She just wants you at her beck and call. Her little lapdog. If she really liked you, wouldn't you be with her now? Sharing a bottle of wine? Sharing her bed?'

Mattie looked at Heidi – really looked at her, as if for the first time. As if someone had just taken the blinkers off his eyes so he could see her clearly. She was attractive for her age, yes – she didn't have many lines or wrinkles. But it was her eyes that caught his attention now. They were so dark and cold. He felt as if she were staring straight down into the depths of his soul. It scared him.

Then, in an instant, her face changed back to its usual warmth. She smiled at him, leaning forward to kiss his face where he could feel that she'd left a red mark.

'Sorry, darling,' she said. 'I've had a terribly busy day. You know how jealous I get of her – of any woman, really, who I see as competition. I can't help it. She's so young and pretty, and I'm so much older than the both of you. Here, have a glass of wine.'

'You have it all wrong,' Mattie said. 'Me and Lucy – well, we're just really good mates. Look, I found out today that you're Lucy's daughter's support worker. I understand why you didn't tell me that – client confidentiality and so on. But why did you tell me you were called Heidi, when Lucy knows you as Jane?'

Jane sighed. 'My full name is Heidi Jane Toppan. I prefer to use plain Jane for work – it's just easier.'

She'd poured him a large glass of some sparkling wine. Mattie prayed it was Prosecco and not champagne, because he was already going to have to sell his soul to pay for tonight. And he didn't even want to be here – all he really wanted to do was to go and see Lucy.

The waiter came over to tell them their table was ready. Heidi stood up, slipping her hand inside Mattie's, and tugged him towards the restaurant. He picked up the wine glass with his other hand and downed the contents. The waiter showed them to a cosy table in the corner. Mattie was relieved the lighting wasn't very good, because he didn't want to have to look at Heidi. He had a bad feeling about tonight. He wondered if he should just apologise, throw her a hundred quid and walk out of here. Out of her life.

Only that wasn't who he was. He had been brought up with better manners than that. So he found himself sitting down, and the waiter poured him another glass of that fizzy stuff –

which was actually quite nice, meaning it was expensive. Thank god, Mattie thought, that he had his credit card on him, because it wasn't pay day for another week yet. Two bowls of soup were placed in front of them and Mattie looked down at his. He hadn't even seen the menu.

'I hope you didn't mind me ordering for you?' Heidi asked.

Mattie did mind. He minded a fucking lot because he never ate soup, and if Heidi had bothered to ask him, she would have known that. A burning rage filled his insides. He shook his head, but the room began to spin a little so he stopped. The wine must have gone straight to his head.

Instead of standing up and telling her to fuck off, like he was tempted to, he picked up the spoon and began to shovel soup into his mouth. He was relieved to find that it tasted better than it looked. He picked up a bread roll, ripped it apart, and stuffed it into his mouth. He saw Heidi cringe, which gave him some feeling of satisfaction, so he did the same again. The room was still spinning and he wasn't sure if he was going to puke or not. Better get his money's worth before he did. This thought made him laugh, and he looked across at Heidi, who was sitting there not touching her food. He gulped down his bread roll and pointed at her soup.

'What's up? Not hungry?'

'Not any more.'

'Why not? You took the liberty of ordering my food so that it arrived faster. You must be starving.'

'What's wrong with you? You're acting like an animal.'

'I'm just getting my money's worth.' He picked up the wine glass and downed the contents. Suddenly, the room lurched violently and he thought he was going to pass out. 'I need to lie down,' he said. 'I don't feel well.' The words sounded as if he'd tried to speak through a mouth full of cotton wool.

Heidi put her napkin down and stood up. Walking over to him, she linked her arm under his elbow and tried to help him up off the chair. Mattie tried to stand, but his legs didn't want to hold his body weight. The waiter came rushing over to help.

'Is everything OK, sir?'

Mattie heard him. His mouth opened to answer – only, nothing came out.

'I don't think he's very well,' he heard Heidi say. 'Can you help me get him up to our room, please?'

The last thing Mattie wanted to do was go and be sick all over the hotel room. He tried to mumble this to the pair of them, but it was unintelligible. He felt them take an arm each and march him out of the restaurant to the lift. Within a matter of minutes, he was being laid down on a king size bed. He could hear Heidi thanking the waiter as he lay there, trying to stop the room from spinning. He felt his shoes being tugged off his feet and his trousers being removed. His tie was loosened and his buttons undone, and then everything went black.

CHAPTER FORTY-EIGHT

As Lucy rushed through the side door into the station, she was surprised to see Browning in the process of putting his radio away in the locker room. It was late, and he'd started earlier than she had, yet he was still here and only just about to leave. Fleetingly, she felt bad – there must be some reason why he was still here – but she carried on past him and went upstairs to the empty CID office.

Lucy flopped down onto the chair behind her desk and typed her username and password into the computer, hoping it wouldn't take forever to log on like it normally did. Out of the corner of her eye, she saw Browning come back into the office and begin hovering around his desk. She didn't acknowledge him. She knew what he was up to – trying to find out why she was here. Wouldn't she be the same if it were the other way around? She knew without a doubt that she would.

The blue screen finally filled with icons and Lucy double-clicked on the email envelope. The message from Chris was the newest one in her folder and she opened it, trying not to swear loudly or drum her fingers on the desk as it took an age to load. She could feel the meal she'd eaten earlier lying heavy in her stomach, and she wished that for once she'd eaten a salad. The computer was playing up and it wouldn't open the attachment. Thumping her fist on the desk, she turned the computer off and stood up. She needed to find another computer, one that wasn't frozen. She looked at Mattie's – his was free, so she logged in once more. It was taking forever, and Browning was still hovering around by his desk.

Finally, the attachment began to open. Lucy hadn't realised she'd been holding her breath until the image was fully loaded onto the screen, when she gasped so loudly that Browning shouted: 'Are you OK over there, Lucy? Don't want you having a heart attack when I'm about to go home.'

Lucy peered at the screen in horror. She couldn't say it was her one hundred per cent –

the hair colour was different, and the woman she knew had fewer lines on her face – but the likeness was uncanny. She stared at it, hoping to god that it wasn't true. Only, the more she studied the face staring back at her, the more she was convinced it was her.

'Browning,' she said, 'I need you to come and look at this now. I know who the killer is.'

Heidi stood and watched Mattie for a little while, so she could catch her breath. Getting him on the bed had been hard work, even with the help of the waiter. It had left her quite flustered. She hadn't expected the drugs to work so quickly on him.

He was so handsome. As she looked at him lying there, almost naked and in a deep sleep, she felt quite sad that this relationship was over. It had been fun. He was a nice guy – but she no longer had any use for him.

His phone began to ring with an unknown number and she picked it up, sending the call straight to voicemail. It rang again, then vibrated to say there was a voice message. Intrigued, Heidi dialled through the voicemail and heard Lucy's voice. The panic in it was quite refreshing to hear. She had thought that Lucy Harwin had everything under control, but judging by that message, it seemed not.

Heidi deleted the message. So, the clever Lucy had figured out who the killer was. How kind of her to warn Heidi like this

– in doing so, she had just sealed her own fate. It was just as well Mattie was out for the count, Heidi thought, because if he'd got an inkling that Lucy was in danger, she didn't think he'd have thought twice about killing her.

Bending down, she kissed his cheek. 'It was good while it lasted. Thank you.'

As she left the room, she hung the 'Do not disturb' sign on the door handle, and smiled as she walked away.

CHAPTER FORTY-NINE

The woman Lucy was looking at bore a very strong resemblance to Jane Toppan. *Oh, god, Mattie. Mattie!*

She waved Browning closer. There was no time to mess around. She was convinced that Lizzy Clements had grown up to be Jane Toppan, which meant that Mattie could be in serious danger. He was probably with her right now.

Browning looked at the artist's sketch on her screen.

'It's pretty good. What are you doing, taking up portrait drawing in your spare time?'

She shook her head. The lump that was forming in her throat was making it hard to speak.

'This is an artist's impression of the Clements' daughter, Lizzy, as an adult. Did you not listen to the briefing?'

Browning shrugged.

'She was put into the asylum at nine years old and the Clements never saw her again. Supposedly she died in 1990 of a drugs overdose.'

'And?'

'Well, this is an age progression portrait drawn up by a forensic artist. The woman in the portrait looks very much like my daughter's youth offending key worker, and more importantly, that is who Mattie just so happens to be dating at the moment.'

Browning studied the picture whilst trying to digest what Lucy had just said. He looked at her. 'Sorry, it's late. Forgive me, but what exactly are you saying?'

Lucy took a deep breath. 'This is our killer. We know who she is, and I think that Mattie might be in danger.'

She looked for her phone to ring Mattie and realised that she'd put it down on her hall table when she'd turned to speak to Stephen. Picking up the desk phone, she dialled the only number apart from her daughter's that she knew off by heart. It went straight to voicemail.

Browning had disappeared and she didn't know where he'd gone – she just hoped it was to do something useful. She tried Mattie again, this time leaving him a message:

'Mattie, it's Lucy. This is really important. I need you to ring me back as soon as you get this. I know who the killer is.'

Browning appeared at the door with one of the student officers from the parade room. 'Inspector, this is Luke. He's a bit of a computer whizz, aren't you, Luke?'

Luke nodded.

'He's going to do some background searches on our suspect until Col can get back to take over – social media, whatever – whilst we try and get hold of the boss and tell him we need an arrest team assembling asap.'

Lucy felt a wave of relief rush through her that Browning had taken her seriously. 'Thank you. That's brilliant.'

Luke, who looked as if he was about twelve and had dressed up as a policeman especially for World Book Day, had turned beetroot red. Browning ushered him towards the nearest desk and told him to get started. Lucy tried Mattie's mobile again, before looking up his details on the system to get his house phone number. She'd never had to ring it before because he always, always answered his mobile phone.

A quarter of an hour later, Lucy was pacing up and down the office waiting for the DCI to arrive and get the ball rolling. She'd already put in a request for cell site analysis of Mattie's phone. If they could ping the phone masts and get a location of where he'd last used it, they would be able to narrow the search down to a specific geographical area within a three-kilometre radius. The control room inspector had promised they would start on this just as soon as Mattie's house had been searched to make sure he wasn't tucked up in bed. Lucy had wanted to tell him to go fuck himself. Mattie would never not answer her calls.

A voice in her head whispered: *Not usually, but you pissed him off today with your judgemental accusations, didn't you?*

She heard a cough, and looked up to see Luke standing there, holding some sheets of paper.

'What have you got, Luke?'

'Well, ma'am—'

She lifted her hand up. 'Lucy. Call me Lucy.'

He nodded, his cheeks glowing even redder. 'Lucy. I couldn't find anything on social media – Facebook, Twitter, Instagram – for a woman called Jane Toppan. I did find her address, though – and this is off Google.'

He handed her the sheet of paper and she looked down at a grainy black-and-white photograph of a woman.

'Who's this?'

'She's called Honora Kelley. She was an American serial killer who changed her name to Jane Toppan.'

Lucy read the printout. Honora's father, Peter Kelley, had been supposedly insane and an alcoholic. Her mother had died when Honora was very young, and in 1863 Kelly had taken his two youngest daughters, Delia and Honora, to the Boston Female Asylum. He never saw them again. When Honora left the asylum, she changed her name to Jane Toppan, became a nurse, and began poisoning her patients and the people who got close to her. She confessed to thirty-three murders in 1901.

Lucy felt the hairs on the back of her neck begin to prickle as she finished reading. Somehow, Lizzy had found a kindred spirit in Jane Toppan, and had named herself after her. Lucy had never heard of the poisoner, and she wondered how Lizzy Clements had.

'Thank you, Luke,' she said. 'This is very useful.'

She dialled Mattie's phone again. What if they were already too late? She'd never be able to live with herself. A cold feeling gripped her stomach as she realised that he'd tried to call her earlier and she hadn't returned his calls.

'Lucy, what the fuck is going on?'

Lucy looked up to see Tom standing there in a pair of jogging pants and a faded T-shirt. She'd never seen him in anything other than a suit and tie before.

'I believe Mattie's girlfriend, Jane Toppan – aka Lizzy Clements – is our killer. She also works with my daughter at youth offending. Mattie's been seeing her for a while now and I can't get hold of him. I have two addresses that I want searching simultaneously – his and Jane's.'

'And this is based on what?' Tom asked.

Lucy pointed to the image on her computer screen. 'I took the liberty of engaging the help of a forensic artist, who very kindly drew this age progression portrait from a childhood photograph of Lizzy.'

'Jesus, Lucy, anything else you might want to tell me? Do you know how long it will take to get Task Force assembled to make up two entry teams? They all went off-duty at ten – they won't be ready in the next thirty minutes. That I can guarantee.'

'No, I don't know, and I don't fucking care, sir. I want to be ready to go as soon as possible. This is a matter of life and death.'

Browning appeared behind Tom. 'I'll take a Taser-trained officer with me and go and sit outside Toppan's address in a plain car until Task Force can get there. Lucy, you take another and go and sit outside Mattie's house, then we can coordinate from there.'

'Oh my god,' Lucy said, as something else occurred to her. 'Ellie. Jane knows where she lives.'

Tom sat down in the chair opposite Lucy, rubbing his chest. He turned to Browning. 'I think I'm going to have a heart attack.'

'No you're not, sir. It's probably indigestion. Now, you know how much she gets on my nerves' – he pointed to Lucy – 'but there's no denying that she is on to something, and I seriously think we need to do what she's telling us. I'd hate for one of our own to get hurt by some sick psycho bitch.'

Lucy, ignoring them, was busy dialling Ellie's number. Ellie answered.

'Where are you, sweetie?'

'In bed, why?'

'Just wondered. Can you go and get your dad for me, please?'

'Why didn't you ring him instead? I don't know if he's back yet; he was taking Rosie out for a meal.'

'I need you to go and see if he's back. It's really important.'

Ellie let out a huge sigh. 'Yes, Mum.'

Lucy heard her daughter clambering out of bed and walking downstairs. There was some fumbling and then George's deep voice came on the line.

'Lucy?'

'Is Ellie next to you?'

'Yes.'

'Give her phone back to her, then can you ring me on my work phone? It's very important.'

She ended the call and started drumming her fingers on the desk. Browning looked at her.

'Toppan is Ellie's key worker,' Lucy said. 'What if she decides to go after her?'

'Why would she?'

'Because she doesn't like me and I don't like her. She might go after her because of me.'

Tom appeared at the door. 'Browning, get a patrol sent to sit outside Ellie's house until I tell them they can leave.'

The phone began to ring.

'It's late, Lucy,' George said. 'What's wrong?'

'I think the killer is Ellie's key worker. Whatever you do, don't tell Ellie though, I don't want her frightened until we've caught her. I don't think that you're in any danger, but I don't want to risk it. Will you please make sure everywhere is locked up? And do not open the door to anyone until I tell you that it's safe to do so. There's a patrol car on its way to sit outside your house, but if anything happens you must ring 999.'

'Dear god.'

'I know, and I'm sorry.'

'Be careful, Lucy,' George whispered.

Tom was on his phone, mid-argument with the Task Force sergeant. 'Yes, I bloody do authorise the overtime. Would I be asking you to get your men together if it wasn't serious?' He slammed his phone down. 'Bloody idiot. Won't call his team unless I guarantee that they're all getting paid. Right, what's next?'

'Sir, you can run it from here,' Browning said. 'We need someone to coordinate who has half a brain.'

'Yes, I suppose so. Lucy, full protective gear. I don't care if your body armour creases your shirt, get it on – and don't go into Mattie's house until Task Force have been in and cleared it. Do I make myself clear?'

'Yes, sir.'

Lucy took off down to the locker room to get her body armour – not that she was going to wear it until she had to. Browning followed her. He opened his locker and pulled out a pristine fluorescent yellow vest that had clearly never been worn. Lucy looked across at him to see if he was going to put it on, but he flung it over his arm.

'Doesn't fit,' he said. 'It never did, and I was too embarrassed to order a bigger size.'

Lucy felt a sudden rush of warmth towards the man. Maybe he wasn't such an arsehole after all. 'Neither does mine. I've put on weight since it was issued.'

He looked across at her and arched his eyebrow.

'I swear I have,' Lucy protested. 'I used to be able to eat what I wanted. Now all my trousers are too tight. Don't tell Mattie, though – he's always trying to get me to go to the gym.' Pain shot through her heart at the mention of Mattie's name.

'You're getting older,' Browning said. 'It happens to the best of us. Come on, let's go and find Mattie, young whippersnapper that he is, and kick his arse for giving us both heartburn. I hope he realises that I'm missing *Gogglebox* for him.'

Lucy nodded, feeling her eyes glisten with tears that she had to blink back. Two uniformed officers were waiting for them just outside the locker room. They looked at Lucy and Browning with their vests thrown over their arms, but never said a word. Lucy followed her officer to the waiting unmarked car. Then, turning, she looked at Browning.

'Thank you.'

He nodded. 'I'd do the same for you – even though you do get on my last nerve.' He winked at her and despite the seriousness of the situation, she couldn't help laughing.

As she climbed into the car and put her seat belt on, she couldn't stop her hands from shaking. All she wanted was for Mattie to be safe. If it meant he didn't speak to her ever again, she could live with that, just as long as he was alive.

The car stopped a few doors down from Mattie's house, which was all in darkness. Lucy looked around the street for his truck, but couldn't see it. She opened the door, and Scott, the copper behind the wheel, whispered, 'What are you doing? We have to wait for Task Force.'

'I'm just going to do a quick check of the perimeter,' Lucy told him. 'Make sure there's no blood or open doors. Don't you dare radio Control and tell them. This is my best friend we're looking for. Don't tell me you wouldn't do the same if it was yours?'

Scott shrugged, clearly not about to argue with a superior officer, even if she was acting like an idiot. Lucy slipped through Mattie's wooden gate and ran the short distance to the front door. She pushed at it with the heel of her hand – it didn't move. She moved across to see if she could see anything through the wooden blinds at the living room window. They were fully closed, with no gap to peer through, so she listened at the window instead. This was the room where Mattie had his sixty-inch television and Xbox. It was too quiet: he wasn't here.

She got back inside the car, and pointed to the officer's radio. 'Ask Control to run ANPR checks on DS Jackson's number plate to see if it's been through any of the cameras tonight.'

While Scott did as she asked, Lucy used her radio to contact Browning. He answered on the second ring, out of breath.

'Jesus, I was just scouting around the outside of her fancy gaff when my bloody radio started ringing. You gave me a heart attack – I had to run back to the car, and I don't do running, Harwin, so bear that in mind, will you?'

'Sorry,' Lucy said. 'Mattie's house is all in darkness, and his truck isn't here.'

'No sign of life here either. Do you know what kind of car she drives?'

'A black Merc, pretty new.'

There was a slight pause – Browning was looking around. 'No Mercs in this street,' he said.

'Where the bloody hell are they?'

'For all we know they might not even be together,' Browning pointed out. 'You and I might just be prematurely aging ourselves over nothing.'

'Yeah well, I'll take a couple of extra wrinkles as long as he's OK,' Lucy said.

'Speak for yourself – have you seen the state of me lately?'

She couldn't help but smile. 'You missed your calling, Browning; you should have been a night club comic.'

'Funny you should say that…'

'What, were you a nightclub comic?'

'It's a long story, I'll tell you about it one day.'

They were interrupted by the arrival of the armed response officers. Lucy ended the call, getting out of the car to walk down the street to speak to Robbo, the sergeant, who climbed out of the van to greet her.

'What the hell is going on?' Robbo asked her. 'Does anybody actually know? Is it true you think that Mattie is with the killer?'

'Yes, I do, I don't just think it – it is true. I don't think there's anyone in Mattie's house, though; he normally falls asleep with the television still on.'

Lucy went back to the car – she was only in the way. Robbo would now have to coordinate two teams of officers to enter both premises simultaneously to minimise the risk to Mattie. She felt sick: if they found him inside and it was too late, what would she do?

She watched as the armed officers approached the house, all dressed in black. One of them was carrying the heavy red whammer, ready to put the door through. Robbo knocked on her window and she put it down.

'Are you sure you don't know where there's a door key?' Robbo asked. 'It would make life a lot easier.'

Lucy shook her head. How many times had she told him to get a spare key cut in case he lost the main one? 'No, there's no spare.'

Seconds later, Robbo gave the orders and Mattie's front door was put through – while Jane's was put through at the same time elsewhere. Armed officers flooded into Mattie's home, and Lucy jumped out of the car, unable to watch any longer. There was a lot of shouting 'Clear', and that was it. Minutes later, they came back, out the lead officer shaking his head.

'Empty. No one's home.'

'What about the other address?' Lucy asked.

The sergeant radioed the other team and shook his head. 'Empty.'

Lucy took off running. She had to check for herself. What if the team hadn't looked properly? She pushed past the last officer on his way out of Mattie's house, and began to check every room. After looking downstairs first, she ran upstairs to Mattie's bedroom where she threw open the door. It was untidy; his bed was unmade. She lifted the corner of the duvet to look underneath the bed, but there was only one odd shoe and a rolled-up pair of socks. She checked the bathroom and the spare bedroom, feeling more and more panicked that he wasn't there. All she wanted was to know that he was safe.

She went back outside, where the sergeant was waiting for her.

'Someone is going to have to wait here for the joiner to come out and make it secure,' Robbo said. 'I hope you're right about him, because he's going to be pissed off when he comes home and sees the state of that door.'

Lucy bit her tongue to stop herself from telling him to get fucked. She was tired and angry, not to mention beside herself with worry. 'Well, you'd better get one of your officers to stay until the joiner turns up,' she said, 'because there's still a chance that she could come here with Mattie. So it will need to be an armed officer.'

The look on Robbo's face made her smile.. Task Force officers seemed to think they were above the day-to-day duties of waiting for joiners to arrive. She walked back to the car and got inside.

'Take me to the station; I need to see the DCI. Please.'

'Don't you want me to wait for the joiner?' Scott asked.

'Nope, let one of them do it. I need you to help me tonight.'

He began to chuckle. 'My pleasure, boss.'

They congregated back at the station. Lucy was there first. Col had arrived in his Batman pyjamas and was on the computer, frantically typing away. She smiled at him: if anyone could track Lizzy Clements down, it would be him. Tom was in her office on the phone. She walked in and he ended his call.

'No sign of either of them?' he asked. 'Your ANPR request didn't come back with any hits. Wherever they are, they haven't passed through any of the cameras.'

Browning walked in as Tom was saying this, slightly out of breath. There was a fine film of perspiration on his brow. He took a tissue from his pocket and dabbed his forehead. 'Well, that's technically a good thing, isn't it?' he said.

Lucy looked at him. 'How?'

'It means that they're still in the area. The cameras are on all the main roads both in and out of Brooklyn Bay. They can't have left town. Did Mattie mention if he had any plans tonight?'

'He didn't say anything,' Lucy admitted, 'because we had a bit of an argument.'

Tom looked at her. 'Why didn't you say that before?'

'Because it's not particularly relevant, is it? He was angry with me – it didn't stop him going and meeting her, did it?'

'Lucy,' Tom said, 'please tell me you're not having us running around on some wild goose chase because you feel bad that you two fell out?'

Anger flooded Lucy's chest, making it hard to breathe. 'No, sir,' she managed. 'I'm not having you running around because of that.'

Browning stepped between them to defuse the situation. 'Maybe they went out for a meal? Let's get checking all the local restaurants and pubs.'

Lucy looked at the clock. 'I think they shut long ago.'

'OK, what about hotels? Let's get a patrol to check all the hotel car parks and see if either of their cars are in one.'

Lucy nodded. 'That's a brilliant idea. Much better than sitting here doing nothing.'

'Let's hope this works,' Tom said, 'because we're running out of options.'

'Can we ping his phone now, sir?'

'We sent the order to do it as soon as the house was checked.'

Tom left and Browning went to make coffee. Lucy sat down at her desk. There wasn't anything more she could do for the moment. It would take time to contact Mattie's phone provider. She was so tired. She leant forward, putting her head on her arms and closing her eyes. She just needed five minutes to think.

Lucy opened her eyes as she felt her shoulder being gently shaken. She looked up to see Browning standing there with a mug of coffee in his hand. She felt grateful towards him for the help he was giving her tonight.

'Anything?' she asked.

'No, not yet. Look, you need to drink this, then get yourself home for a shower and a bit of sleep. There's nothing more you can do here. As hard as it is to accept, it's out of our hands.'

Lucy knew he was right. Her neck was stiff and she felt like crap. 'Thanks for the coffee,' she said. 'You should go home as well.'

'Oh, don't worry about that, I'm going,' Browning said. 'I need food and sleep. I get really angry when I'm hungry. Tom's going to let us know the minute they find him.'

Lucy took a sip of the lukewarm coffee, then stood up.

'I'm not leaving unless you do,' she said.

'I'm ready to go. I stink.'

'So do I.'

They walked out to the rear yard together. The fresh air hit Lucy, waking her up. She felt a little brighter, but her heart was still aching with the worry of not knowing where Mattie was.

Browning opened his car door and turned to her. 'Lucy, this isn't your fault. You know that, don't you?'

She nodded.

'Whatever happens, none of this is down to you.'

She tried to smile at him, but couldn't. *Where was Mattie?*

CHAPTER FIFTY

Lucy went home. Even if she weren't exhausted, she needed to go back anyway, to check her phone in case Mattie had tried to get hold of her. She'd look a complete idiot if he had and he was OK – but that was a price she was willing to pay.

Her whole body ached, she was so tired. She opened her front door, expecting to see her phone there on the hall table, with its little green light flashing. It wasn't there. She checked the floor, in case it had fallen off the table as she had rushed back out of the house. It wasn't on the floor, either.

She'd been so sure that was where she had left it. *How strange.* She ran back to her car to check whether it had fallen under the seat. It hadn't. She went back inside the house, locking the front door behind her, and ran upstairs to check the bathroom. *You never went up here though, did you?* Warning bells were ringing in her head, but she brushed them to one side. She was so tired she couldn't spell her name right if she'd been asked. She must have left it somewhere silly and forgotten about it. It would turn up.

She pushed open her bedroom door and let out a small scream: her room had been ransacked. Someone had been in her house. The bed, which she'd made before she left for work this morning, was a mess. The bedside table where she kept her diary had been overturned. The mirror above her chest of drawers was smashed into pieces. Who would do this? The only person she could think of was Ellie – but hadn't she and Ellie come to some sort of truce this afternoon?

Lucy stepped over the mess to pick the house phone up off the floor. She dialled George, who answered on the second ring. Good old dependable George. Even though he'd left her, he still answered all her calls as if they were still married.

'Morning, Lucy.'

'Is Ellie there?'

'Yes, she's in bed. We all are. Did you catch your killer?'

Shit. She should have realised that she hadn't even updated them She was so crap at this being a mother job it was unbelievable.

'Not yet,' Lucy said. 'Has everything been OK?'

'Yes.'

'Do you know if Ellie's been to my house at all yesterday – maybe last night sometime? Whilst I was at work?'

'No, she was working herself all day, then she came home and didn't go back out. Why?'

'Nothing,' Lucy said. 'It doesn't matter.'

'Well, quite clearly it does. I can tell when you're upset and right now you sound as if you are.'

'Someone's been in my house. They've trashed my bedroom and I can't find my phone.'

'Well, have you considered calling the police? You might have been burgled.'

Lucy started to laugh. 'George, I am the police. No, the rest of the house is fine, as far as I know. This seems to be something personal, which is why I thought it might have been Ellie. I know she's been angry with me, but I thought we'd sorted that out today. I really need my phone in case Mattie has tried to get hold of me.'

'Haven't you found Mattie?'

'Not yet.'

'Well then, you need to ring the police. You put a car outside my house because you were worried about our safety, and now I'm worried about yours. Don't you think you should call this in?'

'I will.'

Lucy put the phone down and looked at the mess. Then she dialled her mobile number and waited for it to connect. Maybe it was hidden somewhere in here. It began to ring out on the line, but she also heard the faint, annoying ring tone coming from somewhere downstairs.

Leaving the house phone off the hook, she ran downstairs, following the sound. As she went into the living room and turned on the light, she lifted her hand to her mouth. This room was a mess, too. All her photographs had been smashed to pieces on the floor.

Her phone was ringing from the kitchen. She sprinted in there to see it vibrating away in the middle of the breakfast bar. She definitely hadn't left it in here.

Just as she was starting to realise what was going on, Lucy caught a faint whiff of perfume in the air. Then a heavy metal pipe connected with the side of her head. Her legs gave way and she fell to the floor.

CHAPTER FIFTY-ONE

Lizzy smiled. She'd tried her best not to hit the woman too hard. She'd only needed to render her incapable enough to do what she had to do. Lucy was on her side, with a decent-sized pool of blood seeping from the wound. Folding up a tea towel, Lizzy rolled Lucy onto her back and pressed the cloth against her bleeding head. Then, opening the fridge, she took out the bottle of vodka. She unscrewed the cap and began to pour the clear liquid down Lucy's throat. Most of it was dribbling down her face and chin, but it didn't matter. As long as she smelt like a brewery and had enough alcohol in her veins so she was over the limit when they did the post-mortem, all would be good.

The vodka smelt too sweet and sickly, mixed with the coppery smell of the blood. Lizzy had to try not to breathe it in. She sat on one of the bar stools to catch her breath, then started when she heard a knock on the front door. Her heart skipped a beat. She ran over to the kitchen tap, washed her hands, and dried them on her trousers. As long as whoever it was didn't come around the back it would be fine.

There was a pause, and then a familiar voice shouted through the letter box: 'I know you're in there. Your car's here. Mum, let me in. I need to talk to you.'

Wondering what to do, Lizzy paused until she heard the sound of the key being turned in the lock. Then she ran to the front door and threw it open before a bleary-eyed Ellie could.

'Oh, Ellie, thank god you are here. I came to tell your mum something important and…well, I don't think you should go in there.'

'Why, what's the matter?'

'She's had a bit of an accident.'

Ellie pushed past her and ran towards the kitchen, crying out to see her mum lying on the floor with a blood-soaked cloth against her head and an almost empty bottle of vodka on the floor next to her.

'I found her like this,' Lizzy said. 'The door was ajar so I walked in. It's a good job I did.'

Ellie bent down and let out a sob as she clutched hold of her mother's hand. 'Have you rung an ambulance? She only phoned my dad a little while ago. How has she got in this state? I knew something was wrong – that's why I sneaked out and got a taxi here. What about Mattie? Ring him, Jane. He'll know what to do.'

Lizzy had to try her best not to sneer. *Yes, bloody love-sick Mattie would know what to do. He'd sweep her up into his arms, rush her to the hospital and save her life.*

'Of course I've rung an ambulance,' Lizzy said, 'but there's been a major accident on the coastal road and it's going to be some time before they can send one.'

Ellie looked at her mum. The last few shards of anger and bitterness she'd felt for her were draining visibly from her face. 'Well, we have to take her to the hospital ourselves then. We can put her in your car if we both carry her.'

'I walked.'

'Then we need to put her in her car,' Ellie said. 'You can drive. I'll sit in the back and hold her head still. Come on, Jane, she might die!'

While Ellie was busy with Lucy, Lizzy rolled her eyes, furious with the interfering kid. Yes, Lucy might die – that was the whole fucking point. Between them, they managed to manhandle Lucy off the floor and half-carry, half-drag her to the front door. Ellie picked up her mum's car keys off the hall table, and they bundled Lucy into the front passenger seat. Ellie climbed over into the back behind her mum and sat holding her head as still as she could, keeping the blood-soaked cloth pressed against the wound. Lizzy got into the driver's seat and started the engine. Poor Ellie was in for a shock, she thought, because there was no way they were going to the hospital.

Lying in bed, Sam had heard more car doors slamming shut in the last ten minutes than there normally was all day. He had tried to ignore it, but he couldn't help but wonder what the hell Lucy was doing so early in the morning. Out of curiosity, he got up and drew back his curtains – only to see Ellie and some woman dragging an unconscious Lucy to her car.

He began to hammer on the window to ask what was happening, but they were too preoccupied to hear him. He ran to grab his phone off the bed, then went back to the window to see the tiny green car being driven away at speed. He dialled 999.

'Police, please.'

CHAPTER FIFTY-TWO

Mattie opened one eye and looked at the clock on the bedside table. He didn't have a clue where he was – or why he couldn't remember where he was. He sat up and his stomach lurched. He was starving, and his head felt as if someone was inside it with a pickaxe. As he looked around the hotel room, bits from the night before began to come back to him. He'd been so angry with Heidi. He looked around to see where she was, and felt nothing but relief that she wasn't here. *Phew.* It was over, and he wouldn't be in a hurry to find another woman after this one. It was time to move on.

There were sixteen missed calls on his mobile from an unknown number. Lucy. She was going to be so pissed off with him. Something must be going down if she needed to get hold of him so urgently, but she was going to have to wait. He felt rough as hell.

He got up and went into the bathroom. Filling the tumbler from the sink with ice-cold water, he drank glass after glass until he'd quenched his thirst. After a shower, he got dressed and decided he might as well make the most of being here: he would be paying enough for it. By the time he'd eaten his full English breakfast and had driven to the station, he almost felt like a new man.

He walked past the duty sergeant's office to the stairs. Something was wrong, he noticed – something strange. Everyone he passed in the station was staring at him.

The sergeant came running out of his office.

'Oh my god, where the fuck have you been, Mattie? Lucy has had most of the shift out searching for you.'

'Why?' Mattie frowned. 'I'm allowed to sleep, you know; it's not against the law.'

The sergeant looked confused. 'What, you mean you were at home all this time?'

'No, I was at a hotel. Why, what's going on?'

'Lucy had you down as a high-risk misper: she thinks your girlfriend kidnapped you. She also thinks your girlfriend is the killer of that stack of dead bodies you have up at the mortuary.'

Mattie began to laugh. 'Seriously? She's lost the plot, mate, I'm telling you now. That's plain ridiculous. She's just pissed off with me because we had an argument.'

The DCI leant over the balcony. 'Jackson? My office, now.'

Mattie stopped laughing. 'Shit, she's really mad at me,' he said to the sergeant. 'You'd better call off the troops; I'm safe and well, thank you.'

He ran up the stairs to Tom's office. The DCI was pale with dark stubble across his chin and big black circles under his eyes. Mattie had never seen him looking so dishevelled.

'Boss, I don't understand what the problem is?'

'The problem is you didn't answer your bloody phone and we've had Task Force out searching for you.' He handed Mattie a printout. 'Lucy had a forensic artist draw this up of Lizzy Clements as she would look now.'

Mattie stared at it, open-mouthed. He was looking at a picture of Heidi.

'Lucy said that this Jane Toppan, who I believe you're in a relationship with, is the same woman as the one in the picture. Col has done some digging and discovered that Lizzy Clements died the same day that Jane Toppan mysteriously appeared on the scene. And the DNA from the hair sample that Jack got from the Stone murder scene came back as a match for Mr and Mrs

Clements. I'm sorry to tell you this, son, but it looks as if this Jane and Lizzy are the same woman. Now that you've turned up safe and well, we can concentrate on finding her. As I'm sure you realise, she's extremely dangerous.'

Mattie couldn't get his head around it all. How had this happened?

'Why didn't Lucy tell me earlier?'

'She couldn't. By the time she realised, we couldn't find you anywhere and it was panic stations. Lucy thought that you'd come to some harm.'

A sinking feeling filled Mattie's heart as he processed everything he'd just been told. All the questions that Heidi – or, as it turned out, Lizzy – had been asking him were running through his mind. *Do you like Lucy? Have you ever slept with her? Do you wish she wasn't your boss?*

'Boss, where's Lucy now?'

'I sent her and Browning home to get some sleep. She was exhausted after running around all night trying to find you.'

'I think she's in danger,' Mattie said, feeling a surge of panic. 'We need to find her. Now.'

Tom ran his fingers through his hair. 'Please tell me I'm having a bad fucking dream, because this is exactly what she said about you last night.'

'No, I honestly do think she's in danger. I don't want to believe that I've been having a relationship with a cold-blooded killer because it seems so ridiculous. But Heidi – she told me her name was Heidi – hated Lucy. She went mad at me yesterday about her. If she knows that Lucy is on to her... Well, I don't even want to say it out loud. Oh, god.' Mattie took off running towards the office, where Colin was in the process of pulling on his body armour.

'I heard all of that,' Col said. 'You never shut the door. So, where's the boss? Where are we going first?'

The duty sergeant came running upstairs. 'We've just had an IR for Lucy's address, neighbour saw her getting dragged into her car by two females. It's driven off. I've sent officers there now.'

Mattie rang Lucy's phone number. It went straight to voice-mail. 'OK, Tom's getting a search team to check Lucy's, mine and Heidi's – Jane's. We need to find out where they've taken her, and who the other woman is. An accomplice?'

Colin shook his head. 'I hate to state the obvious, but this is a right fucking mess, Sarge.'

Tom rushed in. 'Right, I've put observations out for Lucy's car. It shouldn't be that hard to find; it's quite distinctive. I've got all patrols out looking for it.' He noticed Mattie and Col heading for the stairs. 'You two come back here and wait for the briefing. I've assembled one for fifteen minutes' time.'

'Sorry, boss, can't do that,' Mattie said. 'You know we can't waste that much time.'

All Mattie could hear in his mind were the words he'd said to Lucy about her being a bad mother. *If the cap fits...* He hadn't meant it. She'd just made him angry, and he'd lashed out with what he knew would hurt her. If anything happened to her, he would never forgive himself.

CHAPTER FIFTY-THREE

Jane was driving too slowly. Ellie kept telling her to hurry, but Jane just shook her head.

'I can't drive too fast. We shouldn't have moved her. She might have brain damage or something and we could be making her worse.'

Ellie was frantic with worry. She wished that Jane would hurry up – ambulances went fast, didn't they? She just wanted her mum to be at the hospital, being taken care of, as quickly as possible.

All of a sudden, Jane slammed her hand against the steering wheel, and Ellie jumped.

'Sorry, sweetie,' Jane said. 'I'm just so mad at your mum. What was she thinking, doing this to herself and getting into such a state when she's got you to think about? If she loved you, she wouldn't behave like this, would she?'

Ellie felt a wave of hurt crash over her as she heard Jane's words. Jane was looking steadily at her in the rear-view mirror. Ellie looked away, feeling uncomfortable under the woman's gaze. Something wasn't right. Something was bothering her…

'Jane… What were you doing at my mum's so early in the morning? You've never been there before. What did you have to tell her that was so important?'

Jane shook her head. 'I can't really tell you. It's grown-up stuff.'

Ellie frowned. What was the woman talking about? She knew Jane didn't like her mum from the things she'd said about her. So why would she put the effort in to go to her house so early in the morning? It didn't make sense.

She looked out of the window. Where were they going? Jane was driving in the opposite direction to the hospital. She shifted position in her seat, and noticed for the first time that her arm felt wet where her mum's weight was leaning against it. She let go of her mum's head with one hand, and twisted her arm around to see the huge damp patch running along her sleeve. Lifting it to her nose, she detected the sweet smell of the vanilla vodka that was her mum's favourite. Her mum's top was soaked with the stuff. Ellie frowned. She knew her mum liked a drink, but she'd never known her to drink this early in the morning. And if she'd been drinking her favourite vodka, she wouldn't have poured it all over herself. Had there been a glass in the kitchen? Ellie didn't think there had. And her mum definitely wouldn't have drunk from the bottle: it just wasn't her.

Ellie felt sick as she had the dawning realisation that Jane must have hurt her mum. Feeling terrified now of the woman in the front of the car, she tried to slip her phone from her pocket without making a sound. Thank god she'd forgotten to turn it off silent after she'd finished work yesterday. She typed a message to Mattie:

Help, Jane's hurt mum. In mum's car don't know where we're going.

The car stopped suddenly and Ellie's phone flew out of her hand, landing under the seat with a thud.

'What was that?' Jane asked sharply.

'I don't know,' Ellie said. 'Probably something rolling around under the seat. Jane, can we go a bit faster, please?'

Jane didn't answer. Ellie looked anxiously at her mum. There was a fine film of sweat forming on her pale skin. As Ellie watched, a small groan escaped from her lips and Ellie felt a huge wave of relief.

'Mum? Mum? It's OK, we're taking you to the hospital.'

* * *

Lucy felt as if her head was on fire. If she tried to move, the whole world began to swim. She had no idea what had happened. What she did know was that she was in a moving car, and she'd just heard Ellie's voice. There was a strong smell of neat vanilla vodka – it filled her nostrils when she inhaled. Why could she smell vodka? She hadn't been drinking, had she? She'd gone home for her phone…

Ellie's voice came again. 'Mum, it's OK. Jane is driving us to the hospital.'

At the mention of Jane's name, Lucy felt the thick fog in her mind clear. She didn't dare open her eyes, because then Jane – Lizzy – would know she was awake. But she needed to somehow get Ellie out of the car, out of danger. Lucy didn't care about herself, but she loved Ellie more than anything and she wouldn't let her get hurt. She would wait until the car stopped, then tell Ellie to run.

She tried to rub her cheek against Ellie's hand to let her know she was OK. Ellie had Mattie's number. Once she was out of the car, she would be able to phone Mattie to come and get Lucy. Except… A burst of sharp pain filled her heart as her memory came back to her: they'd been looking for Mattie and hadn't found him. What if Lizzy had already killed him? The thought filled her with fear.

As the car took a sharp turn, Lucy half-opened one eye to see where they were. She was relieved to see that Lizzy had just turned onto the promenade: traffic-light central. Lucy would be able to tell Ellie to run any time soon. Once Ellie was free, Lucy's biggest worry would be the fact that the hospital Lizzy was driving in the direction of wasn't the general. She was driving towards the asylum.

CHAPTER FIFTY-FOUR

Mattie and Colin arrived at Lucy's house in record time. Sam, the neighbour, was outside waiting for them, waving his arms around as soon as they got out of the car, telling them what he'd seen. Col told Mattie to wait outside, but he couldn't. He ran inside and went straight upstairs. He heard Col follow him in and take the downstairs. Just as he opened Lucy's bedroom door and saw the mess, Col shouted: 'You need to come and see this, now!'

Mattie raced back down and into the kitchen, to see the large pool of blood and the almost empty vodka bottle next to it.

'Where have they taken her?' Col said. 'That's a lot of blood.'

Mattie couldn't speak. His brain couldn't put into words his worst fear. Just then, his phone beeped. It was a message from Ellie. He read it with a mixture of panic and relief.

'Get response and CSI here now,' he told Col. 'We also need a welcoming party at the hospital, in case Lizzy takes Lucy there. You can wait here until someone arrives to take over scene guard.'

'Whoa,' Col said. 'Where are you going?'

'I'm going to see if I can find them before they get there.'

'Be careful – don't you think you should wait for backup?'

But Mattie was already running out to his car. Backup could sod off; he wasn't waiting for anyone.

Lucy tried to count the traffic lights, but her brain was still foggy. As the car slowed down, then came to a stop, she whispered to her daughter who had her head between the passenger window and her head: 'Ellie, get out of the car and *run*.'

For the first time in her life, Ellie listened to her mum's order. She clambered between the small gap between the seats and fell into the front of the car, knocking both Lucy and Lizzy at the same time. The car swerved across the road. Lizzy, clearly realising what was about to happen, put her foot down on the accelerator as Ellie climbed across her mum's lap and jumped out of the door. Lucy watched her daughter in the wing mirror as she fell to the ground and rolled to a halt. A crowd of people ran to help Ellie up and relief flooded through Lucy as she grabbed the car door and slammed it shut. The car was going too fast for her to try and jump out after Ellie.

'You sneaky cow,' Lizzy said. 'How long have you been awake?'

'Long enough to realise that you're not going to take me to the hospital,' Lucy said. 'It's over, Lizzy. We know everything about you; we know that you killed them all. If you hand yourself in now and tell us what really happened, it won't be as bad as you think. The judges love a good sob story.'

'Fuck off,' Lizzy said. 'I'd rather die than get locked up again.'

She put her foot down. Lucy watched out of the window, helplessly. If it all went wrong at least she would die knowing that she'd put her daughter's safety first. They were heading as fast as possible in the direction of the asylum.

CHAPTER FIFTY-FIVE

Mattie turned onto the promenade, passing the speed camera at sixty. A brilliant white light flashed in his rear-view mirror, but he didn't care. He drove straight through the first three red lights, then spotted a crowd of people in the distance gathered around a girl. He slowed down, recognising a scraped – but safe – Ellie. She recognised him, and pointed frantically down the prom. He saw the small speck that was Lucy's car in the distance, and radioed for more patrols, giving them the direction in which to head.

Lizzy pushed the little car until it was doing ninety, taking a sharp bend so tightly that Lucy thought there was a good chance they were going to die in a head-on collision before they even reached the asylum. As the huge, abandoned hospital came into sight, Lucy wondered if she'd be able to fight Lizzy off. Her vision kept swimming in and out of darkness.

To Lucy's surprise, Lizzy drove straight past the hospital gates and headed for the old cemetery. The building work there had been ordered to stop after the discovery of Edwin Wilkes's body, so it was empty. Rain began to fall in big wet splotches on the windscreen. Slamming the brakes, Lizzy skidded the car to a halt near the small pedestrian entrance to the cemetery. Then Lizzy threw out her fist and punched Lucy on the side of the head where the open wound was. Lucy's head snapped back, and for the second time, she lost consciousness.

* * *

Getting out of the car, Lizzy knew she didn't have long. She opened Lucy's door and dragged her out of the car. She was only little, but she was heavy. Putting her hands around Lucy's waist, Lizzy threw her over her shoulder as best as she could. Lucy groaned.

Lizzy began to walk as fast as she could manage under Lucy's weight to where she knew there was a deep hole in the ground. It was tucked away in the far corner. The rain was torrential now, making the ground slippery underfoot. Lizzy could feel herself sliding with every step. Barely managing to keep her balance, she finally reached the hole and peered over the edge. It had been full of water anyway: the extra rain would make it so slippery it would be impossible for Lucy to climb back out.

With one final heave, Lizzy pushed the unconscious woman from her shoulders. Lucy fell down into the muddy water with a huge wet splash. Lizzy turned and ran as fast as she could. There was no point in driving Lucy's car: they would find her. She ran towards the asylum. She knew plenty of places to hide inside there until things had calmed down.

As Lucy's body hit the cold water, the shock of it made her eyes open. She tried to stand up but she couldn't find the bottom: it was far too deep. It was so dark and cold wherever Jane had just thrown her. The rain was falling into her eyes, blinding her. Doing her best to tread water, she gulped in mouthfuls of the dirty water. She tried to look around for something to grab hold of to pull herself out of the hole, but there was nothing. The earth walls were too slippery.

As she tried to stay afloat, her legs touched something cold and hard in the water and she let out a scream. She was in someone's grave… *Oh god, please don't let that be a body.*

She was shivering so much that her teeth were chattering. She didn't know what to do. She screamed again, hoping desperately that someone would hear her.

She was getting more tired and cold by the second, when she heard a voice in the distance, shouting her name.

'I'm over here!' she cried. 'Help me!'

Mattie screeched to a halt behind Lucy's car and jumped out. He could hear sirens in the distance and hoped that backup wouldn't be long. The passenger door of Lucy's car was wide open. He looked inside, and his stomach lurched to see the blood that covered the head rest. Where were they?

He ran towards the cemetery, shouting: 'Lucy? Lucy? Where are you?'

He heard a faint response: 'I'm over here! Help me!'

'Lucy?'

But there was no more response.

Mattie ran frantically backwards and forwards through the cemetery, calling Lucy's name. Where was she? Why wasn't she responding? Finally, he ran towards the large hole in the far corner and peered over the edge – only to see Lucy's head as it went underwater.

Screaming down his radio for help, he heard heavy footsteps behind him, heading in his direction. Stripping off his jacket and shoes, he jumped down into the hole to the sound of the DCI's voice bellowing at him to stop.

The water was cold, and much deeper than he'd imagined. He took a deep breath, then ducked under. He felt for Lucy, and grabbed at her shoulders under the water. Pushing her up, he managed to lift her head above the water. By this time, two officers were leaning down into the hole, and Mattie tried his best to lift Lucy's unconscious body towards them, straining and pushing with every ounce of strength he possessed. The officers managed to grab her arms and dragged her out while he trod water.

Tom was standing on the edge of the hole, shouting at Mattie to get out of the water. Another two officers leant down to grab him – only he couldn't. He'd felt something else in the water. He dived back down again, struggling to lift up what he already knew was a dead body. It was female: he could guess from the shape, and from the long hair streaming across his face in the water. He couldn't leave her down there.

He managed to push her up, and the two waiting officers recoiled and drew back their hands. It was Tom and Browning who bent down and grabbed the dead girl, pulling her up. Browning leant down and pulled Mattie up next. He felt a foil blanket being wrapped around his shoulders while he looked at Lucy lying on the ground beside the hole, the dead body nearby. The paramedic from the crime scene yesterday was now performing CPR on his best friend.

Mattie stood with his fingers crossed behind his back as he watched them pump Lucy's chest. *Come on, Lucy. Don't you dare die on me.* It felt as if time was standing still as he watched every single chest compression. Finally, she took a breath and began to cough up dirty great mouthfuls of muddy water. They turned her onto her side, so that she was facing the dead woman.

'Lauren…' she said. 'That's Lauren Coates.'

'All right, Lucy,' Mattie said, bending over her. 'It's all right. We're dealing with it.'

Lucy lost consciousness. As she was loaded into the back of the ambulance, Tom looked at Mattie. 'Come on, let's get you inside a car before you upset any nice members of the public. I want you checking out at the hospital – god knows what contamination was in that water.'

'Lucy thinks that body is Lauren Coates,' Mattie said. 'Where's Heidi? Lizzy, I mean.'

'I have no idea where she is. She can't be far if she's on foot, though. My best guess is she's gone into the hospital. I've requested a dog handler; they'll be able to catch her scent. We'll get her. I've got every available officer surrounding the hospital and grounds until the dogs get here.'

'Good.'

The ambulance drove away with Lucy inside, its blue lights flashing. Mattie watched it go. The relief that she was alive was unlike anything he'd ever known.

He looked around as a lot of shouting went up from the hospital grounds. Officers were running and pointing upwards. Mattie's gaze followed where they were pointing to see the small figure of a woman standing on the top of the asylum roof. Before anyone could do anything, the woman threw herself off and hurtled towards the ground, landing with a loud thud.

Mattie flinched. Out of the corner of his eye, he saw Tom motion for Browning to take him, but he pulled away and began running towards the crowd of officers that had gathered around the body on the floor. They stepped to one side to let him through, and Mattie stared at the bloodied mess that had yesterday been his lover.

Tom had followed him. 'Is that her?'

Mattie nodded. 'Yes, it's her. I can confirm that is the woman I knew as Heidi Jane Toppan.'

He turned and walked back to where Browning was waiting at the car for him.

'Come on, Matthew,' Browning said. 'Let's get you to the hospital so they can give you a tetanus shot or something. You did pretty good, lad.'

Browning patted his shoulder as he got into the car. Then they drove in silence towards the hospital and Lucy.

CHAPTER FIFTY-SIX

Lucy could hear the steady beep of the machine she was hooked up to. The noise of it was a relief: at least it meant she was alive. Just as she was wondering where Ellie was and if she was OK, she felt a warm hand squeeze hers. Her daughter was there, beside her.

Lucy opened her eyes, and was surprised to see George and Mattie beside her as well. As she smiled at them, Ellie let out a shriek, jumping up to kiss her on the forehead. Then she bent close and whispered: 'I love you, Mum.'

Lucy felt her eyes fill with hot tears. She was so grateful that she'd been given a second chance to prove just how much she loved her daughter. She croaked back: 'I love you more.' It hurt her parched throat to speak.

George bent down, kissing Lucy's cheek. 'You had us all scared there. I'm so glad you're OK. I'm going to take Ellie home now so you can get some rest. If you need anything, you know where we are. The nurses have our number.'

Lucy smiled at them both. She watched them walk out of the door, then turned to face Mattie, who was dressed in a set of blue hospital scrubs. She pointed at the jug of water on the bedside table. He poured some out and held it up to her lips while she sipped. When she'd finished, he put the glass down and wiped her lips with a tissue.

'That was close. You almost…' His voice tailed away. He looked awful.

'Thank you.' Lucy clasped his hand.

The door opened and Dr Stephen King popped his head in. Lucy noticed that Mattie pulled his hand away from hers.

'I'm glad to see that you're back with us, Lucy,' Stephen said. 'You didn't half give us a fright when they brought you into resus. How are you feeling?'

'I have a terrible headache and I can taste muddy water – apart from that, I'm fine.'

'All your scans are good. I've spoken to the doctor in charge of your care, and there's some swelling to the brain around your injury, but it doesn't look like there's any permanent damage. If you need anything at all, tell them to bleep me. I'm on duty until tomorrow morning.'

'Thank you,' Lucy said.

Dr King left, and Mattie took hold of her hand again. 'You know he likes you, a lot,' he told her. 'You should go out on a date with him.'

Lucy smiled. 'What about you?'

'I'm OK thanks; I don't think he likes me that much.'

'That's not what I meant.'

She watched his cheeks begin to turn red as he realised what she was implying. He squeezed her hand. 'Let's just say I'm glad you didn't die, Harwin. Do you know how much paperwork there would have been?'

She nodded. 'Yes, I do. Oh, thank god you found me. Where is Lizzy Clements? Did they arrest her?'

'She's dead.'

Lucy stared at him. 'How?'

'She left you for dead and ran across to the asylum. She got into the hospital and somehow managed to get up onto the roof. She jumped.'

'Oh Mattie, what a mess. I'm so sorry. Are you OK?'

He squeezed her fingers. 'It's fine, really it is. We were over anyway. Oh, and you were right.'

'About what?'

'Lauren Coates. She must have been in the wrong place at the wrong time when Audrey Stone was killed. I felt her body in the water when I was in the hole, and after I got you out I went back under. Browning and Tom dragged her body out. Her parents flew back from their holidays last night and identified her body an hour ago.'

Lucy sighed. 'You know, for once I wish I'd been totally wrong.'

Mattie bent down and kissed her cheek. 'I'll see you tomorrow. Get some rest. In the meantime, try not to be a pain in the arse, Lucy Harwin.'

He walked out of the room. As the door softly closed behind him, Lucy let the tears flow: for herself, for Mattie's loss – and for Lauren Coates, who had somehow got caught up in this whole mess and had ended up paying with her life.

A LETTER FROM HELEN

I really hope you enjoyed meeting DI Lucy Harwin and DS Mattie Jackson and I hope you will follow them on their next adventure.

For me writing this series was a new beginning and one which at first I was a little daunted by, but I thoroughly enjoyed getting to know Lucy Harwin and can't wait to see what happens to her next.

I've worked for the police for the last ten years and I'm hoping that Lucy, Mattie, Col, Browning and Tom are pretty believable characters. Although I've had to bend the rules slightly to make the book flow, real life is much slower and seldom as exciting as my colleagues in Cumbria Constabulary well know.

I'd like to send a huge thank you to each and every single one of my readers, your support is invaluable and so very much appreciated. I'd also like to thank the many book bloggers and clubs who read and share my work, you're all amazing.

I always enjoy hearing from you and if you would like to get in touch my links are below. And if you loved the book please post a review if you can.

Love always,
Helen xx

www.bookouture.com/helen-phifer

www.helenphifer.com

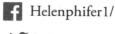 Helenphifer1/

 helenphifer1

ACKNOWLEDGMENTS

I am extremely grateful to Oliver Rhodes and the amazing team at Bookouture for giving me the chance to bring this book to life. Thank you all so much from the bottom of my heart.

I would like to thank my editor, the amazing Keshini Naidoo, who has worked so hard to make this book what it is. Your insight has been invaluable and I can't thank you enough. A huge thank you to Kim Nash for her never ending enthusiasm and hard work, it truly is appreciated. And a very special thank you to my lovely copy editor, Gabrielle Chant, for all her hard work.

I'd like to thank Caroline Mitchell, Angie Marsons and the rest of the fabulous writers, too many to mention at Bookouture, for your amazing support and for always being there. I feel privileged to be in such esteemed company.

A huge thank you also to Annie Lyons and Liz Tipping. You two gorgeous ladies are the light in my ever so dark writing life and I love you both for making me laugh out loud on my darkest days.

I am forever indebted to my amazing readers, I can't thank you enough for taking a chance on a writer called Helen Phifer. Your support is everything and I'm truly grateful to each and every one of you.

I'd like to thank my husband Steve and my amazing children for understanding that when I have to write it's best to keep out of the way. I love each and every one of you more than you could ever know.

Last, but definitely not least, I'd like to thank my wonderful friends and colleagues at Cumbria Constabulary. Sam Thomas, Tina Sykes, Tracy Livingston, Gail O'Neill, Phil Sullivan, Iain Richards, Caroline Kendall, you've been there from the start. I love you all for making me laugh and keeping me sane in our sometimes, crazy world.